GOLDEN SEA

Book Two in the Mapmaking Magicians Series

EMMA STERNER-RADLEY

SIGN UP

Thank you for purchasing Golden Sea.

I often hold sales and giveaways, to find out more about these great deals (and what I'm working on) please sign up to my mailing list by clicking the link below:

https://www.subscribepage.com/emmasternerradley

To any reader daring to venture, and love, beyond the usual.

ACKNOWLEDGEMENTS

Thank you to everyone who has been involved in this novel's editing, proofing, and sensitivity/continuity reading: Jeanette Rodriguez, Tova H-L, James Tapiwa, Kit Eyre, and Cheri Fuller.

As always, thank you to my patient family. And, of course, my wife Amanda who STILL lifts me so I can reach for my dreams. (And the cookies on the top shelf.)

As always, in memory of:
Malin Sterner
1973-2011
Who never liked fantasy books but who would've loved Eleksander.

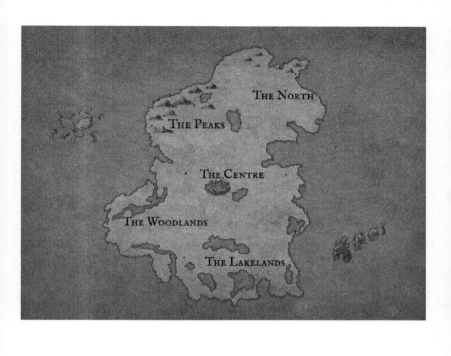

Chapter One

START OF TERM

At the start of something new, was it right to be excited or terrified? Or both?

Sabina Rosenmarck sure as snow didn't have a clue. Currently, she stood wondering about that in the Hall of Explorers' empty courtyard. A murder of crows cawed in the tree behind her, the sound forlorn but also ominous, a reminder that she had stepped back into danger when she returned to the academy.

Sabina gave the crows a challenging glare, then buttoned her coat up. The winters here at the Hall of Explorers were mild compared to back home in the North, so it was probably the loneliness biting at her more than the cold. She was the first in her class to arrive back from Winter Solstice, and, even accounting for her early arrival, it was unnervingly desolate around her. Where was everyone? Only a couple of servants passed her in the courtyard, dignified and busy. She should get about her business too. The sensible thing to do would be to take her luggage, get situated in the bedchamber, and change into her uniform. Maybe start sparring or perusing the books they'd be using this term? She wouldn't do either of these things, though, because if she started to unpack her bags, she'd only take out Avelynne's letters.

Eight weeks they had all been home for Solstice and in that time, she'd received ten letters from the lass she had fallen for. More letters than she could've dared asked for. She only wished their contents had been different.

She kicked the sundial in front of her, prompting Kall to swipe a massive paw at the ornate stone structure, warning it to not attack his mistress. There was no more defensive animal companion than a snowtiger. Shame that Kall didn't know that Sabina's pain didn't come from the sundial but from her heart and mind. Sure, Avelynne's letters had been wonderful and sweet. However, they'd also been decidedly less flirty or intimate than their interactions in person. Sabina shouldn't be surprised, Avelynne had always said that she had no time for romance. Still, at least Avelynne could've kept up the sexual tension between them?

Sabina would have settled for that.

The silence of the courtyard was broken by heavy steps. Tutor Rogan approached with a polearm in one hand. Sabina stiffened, thoughts of romance and friendship all gone. The man approaching had been in her nightmares these past weeks. He was so clearly connected to the king and his covert scheme to shape the Hall of Explorers' mapmakers into cruel colonisers. What made it even worse was that his emerald tutors' robes reminded Sabina of the death of Tutor Rete.

"Northerner," Rogan roared. "Why in the name of the shitting silver beasts are you just standing there? Where are the rest of the second wave?"

"They have yet to arrive. I'm early."

He clenched his free fist, silvery magic glinting around his bruised knuckles. "Well, if your little classmates deign to show their snotty faces, at least we'll have *some* of you terrible toddlers to train."

Combat training was Coth Rogan's primary subject, something impossible to forget with his violent nature and unnecessary but constant aggression.

"Some?" Sabina dared ask.

"Yes. The first wave will spend the term in the dockyard, learning how to rough it and how to take care of their longship when it's not at sea." He harrumphed. "The spoiled little scholars whinged

3

when they were told they had to sail in winter. Brats."

The first wave had made practise sails around the coast during last term but weren't meant to start longer journeys until the end of this year, with the second wave following suit the next term. No one had said anything about sailing winter seas, though. That was perilous enough to be downright reckless. Sabina ground her teeth. Perhaps what they had feared last year was coming true: the schedule might be moved up, despite the danger that put the untrained students in.

Sabina put a hand on Kall's head, keeping the snowtiger back from Rogan, lest he growl at the tutor. "Even with the first wave at the coast, won't we have more recruits around? I mean, won't a third wave start their studies now?"

He shook his head, seeming irritated at the question. "No. We have delayed taking on new students. There is to be more doing and less studying at this academy."

Sabina was about to ask if academies weren't meant for learning and training but bit her tongue.

Hooves and the clanging of a large carriage sounded. Rogan and Sabina both peered through the gate. The carriage had the emblem and colours of the Grand Count of Ironhold.

Rogan sneered, then strode off muttering, "Looks like her ladyship, in all her uselessness, has arrived."

Tutor Rogan was from the Peaks, just like Avelynne, and despised her worst of all the "scholarly toddlers." Probably because she was of higher birth than he and, despite her sweet nature, refused to be cowed by his bullying.

He was wrong about Avelynne being useless, though. While she did illicitly get into the academy through her parents—who against Avelynne's will cheated the tests to stop a civil war and advance their own house—she had worked so hard to catch up on her sparring, arithmetic, navigation, magic skills, and everything else the Hall of Explorers taught. Besides, the emotional support and nurturing she gave those around her would be vital for their future mission, as it was for their wellbeing now.

Someone like Rogan would never understand that. He only saw strength, power, and success as admirable features and dismissed all the work that those who nurtured the strong, powerful, and successful put in.

Sabina watched him, all resentment and emotional stuntedness, stride off and pitied him.

She returned her focus to the carriage, from which Avelynne now departed with her perpetually bored maidservant, Myllie, in tow.

Countess Avelynne Ironhold of the Peaks was as

beautiful as Sabina remembered. Her slim frame moved as gracefully as always, but her sleek reddish-black hair was longer now. She spotted Sabina and gave that bashful smile which exposed her dimples and made her eyes crinkle, eyes which were meticulously lined with black today. In general, her features were perfectly painted and her clothes exquisite. Sabina was suddenly aware of her clean-scrubbed face and crumpled, old clothes.

Avelynne ran into her arms. "Snowdrop, I've missed you so much! Are you well?"

"I'm fine, *little Countess*," Sabina replied, nuzzling into the shorter woman's hair, happy they fell straight into their nicknames as well as each other's arms.

"How are you? How was your journey?" Sabina asked as Avelynne placed a kiss on her cheek and stepped out of the embrace.

"Long," her maid Myllie grumbled before walking past them with the luggage.

Avelynne tried to take one of the bags from her but Myllie pulled it out of reach. "No. Carryin' is my job. Tell the Northerner about your parents' farewell instead. I'll go in and sort out your room."

"Yes, please do," Avelynne said with sadness. "And then, as we discussed, you must decide if you wish to remain with me or return to Ironhold castle."

"Oh, I'll be goin' back," Myllie called over her shoulder.

Avelynne's face fell but she said nothing.

"What was that about a farewell? And why is Myllie leaving?" Sabina asked.

"Well," Avelynne said on a deep inhale. "As I said in my last letter, this Solstice made it clear that I shall have to take my future holidays here at the Hall. I'm... no longer welcome at Ironhold castle."

"Because you stood up to them?"

"Yes. Apparently, it is despicable of me to tell them that I will no longer blindly follow their orders and that I'm too old for them to control. Or to imprison at their whim."

"They took it badly enough to not want you to come back for the Spring Feast? Or the Summer Solstice?"

Avelynne brushed down her dress, putting on a brave smile. "They took it badly enough for them to not want me to ever return."

"Ever?"

"Mm. I have been disowned. I'm no longer a countess. My cousin will inherit the castle and title while I get nothing. I'm not welcome back to the castle, or the Peaks in general."

"What?! They can't keep you out of your native county!"

"They can make sure I will find no home or work

there, so I suppose they already have. I'll have to make my future elsewhere. Which should be fine since I will be sailing and then hopefully settling in the new land we find."

Sabina took her hand and held it tight. "Well, you'll always be a countess to me. And I'll happily stay here with you during holidays."

She didn't say that she'd happily come to live with Avelynne in the new land, or wherever Avelynne went, too.

One thing at a time, she reminded herself.

"Thank you," Avelynne said. "I am so lucky you put up with me."

"I don't put up with you. I value you." Sabina brought Avelynne's cold hand to her mouth and placed a kiss on the knuckles. "Your parents couldn't handle you. So, they tried to file you down to something that fit their slot for you, something smaller and less unique. You didn't let them. Take pride in that."

"Filing me down would be better than using me as a puppet." Avelynne waved that away. "Never mind me. How are you? Did you get a chance to speak with your uncle?"

Uncle Ossian. That was who she and Avelynne, through their letters, had decided Sabina could confide in about her guilt over killing Tutor Rete.

"Yes, we've talked. He said the same things you

did. I had to do it, or he would have killed you and then me, Hale, and Eleksander."

Avelynne surveyed her through those blackened lashes of hers. "And did that help?"

"It was nice to hear an outsider confirm that I did nothing wrong."

"That didn't answer the question, snowdrop."

"It helped a little. Time will do the rest," Sabina said, curtly enough to cut off the topic.

There was no point in trying to explain how she felt. It didn't help, didn't stand a chance against the voice in her mind screaming about how this was her responsibility, her guilt to carry, and that she should do better. That she owed something for everything she had ever done wrong, but especially for the life she took.

Sabina was about to ask Avelynne something else, about where they stood, about their relationship. Or lack thereof. But the hammering of hooves was heard again. This time the carriage was clearly from the Lakelands, beautifully decorated, lavish and, of course, in the famous powdery Lakelander-blues.

Therefore, it was no surprise to see the second waver from the Lakelands, Eleksander "Sander" Aetholo, step out of it. He tucked a book into a pocket of his surcoat and pulled the garment more neatly over his broad shoulders. What was, however, surprising was that after him, the fourth member of their class and the recruit from the Woodlands, Hale Hawthorn, leapt out.

"Hale! Sander! You arrived together?" Avelynne called as she hurried towards them.

"Yes, Ellenaria and I spotted these two stragglers on the way and had to rescue them," Eleksander said, pointing to Hale and his mentor, the old fighter Ghar.

Eleksander's sister and the less kind of the two siblings, Ellenaria chuckled. "I thought they'd walked the entire way considering how dusty they are. But apparently their rented carriage broke down halfway from the Woodlands," she said before heading to the servants' quarters with Ghar.

"Of shitting course," Hale said. "Otherwise I would've been here first!"

Good old Hale, always crowing, always with something to prove, always with the worst language, Sabina thought to herself.

Unlike Eleksander and Avelynne, he had not sent many letters. Only a scrawled note to say that he adored Sabina but did not adore letter writing.

Avelynne embraced Eleksander, while Sabina and Hale shared an awkward one-armed hug. The two warriors weren't as cuddly as their more emotional friends.

Sabina tugged at Hale's tunic, underneath which

there was a hint of black ink. "Why in the name of the ice are you not wearing a coat?"

He grinned, deliberately halting his shivering. "Dressing for the weather is for weaklings."

Eleksander laughingly shook his head while Avelynne smiled maternally. It fell to Sabina to give Hale a stern look. One which made Hale groan, "Fine. Dressing for the weather is smart. I simply wanted to show off my new tattoos. Would it kill you to give me a break, older sister?"

She reached up to ruffle his hair, proud of the honorary sibling title. "I'll give you a break when you've earned one."

He clapped her on the back. "Just as expected. Now, I know I can trust you to have gotten the lay of the land, Northerner. How are things back at the good old Hall of E?"

Sabina explained about the first wave having left for the coast, there not being a third wave, and Tutor Rogan being in his usual foul mood.

"Rogan. Ugh." Hale spat on the ground. "I've spent most of the Solstice break on my own, I'm not ready to have to obey adults again."

"We'll all turn nineteen this year, Hale. *We're* adults," Sabina said.

"You are," Eleksander said. "And Ave is. But I doubt you can call me or Hale adults."

"Dearest Sander, still as hard on yourself? Please

don't put yourself down," Avelynne said, making the Lakelander shuffle his feet with embarrassment.

"Also, you're as adult as the rest of us, Hale. You just don't act like it," Sabina said, bumping the Woodlander with her hip.

"Anyway, let's move away from where Rogan might get to us," Eleksander said. "How about we go inside, drop off our bags, and get into uniform?"

Avelynne lit up. "Yes. Then we can sit down and catch up."

"Maybe play some bottletop?" Sabina suggested, eager to relax and have some fun.

"I'll race you all inside," Hale said, ignoring the whole conversation.

They all sighed with a smile and followed him in.

Chapter Two

ONE MONTH INTO SPRING TERM

Eleksander jumped as the window blew shut with a bang. Despite the wintery winds, Tutor Myle had decided they needed some air in the stuffy lesson room to help them focus as he tried to teach them about navigating at sea. This wasn't Ithikiel Myle's topic. It showed.

Eleksander buried his second-hand embarrassment as the tutor, more comfortable with a quill, dropped his oversized compass for the third time.

Hale leaned back towards Eleksander's bench and whispered, "I miss Tutor Santorine's nautical navigation lessons. Why haven't they gotten in new tutors for the subjects the insurgent tutors taught?"

"You know why. The king wants only staff he's sure are utterly loyal and under his control. And he doesn't care about our education other than that we know enough sailing to stumble upon some land, and that we can fight for him. The mapmaking and science of seafaring bores him."

Hale grunted and bent back over his own desk.

They'd been back for a few weeks now but had barely spoken about the king's conspiracy. Or what happened with Tutor Rete and Tutor Santorine. Or even about the Twelve in general. They had doggedly kept to talking about their lessons or the Solstice break: who they had met during it, what they had done, what books they had read, who had written letters to whom and who—Hale—had forgotten to write more than a couple of letters.

Now, as academy life returned to normal, it was impossible not to talk about the things that kept them from being regular eighteen, going on nineteen, year-olds. Impossible not to speak of the dangers and the duty.

Tutor Myle put the huge teaching compass down. "I believe that is all I can teach you regarding that. Now, we have a while left before you break for your midday meal. King Lothiam," his voice went up in falsetto for an instant, "wanted me to speak to you about the people you may encounter when you sail."

They all sat up straighter.

"During your voyages, your primary goal is, of course, to find new lands, ones without the terror of the silver beasts." Myle cleared his throat. "However, should you come across lands that are already inhabited..."

"We are to make ambassadorial advances — if we can communicate with them in the manner we'll be taught next term when we cover trade and diplomacy," Avelynne said in her usual deferential way, but there was a hint of confidence in her voice which hadn't been there in their first term. "If we cannot communicate with them or if they are hostile, we are to withdraw and sail on."

Eleksander's skin crawled as he anticipated Myle's answer to that. They all knew what the king wanted. Had he finally come out into the open with it?

Their tutor squirmed where he stood. "Yes. Those were your instructions. However, they have changed."

And there it was.

Myle wasn't making eye contact. "The new orders are still to try the diplomatic route first. However, if the foreigners are not as acquiescing or generous with their information and resources as we Cavarrians would like, you are to use force to make them more accommodating."

Sabina grunted something under her breath. Eleksander was pretty sure it was a curse word and echoed the sentiment. His heart was racing, rage and indignation making him sweat.

His gaze went to the door. Should he walk out and never come back? No, this was *the grand Hall of Explorers*, you didn't do that. He wasn't even sure what would happen to him if he tried. Would they let him leave? Furthermore, he was a dutiful son and his parents had been so proud when he was accepted to the most prestigious institution on Cavarra. He wouldn't shame them by failing to finish what he had started. Neither would he force foreigners, or anyone, to give up something they did not want to, though.

Myle met his eye, only for a moment, and apologetically mumbled, "Our honoured King Lothiam is... full of surprises lately. Having seen more of him during this Solstice, it strikes me that he might have more secrets than any one of us could guess."

Eleksander's ears pricked up. "May I ask what you mean by that?"

Myle couldn't be referring to the king's desire to conquer and lack of respect for others. He had warned them about that last term himself. What else had come to light?

"Oh. Um. Nothing. I was thinking out loud," Myle squeaked, back to the usual mousy behaviour reminiscent of Tutor Hathleen's. Why did the tutors with backbone have to be violent rebels, now dead or imprisoned? Eleksander didn't count Rogan, who was more of a violent bully and mouthpiece for the king than a tutor.

"Perhaps we should end this lesson early," Myle said, wiping his pallid brow. "Go on. Head to the hall for your meal."

They packed up their books, quills, and parchment and filtered out with Kall in tow.

"Wow. Someone spoke out of turn," Hale whispered as they walked out. "No way was Myle allowed to hint at our shitty king having secrets like that."

When they were far enough away, Avelynne replied, "No. I think he saw the look on our faces and had to show that he was on our side. Then his cowardice took over again and he retreated."

"Still," Sabina said, putting her leather jerkin on. "It's interesting that he wants to rebel. And that he has noticed the king keeping secrets. I assume he means other than the covert labour camps and assassinations of anyone who dissents?"

"I suppose so." Eleksander couldn't stop himself from adding the question burning in his mind. "Do we want to know about this new secret? If we stay and find out, we get pulled further into this mess. We get wedged between the Twelve and the king once more, risking death from either side."

"I don't think the Twelve are as murderous as the king," Sabina said thoughtfully. "Tutor Rete was unhinged when he killed. It wasn't sanctioned by the other members."

Avelynne hummed. "Still, they did commission one murder."

"Yes, but that was to protect themselves from detection and being executed by the king, Ave," Eleksander said. "Wrong as it was, *some* would argue that it was self-defence."

They all fell silent, hearing only the sound of Kall's big paws and their boots, with the Hall of Explorers emblem imprinted on them, against the stone slabs.

There were things that they knew but that didn't have to be said out loud.

They had no good options.

They couldn't trust anyone.

No one would help them.

No one would listen to them.

What hope did four uncertain eighteen-year-olds have if even the members of the Twelve — respected and intellectual councillors of the long dead Queen — couldn't make the people believe them about King Lothiam's plans to take over the world with force? Or that he was using his tithes and riches to indulge himself and his power instead of fighting the silver beasts or helping the people of Cavarra in general. What could the four of them do?

Eleksander swallowed down his rage and helplessness. "If we leave, they'll take in new recruits for the second wave, ones that might not have any compunction about colonising and killing. Or ones that simply don't know all the facts and so are duped into obeying orders."

"We can't risk that," Sabina said.

Another beat of silence.

"We have another year before we sail. We have time to decide what to do and how to do it," Avelynne finally said, not sounding convinced.

No one mentioned that the king had threatened to speed up their sailing plans.

Hale put an arm around Ave. "You're right. We don't have to decide right now."

She leaned into his embrace, physically affectionate as always.

Eleksander's stomach ached. He'd give anything to have Hale hold him like that. For Hale to look at him with such utter adoration.

It wasn't fair. Avelynne loved them all as friends, but didn't want relationships, didn't want to fall in love. And, yet, both Sabina and Hale had fallen for her and begged for attention at her feet like overgrown puppies.

Meanwhile, here Eleksander was, lonely and so in love with Hale that it hurt. He understood Hale, he could help and care for him in so many ways. It wasn't fair that the wild Woodlander only saw him as a friend and roommate.

This day was getting worse by the moment. No doubt the midday meal would be salted cabbage soup. Again.

Chapter Three

SECOND MONTH OF TERM

Sabina squinted at Avelynne through the greyness of sharp, late winter sun as she and Kall entered the courtyard. Why was Avelynne crouched over like that?

Tutor Rogan was over at the castle for an audience with the king and had told them all to start sparring without him. Combat training had gone from being an hour a day to being nearly half the day and even Sabina, who together with Hale had the most muscle and endurance, was feeling the strain.

Now she saw what Avelynne was doing, she was trying to coax a whitengale into her hands. The white bird flapped on the ground, clearly injured since it hadn't flown off. Sabina rushed over, nearly tripping over the sparring sword that Avelynne had dropped.

Sabina commanded Kall to stay, wary of his hunting instincts kicking in, and then crouched over the bird, too. This songbird, from the North like her, wasn't fully grown. "Poor little mite. Is it hurt?"

"No, I cannot see any bodily injuries," Avelynne said softly. "I fear it was blinded by the sun glinting off my sword, then flew into the tower and concussed itself."

Hale came over to them, resting his sword casually against his shoulder. "Not everything is your fault, Ave. It might just have something wrong with it in general. Like in the head. Or in the eyes."

The bird squeaked and tried to get up but to no avail.

Sabina placed a hand on Avelynne's back, taking the responsibility from her. "If it can't fly, we'll take it to our bedchamber and nurse it until it's better."

Avelynne beamed at her, sending Sabina's heart soaring.

She couldn't help herself; she moved her hand from Avelynne's back up to her cheek for a caress. Avelynne let out a pleased hum and her breath steamed through the morning air. Sabina's gaze stuck on that beautiful steam-breathing mouth, and so she moved her hand again. This time to brush those warm lips with gentle fingertips and whisper, "My love."

Avelynne's eyes went wide and her breath halted.

Crap! That had been too much. Why had she done that?

They could cuddle and show affection, but anything *that* romantic and Avelynne froze. Sabina yanked her hand back and fixedly stared at the whitengale.

The bird fluttered its wings and, slowly, attempted another stand. This time it worked. It took a few steps, shaking itself, and then flew off, nearly hitting Eleksander who now joined them. He seemed about to say something when they were interrupted by a gruff voice shouting, "What in all the shitting silver beasts do you think you are doing?"

Tutor Rogan marched towards them, something like a rolled-up parchment in his hand.

"Um, discussing who spars with whom," Avelynne invented.

Rogan didn't look convinced. "We will get to that later. First, some information. Tomorrow morning, you will travel to the shipyard with me to be introduced to some of your sailors and the physician you have been assigned. And, you have the fortune of seeing your longship, which is almost finished."

Hale did a double take. "So soon? It's still winter. Moreover, we're not sailing until next year?"

"That was the original plan. Now, you're sailing as soon as possible."

They four of them shared glances.

"Are you questioning orders straight from the king?" Rogan bellowed.

"No," Sabina said, before Hale could answer and get himself ten blows with Rogan's belt. Or two-hundred laps around the academy. Or be expelled.

"Good. I will cut off all your heads before I return to the king with the news that I cannot control you." His gaze shot to the king's castle in the distance. "While you were home suckling at your mothers' teats, I got myself a seat by the king's right-hand side. I will not let him down."

Sabina noted the disbelief on the other three's faces. Rogan sounded... reverent? It was like seeing a killer shark roll over to have its belly rubbed.

Rogan shook himself off. "Pick up your weapons. Let's see if we can whip you into some sort of accept-able fighting shape before we send you out into the abyss."

They began their sparring and spent the long lesson getting more or less beaten up by their loathed tutor. After that, the rest of the day's lessons went by in a daze. They were all too focused on the bigger picture to worry about math or drawing perfect topography. Even Hale only half-heartedly teased Eleksander for being a "Lakelander coin hoarder" and Avelynne for being "soft hearted Peakdweller" when the opportunities arose.

Lessons finished early because they had a celestial navigation class after darkness had properly fallen. This meant they had a longer than normal dinner break between their final magic practise and what Sabina preferred to call the stargazing lesson. It sounded less intimidating that way.

They trudged to the great hall for the evening meal without a word.

Until Hale said, "So, sad sacks. How about we get Ghar to sneak us out some brandy after we've eaten?"

"That might just be the best idea your thick head ever came up with," Sabina said, boxing his shoulder.

Hale grinned, clearly too pleased to even come up with a teasing retort.

Chapter Four

A WAVE OUT OF GOLDEN STARLIGHT

After dinner, Eleksander was eager for that brandy, despite rarely drinking alcohol. Their meal had not only been eaten in tense silence but had been sparse and dull. The servants must have struggled to find something the silver beasts had left uneaten to make a good meal. Or perhaps they too were having a strange day and the intended dishes had burned or been ruined.

Dropping her spoon into her bowl of inedible soup and standing, the ever-hungry Sabina asked, "Hale, do you reckon you could get Ghar to smuggle out some of the treats saved for the next Hall of Explorers feast as well as the brandy?"

Those feasts took place once or twice during a term, usually whenever the king decided to come by and check on his mapmaking magicians. Since Ghar believed they deserved the treats more than the spoiled king did, Eleksander was ready to wager he'd be happy to sneak them something.

He'd been right. The trip to Ghar's quarters resulted in a package of not only the bottle of brandy but also parcels of spiced nuts and booze-soaked raisins being delivered to them a short while later. They hid in Eleksander and Hale's bedchamber to enjoy their pilfered treasure. There was quite a while until the celestial navigation lesson since true darkness fell later now that winter was on its last legs, so they took the time to savour the treats.

Eleksander watched as Hale threw a handful of raisins into his rough, lovely mouth.

It had been close to two months since spring term had begun and he was no further into the plan of letting Hale know he cared for him, wanted him, loved him with every part of his being. They just kept on being friends, testing Eleksander's battered heart a little more each day. There had been one or two significant glances during dressing and undressing but that might've been wishful thinking on Eleksander's part. Hale kept talking about Avelynne. Wasn't she warm-hearted? Wasn't she brave for standing up to her parents? Wasn't she just the pinnacle of female beauty? The annoying part was that Eleksander could only agree, loving Avelynne as a sister.

Even now, as they sat eating and drinking, Hale's gaze was fixed only on Avelynne.

Still, Eleksander could console himself with one thing. During the Winter Solstice break he knew Hale had only sent one or two letters to Avelynne and barely a note to Sabina.

However, he had sent quite a few letters to Eleksander.

On the surface, that had been due to him having questions about archery, a discipline of fighting in which Hale was trying to improve and he knew Lakelanders, Eleksander in particular, excelled at it. The letters had been short, as always with Hale, and his abrupt sentences and sparse words never showed much emotion. Nevertheless, Eleksander knew there was emotion in the fact that he bothered sending letters at all. After all, if he only wanted to learn about archery, there were plenty of Woodlanders around him that he could learn from. Or he could've waited until they were back at the Hall of Explorers. No, it wasn't just that. He'd been reaching out and Eleksander appreciated it more than he could say.

He appreciated everything about Hale. Surreptitiously, so the other lad wouldn't see his yearning, he drank him in where he sat, slumped against a bed while snacking and listening to Avelynne and Sabina discuss something about snow.

His frame, shorter and slimmer than Eleksander's own, was filled with cut and corded muscles. Peeking out from under the tunic and his rolled-up britches—Hale wasn't a fan of clothes against his skin, no matter how cold it was out—were the scars making white lines on that coppery tan. Hale was rubbing his eyes. Those mischievous, black eyes that flashed whenever Hale lost his temper, which he did far too often, but somehow managed to also make attractive. Especially now that he had learned to lessen the outbursts and to apologise afterwards.

Eleksander had never had a crush this deep. Pathetic as he found it, he hung on Hale's every word. Tried to decipher his every mood, guessing his needs and wants and fulfilling them. In return, he found Hale relying on him more and more. Even showing with friendly, little gestures that he appreciated him, like remembering what Eleksander wanted for breakfast and preparing it for him, a gesture so unlike Hale that Avelynne had marvelled at it every morning.

Eleksander declined the nuts Sabina was handing him and ordered his face not to smile as he thought of the main way he saw Hale returning his attention: he asked Eleksander to do every workout with him despite usually preferring to do it without company, since no one could keep up with how hard he pushed himself. During the workouts, he even complimented Eleksander on his strength and the movements he could achieve with his broad frame.

That was something Eleksander knew Hale liked about him: the swimmer's build that came from his childhood splashing and swimming with his sisters in the lake on the Aetholo grounds.

Yes, that was something he had and that Avelynne, pretty as she was, could never compete with. Not that there was any competition. If it wasn't for the fact Avelynne had said she only wanted to be friends with them all, and her strong affection for Sabina, he assumed Hale and Avelynne would be a couple now.

Hale yawned, loud enough to startle Eleksander out of his thoughts. The Woodlander's body was slack and casual as he sat on the floor with his head leaning back on Eleksander's bed, running a hand through that short, constantly dishevelled hair and sipping at the brandy bottle before handing it to Sabina.

She reached over Kall, the snowtiger asleep between them, and took the bottle while saying, "One last sip, then we should get going. Like Rogan said to me: 'There is to be more doing and less studying at this academy.' Or something like that."

"Well, technically, we are going to a lesson so that is studying," Eleksander said as he stood up.

Hale chuckled, showing that quick and cheeky smile which always made Eleksander lose himself. "Oh dear, soft heart, she knows that. She was making a point about how Rogan and the other royal lackeys keep hurrying us up."

"Aye," Sabina said, taking a swig and standing as well. "While we were warned this might happen, I still wonder about the reasons behind why we're prepping to sail so soon."

"The king is impatient and wants his new land, not caring if we are prepared for the journey since we are expendable?" Avelynne suggested.

"If we're so expendable, why don't they have a third wave starting their studies?" Sabina sucked her teeth. "No, something else is behind it. There's something we're not seeing."

"Who can say? And, frankly, who cares?" Hale said. "I'm tired of trying to figure out what's going on. I'm going to focus on being a student, and then on being a captain and mapmaker."

"Taking things one day at a time?" Eleksander said.

Hale smacked him on the back. "Yes, exactly!"

The other three shared glances, fully aware that none of them could live like that, even if they wanted to.

Eleksander straightened his clothes and said no to one last swig of brandy. It was fine to be a tiny bit tipsy to cope with your world shifting, but it was not fine to be drunk during lessons.

They all headed out to practise navigating by the night sky. The last lesson before they went to see their ship. Imagine that. Eleksander regarded the cold stars and tried not to shiver, but he failed.

Moments later, they stood huddled in the courtyard, the air thick with that metal and earthy scent of frozen ground thawing.

Avelynne rubbed her hands. "Winter might be on its way out, but it's not giving up without a fight, is it?"

While the night was indeed cold, the brandy still warmed Eleksander's belly. More warming still, and cutting through his feeling of impending doom, was the sensation of wanting to catch every moment and enjoy it as much as possible. Probably due to that aforementioned doom. He saw it in the others as well, a sort of unnatural giddiness.

He put his arm around Sabina, who was nearest. She happily leaned in but received one of his braids to the face in the process. She spluttered, jolted, and eyed the braid with that serious warrior glare of hers, making everyone laugh, including Sabina herself.

Maybe it was his tipsy mind becoming nostalgic, but the delicious treats they'd had combined with their being out so late together, giggling and looking at the sky, reminded him of something from his childhood. The Aetholos would always visit the fair when it came to town. There were games, peculiar animals, and bonfires. They'd eat far too many roasted chestnuts, the distinctive nutty flesh almost dry against his tongue, and bags of butter-fried oakenberries, the latter he would usually donate to his sisters since they loved them. All of it washed down with hot leaf tea and stolen sips of their parents' warmed plum brandy. There was that same sense of magic he couldn't understand, mixed with fear of the unknown. The multitudes of stars above showing that he was but a single, tiny speck in a giant world and that he could not understand anything, no matter how hard he tried.

There was a hint of fate in the air. A sense of important things about to happen. A storm about to break.

The sense of awe faded as a thought hit him. If he died at sea, or if the king had him killed for treason, he'd never see the fair again. His sisters would never forgive him for that.

They all broke apart and stood straight as

soldiers as Tutor Hathleen joined them. She carried a lantern held aloft. It had red glass to not outshine the stars, and under her arm were five long spyglasses. Eleksander eyed them carefully. Were these the ones they'd take on their journeys?

She handed out the spyglasses and they all focused up on the stars, picking up from their last celestial navigation lesson.

"Now, what is it you need to find first?" Hathleen said.

"The cresting wave," Avelynne said.

Eleksander watched the set of stars that, if connected, resembled a rising wave created out of golden starlight. It had always been his favourite. As a child because he found it the brightest and prettiest, and now because the constellation's ever-moving placement in the sky could help him tell the time as well as his longitude and latitude.

"That is it, yes," Tutor Hathleen said in her delicate voice. "And, from its location, you can find the most important single star, especially for sailors. The..."

"Utter Northern Star," Eleksander filled in.

"Precisely," Hathleen said. "Let's move on to the lesser, but equally important, constellations. What else shines bright tonight?"

Hale, clearly drunk on brandy and the beauty of the stars, leaned in close to Eleksander and whispered in his ear. He was so close that his breath tickled into the shell of Eleksander's ear and all the way down his neck.

"Can you imagine when we sail? Standing on deck together like this." Hale paused to clear his groggy voice and Eleksander took the chance to take a gulp of air to calm himself. Hale smelled of the brandy and that constant peppery scent of his skin.

By the waters, how Eleksander *loved* that pink pepper smell.

Hale spoke on, "Watching the same stars but with the ocean around us? Free from the tutors and the king, relying on our own wits."

Eleksander turned his face, getting close enough that his mouth was a fraction from Hale's.

"And on each other."

"Yes," Hale said, the word ghosting breath onto Eleksander's own lips. "Each other."

They kept eye contact, Eleksander's face tipped down a little to be right opposite the shorter Hale's. How drunk was the Woodlander? Usually when Eleksander got this close, Hale made a joke or relieved the tension in some other way. Now, he was quiet, letting the tension linger.

His ink-black eyes seemed to reflect the stars and Eleksander's heart hammered like a mad thing.

Elya Hathleen coughed in a marked, attention-grabbing way. "Master Hawthorn, Master Aetholo, are you two listening to me?"

"Yes, Tutor Hathleen," they both said before returning their focus to identifying stars and constellations.

All while Eleksander's head swam.

Chapter Five

INSPECTING THE LONGSHIP

The next morning arrived, bringing dread and anticipation.

Sabina wanted to yawn but her body was too tense to be properly tired, despite the lack of sleep and their late night yesterday.

The four of them stood by the academy's gates. Waiting. Silent as the tomb.

They were going to go to see their longship. What would it look like? Would it feel like home?

Rogan appeared, badly shaved and smelling of ale. "This way, toddlers. Do *not* dawdle."

As they marched behind him to the Hall of Explorers' carriages, Sabina saw some servants with paint brushes.

"Oh excellent, the place could use a spruce up," Avelynne said, having followed Sabina's gaze.

Sabina, however, stopped dead. The building was made up of grey, utilitarian stone, only one small area was painted. Right above the gates was the Hall of Explorers' black emblem with a khaki ship and in bold emerald green shone the motto of the academy: "To Explore, never Exploit."

The servants, helped along by the academy's gruesome groundskeeper Adelard, were painting over it with the red and gold shades of the King's royal emblem. The reassuring motto disappeared, letter by letter.

Sabina spared a glance at the banners with the academy's emblem flying proud on tall poles. How long before they were taken down?

She clenched her jaw. If the king figured she and the other second wavers would rid themselves of those watchwords as easily, he better think again.

Avelynne gave a worried hum. "Ah, not a spruce up. A cover up. I wonder what it is King Lothiam is trying to expunge the most, our wish to explore or our determination to not exploit or colonise?"

Sabina was about to reply when Rogan bellowed, "I said do not dawdle!"

This was one order Sabina did not mind obeying. She took Avelynne's hand, their fingers interlacing, and then hurried over to the others.

When they arrived outside the shipyard, Hale held the carriage door open for the other members of the second wave and Kall. Tutor Rogan had decided to ride his massive, showy warhorse beside the carriage. No surprise there.

The cold air was heavy with the scent of the sea as well as tar and wood from the ships. The view was even lovelier. The sea back home in the North had been frozen solid when she travelled past it on her way to the academy, thereby hiding its dangerous, giant waves and lethal currents. This sea, while the same body of water, was so different. Winter was faltering here, so this stretch of sea only had a few tiny ice floes dotted across its surface. It wasn't nearly as dark, wave-filled, or unruly either. It was a tranquil lake compared to the sea back home. That was calming, at least. She'd be able to protect the others on a sea like this one.

Eleksander stood next to her, his elbow nigh at her shoulder. It still surprised her that someone so gentle and sensitive could be so big. That was what happened when you grew up in the rich and balmy Lakelands, she supposed. Plenty of swimming, medicines, rest, and healthy food.

She tried to swallow down a hint of bitterness at how different lives could be.

She knew she was muscled and curvy, but those curves always lessened during the food-low winters.

Now her veins showed across her muscles, ones formed out of necessity from chopping wood fast before her fingers froze, and the remainder of the curves were only a heritage from ancestors who had to store more fat to survive the ceaseless winters.

She hoped they'd find new land with plenty of food. Her people went hungry and she was the one sent to fix it. She had to fix it.

Sabina wondered where the other two were and saw them standing close to each other by the shipyard's door, giggling. Hale caressed Avelynne's hair, smoothing it down even though it was as sleek and glossy as always.

Sabina's heart clenched in protest. She couldn't say anything about it, though. Avelynne had made no commitment to her.

"Isn't it odd to think that the first wave have lived here all these weeks?" Eleksander suddenly said. "Not just coming here in daytime to practise sailing but actually sleeping on blankets in the shipyard, next to or on their longship so they could get used to it." His elegant features were struck with wonder.

She smiled at him, glad to have a friend who she could be completely comfortable with, since he was neither her unrequited crush, like Avelynne, or the other person enamoured with said crush, like Hale.

"I suppose it makes sense. We won't have beds on the ship, so we'll sleep either sitting on one of the rowing benches, curling up on the deck, or we have to come ashore and make camp somewhere."

"Get used to sleeping rough," Rogan said, inserting himself into the conversation without preamble. "There shall be no more of your fancy comforts, but salted meat and fish to eat, and drinking only water and diluted apple beer. How will your map drawing and arithmetic skills help you with that, huh?"

He strode into the enormous wooden shipyard without another word.

Sabina scoffed and mumbled, "Maggot-brain," as they followed him. When they got inside, the sight of the first wave's longship — hauled back up into the shipyard for maintenance she guessed — hitched Sabina's breath. The ship was as long as the name implied, with the head of a dragon carved in wood at the bow. The big square sail made her stop mid-step. She'd seen sails on fishermen's boats, but they were never this size. In general, this ship was so much larger than any craft she'd ever seen.

She reached out to touch what must be some sort of barnacle stuck at the front of the ship but pulled back, wondering if it was dead or alive.

"Look," Hale called. "I can see the steering oar!"

He was pointing to the oar fastened to the right side of the ship's stern. Right side? Sabina slapped her thigh, reminding herself to start using the terms port and starboard instead of left and right, even if it was only in her thoughts.

She took the whole vessel in. It gave a sensation of simple robustness, smelling of wood, sea salt, and tar. The rowing benches made uniform lines across the deck in beautiful, clean symmetry. The dragon's head was fierce and ornate, making the longship look like a creature about to take on the waves and cleave them without mercy.

"I should love to draw this," Avelynne breathed next to her.

"Wait until you can draw ours," Eleksander said with his sweet, lopsided smile. "I bet ours will be even prettier."

"Aye, yours'll have something better than a dragon as a wee figurehead," a man with a heavy Northern accent and a deep voice said. "It'll have a proud icewolf's head. I saw to that." The approaching man looked to be in his early sixties, with parchment-coloured skin and a beard that was even whiter, and was followed by an icewolf.

He bowed to them, a hand on his broad and rounded middle. "Ivar Nore. I'm working on your ship, the Wolfsclaw. I'll also be one of your sailors. I've been a fisherman and boatbuilder for forty years, so while I cannot help you with your maps or your orders from our great king, I'll help you brave the waves."

Our great king? Sabina thought. *How can people say that when he has labour camps where people work themselves to death for fictitious crimes? Without a trial or any notice of when or if they might be let out, just put in there to be silenced.*

She supposed she'd answered her own question. Silenced people didn't unveil terrible truths. Their deaths or cut-out tongues left surviving Cavarrians thinking they had a "great" king.

"Thank you," Avelynne said, always the first to be polite. "We shall need your guidance and we're lucky to have someone with your experience and knowledge on board the... Sorry, what was her name?"

"The Wolfsclaw. Named her myself, I did," he said while patting his icewolf. "It will be an honour to sail with you. For our generous King Lothiam. For our beautiful Cavarra. And, of course, to rid us all of those vile silver beasts, which'll be the sweetest revenge!"

"Revenge?" Sabina asked, unsure if she should pry.

He averted his face, blinking fast but speaking slow. "Aye, the wife and I, we... lost a little 'un to those beasts a few years back, never even had time to name the wee bairn. That's why I'm so relieved to be here in the Centre with my family now, where the silver beasts are kept out and it's safe."

Safe. Sabina hadn't thought of the Centre as a

safe place for a long time, hadn't thought about how anyone else living here saw the state of their kingdom.

"Yes, they're kept out. By being pushed into the four counties for others to fight best they can," Hale muttered.

Ivar gave him a blank look. "What do you mean?"

"I mean that the king lies."

The others all tensed. Was Hale really trying this here and now?

"Haven't you ever noticed discrepancies in what he says, Ivar? He demands higher tithes but says no coin is coming into court." Hale didn't sound as confrontational now, more coaxing instead. "Brainwashed youths are being forced out on icy seas, armed to the teeth. Does that sound like a king who cares about his subjects? Like a king who wants said youths to trade peacefully?"

Ivar blinked a few times, as if trying to clear his eyes. They all waited for his reply, like an axe would fall and either cut their bonds or their necks.

"I... I'm not sure what you're talking about, lad. King Lothiam is a good king. He cares about us and he rules us well. He will make Cavarra safe and prosperous again."

As expected, then. Sabina saw the others slump and go still. Only Avelynne moved, as she put a hand on Ivar's sleeve. "We're incredibly sorry to hear about your child."

"Yes! We are," Hale hurried to say, looking embarrassed at himself for not saying that first.

Ivar bowed a little as thanks. "As I said, the best revenge will be to find new land and leave the silver beasts here to die a slow death." He crossed his arms over his broad chest. "When they've eaten all the grain and there is no more magic to sustain them, they'll all starve. Aye, that'll be a fine day!"

"Indeed," Sabina said. Because what else was there to say? How could she rid this man of his hope that all would be fine when they found new land? How could she take away his trust in the king who was meant to protect them all but who only cared about himself? How could she shatter his much-needed perceived safety? Even when Hale had tried, nothing had come of it.

Perhaps their upcoming journey would change that.

Ivar smiled, pulling his icewolf back since it kept sniffing Kall's rear. "Anyway, come look at your magnificent Wolfsclaw. She's all but ready to carry you to the horizon!"

They walked past the first wave's dragon-clad longship and, behind it, found another craft. It had no sail, the tall mast naked and forlorn. Its wood appeared untreated, but the framework of the ship was complete. And, yes, there was the carved head of an icewolf at the bow. Sabina respected any shipbuilder who took the chance to honour their animal companion by immortalising it like this.

Polishing, or perhaps tarring, the wolf's head with a rough cloth was a woman who was older than them but certainly younger than Ivar. In her thirties, maybe?

"This is Taferia Palm," Ivar said. "She has been helping me design and build your ship. She'll be sailing with us, too."

The last name referencing a tree gave away her nationality. So did her vigorous appearance: strong, nimble with a good posture and the weathered face of one who spent much time outside. A Woodlander. Her skin, a few shades lighter brown than Eleksander's, glowed with health, making Sabina suddenly aware of how deathly white and weak she must look in comparison. She had to get her strength back.

Hale whooped. "Another Woodlander on board! That's grand!"

"Mm-hm," Taferia said, not stopping her work. "The Physician is a Woodlander, too. Well, no, he was born right on the edge of the Woodlands and the Lakelands." She clicked her tongue. "Feels more like a Lakelander to me, though. All book smarts and no love for nature."

"You've met our onboard physician?" Avelynne asked.

"I have." There was a tone to her voice, one that the enthusiastic Ivar hadn't had.

"Come on then, tell us what he was like," Hale said. "We're to meet him today, apparently."

"I don't think you will, lad. He's at court, tending to the king. Physician Faville is, well, now, how to say this?" She stopped polishing, weighing the cloth in her hand. "He is... a king's man, through and through."

"Ah. Say no more," Sabina said, glancing back to Tutor Rogan who was shouting at someone.

"Not quite like that," Taferia answered. "No, Faville was quieter and more scholarly about it. Anyway," she said. "It's dangerous to speak too much of such things."

Sabina breathed a sigh of relief. Not all of their sailors had bought into the propaganda coming from the court.

There was a bang as something was dropped over by the first wave's longship.

"Not as dangerous as what awaits them, though," Taferia murmured, indicating the first waver who had dropped an oar and caused the noise.

When had they arrived? As always, the first wave thought themselves too grand to even acknowledge the younger class of recruits. Avelynne had probably been right when she said that the king and some of the tutors tried to poison the two classes against each other. It made Sabina want to go over there and talk to the first wave, not that doing so had ever gotten her more than icy stares and curt replies.

"Are you referring to their upcoming journey?" Avelynne asked.

Taferia frowned. "I mean the fact that they keep sailing beyond the coastline before spring has fully sprung. Ask any fisherman, even if you see no more ice floes, you don't sail that far until the waters are safe for our boats."

"Well, we must all hurry to find new land and it is only wee trips beyond the coastline. It should be safe," Ivar said, sounding as though he was trying to convince himself.

The shipyard's large doors were open, so they could see the vast sea. Its waves were growing with the increasing morning wind, tumbling remnants of ice into their froth.

"I see your point, Taferia," Avelynne said. "I mean, we're used to handling the silver beasts after all these years and the unexplored lands aren't going anywhere. Why not wait a couple more weeks?"

Taferia raised her eyebrows in a meaningful way. "That is a very good question. There are a lot of questions that no one seems to be asking."

She said the last words quietly and then returned to work.

Sabina watched the sea again, watching a wave crest into bone-white spray. She wished she still had the feeling of relief she got when she first saw the ocean today. Sure, it looked safer than the one back home. Nevertheless, if there was one thing Sabina had learned about the sea, it was that it was always more treacherous than you thought.

Chapter Six

ONE LAST ESCAPADE

Some weeks later, in a classroom thawing with the early spring warmth, Eleksander tried not to laugh as Hale put his pen down and caught his gaze to yawn theatrically. They had arithmetic with Tutor Hathleen and were calculating distances, one of Hale's least favourite subjects. Still, Hale's bad behaviour shouldn't be encouraged. Not that Eleksander could stop himself from giggling even if he wanted to.

Tutor Hathleen wasn't watching them though; she was busy reading the piece of parchment nailed on the wall. It had been hung this morning by some unknown hand and proclaimed the excellence of Cavarrians and how they deserved to take all of the bounty of the world for their own, no matter the cost or the methods needed. Subtle as a spike to the head.

Eleksander wondered what Hathleen thought of the decree, her pointy, little face gave nothing away.

The door flew open, distracting them all. A servant rushed in and stuttered, "P-pardon me, ma'am, there is n-news for you regarding your students."

Tutor Hathleen, head of the first wave, jerked around like prey hearing a predator at his words. "What is it?"

The hairs on the back of Eleksander's neck stood up. The first wave had completed a large number of day trips in the last few weeks, increasing the journey's length every time. Had Tutor Myle mentioned that they began a longer voyage last week? Or two weeks ago? Eleksander had been too preoccupied with everything to note what the other class was doing.

The servant murmured something. Elya Hathleen went as white as salt and staggered back.

The servant left and Hathleen stared glass-eyed into the lesson room, as if not seeing the four students.

At length, she grabbed the edge of the desk. "The, um, the lesson is over for now. Return to your bedchambers."

"What has happened?" Sabina asked.

"Do as I say. Return to your chambers."

"Oh, come on!" Hale slapped his palm against his

desk. "Something serious has clearly happened to the first wave! You have to tell us. We're not children, we deserve to know."

Her eyes regained some focus. "Fine. They have not returned from their latest journey; they were scheduled to do so two days ago. Driftwood came in with the tide today, matching the oak their longship was made of, but we cannot be sure that it is..."

"Flotsam from their shipwreck," Avelynne quietly filled in for her.

"Return to your chambers and wait for further instructions," Tutor Hathleen repeated, without any feeling in her voice.

This time, they all obeyed.

In their small room, Eleksander and Hale waited. Eleksander sat on his bed, trying to read but actually watching the other lad chew a thumbnail and pace. They'd been here for quite a while and staying put wasn't Hale's strength at the best of times.

When the door finally opened, it turned out to be Tutor Myle.

"Well met," the tutor said, dragging a trembling hand through his thick hair. "I, um, I have just been to speak with your classmates to inform them, uh, and now you, too, that the king has ordered that the second wave will sail tomorrow."

Hale jolted. "What?"

Myle held up his hands in a placating gesture. "You must try to find and rescue the first wave."

"So, our first sail will be a rescue mission, then," Eleksander said, mentally preparing himself.

Myle squirmed. "Well, the king says that when you have sailed that far, you may as well do some exploration as well." He must've sensed that Eleksander was about to argue because he once more held his hands up. "Obviously, the main objective is to find the first wave and bring them home."

"All right," Hale said, shifting his footing with impatience. "Where do we start? And what tools are we given?"

"We know the coordinates of their devised route and they have been gone for about eight days. They were meant to return after five to six days, depending on windspeeds, but..." Myle blanched. "They clearly did not. Um, so you will follow their course. On your ship, which was finished a couple of days ago."

Hale scoffed incredulously. "Follow their exact route. In an identical ship. With the same bare-bones crew? But with half the experience and training?" He threw his hands out. "So, you're not only asking that we do some exploring and mapmaking while trying to rescue other students, you're also tossing us out there half-cocked into a certain suicide mission?"

Myle was about to answer but Hale wasn't finished.

"And if we go missing as well? That's convenient considering the king thinks we know too much, isn't it? Tell me why we shouldn't tell the king to go shit himself and refuse to sail?"

"You four are the only ones with an accumulation of the various types of talents and education needed," Tutor Myle entreated. "You have your navigational training, the knowledge of the sea, the general survival skills, and the fighting prowess if something goes wrong. You are the best suited. Especially as you are young enough to survive and—"

"Able to handle the malnutrition all Cavarrians have suffered. Yes, we've heard this bullshit before," Hale interrupted, the veins in his neck standing out. "And we know that the king did not want his explorers young because we're healthier and hardier." He pointed a finger at Myle. "Lothiam wanted us young because he figured we wouldn't disagree with him. Or understand that he was brainwashing and using us!"

"Hale," Eleksander warned.

Myle may be on their side but he was also a cowardly suck-up to anyone in power. Besides, trusting their elders had gone terribly for them in the past.

Hale turned to Eleksander. "I'm not going to stay quiet about this, Sander! That shitbag in a crown thinks our age makes us controllable, witless murder-machines." Those veins in his neck stood out even further and his face was reddening. "It's bad enough that everyone seems to think our age means no one'll take us seriously if we tell them uncomfortable truths. Now Lothiam thinks that we're naïve enough to jump into death happily as well. It's not right!"

"No, it's not, but right now I'm more worried about you. Try to calm a little, maybe do the equilibrating breathing I taught you," Eleksander said gently. He didn't mention that he worried about what Hale might tell Myle. Or what the king might do if he found out they spoke like this. He didn't have to.

Hale tried to take deep breaths, but it sounded more like he was forcing masses of air in and out as if he was angry at it.

Tutor Myle, on the other hand, was backing out of the room. "Well, I have completed my task and passed on the message, so I shall take my leave," he snipped with an offended expression. "Prepare yourselves to sail tomorrow and come find me or another tutor when you have calmed down and have *practical* questions."

As soon as he had left, Eleksander and Hale ran for the door and through the hallway until they got to Sabina and Avelynne's room.

They had barely knocked before they were let in.

"We sail tomorrow?" Sabina whispered, her lips bloodless and her eyes unblinking.

Kall was pacing and growling, clearly picking up on the upset mood.

"It's madness! No, it's *utter shit*," Hale snapped.

"It's both," Sabina said, sounding dazed.

"It's not a complete surprise, though is it? Let's all calm down and think this through together," Eleksander said. He was as shocked and worried as everyone else but sometimes pretending to be composed made him feel calmer.

"I say we refuse to go," Hale growled.

Avelynne sat on her bed, fretting with her necklace. "If we don't pretend to go along with it, King Lothiam will simply send fishermen and soldiers to command the ship and the sailors instead. They stand even less chance to survive and find the first wave than we do."

"Aye," Sabina agreed. "Also, Lothiam will no doubt pick violent people who will actually conquer, steal, and terrorise, like Tutor Rogan."

"So, we sail to rescue the first wave and promise to colonise but then just... don't?" Hale said with a confused frown.

"That is what Sabina and I propose. Basically, we follow orders but in our own way." Avelynne held up two fingers. "Firstly, save the first wave. I asked Tutor Myle what we are to do if we find them and he said that we should take them with us to explore and find land."

What?" Eleksander said. "That's ridiculous. The Wolfsclaw can't sail around with two full crews. We'll sink and run out of food! And what if they're injured?"

"Exactly. No one has put any thought or care into this," Avelynne said. "That is why Sabina suggested that we sail straight home with the first wave if we find them, in whatever state we find them. I agree and I think you two do as well?"

They both nodded.

She dropped one of the fingers. "Secondly, if we do come across new land while searching for the first wave and find it inhabited, we try peaceful trade and diplomacy and, if that doesn't work, we leave."

Sabina added, "And don't mention it to anyone when we get back."

"Sounds good," Eleksander said, happy someone had a plan. "And if we find uninhabited land, what do we do then? Follow orders and thereby give Lothiam another country to mismanage?"

"I didn't get that far." Sabina sat slumped on the

floor, patting Kall with a despondent expression. "I'm sorry."

"Don't apologise," Avelynne said, "It's not your job to solve everything."

"Back on topic," Hale growled. Only adding a, "Please," when he saw the others' faces.

"All right," Eleksander said. "So, do we plant the king's flag and give him a new continent to plague, probably dooming this new land to silver beasts and over-farming like here? Or, go along with the Twelve's plan to find land for them to place their secret base for launching their rebellion against the throne?"

"Can we trust the Twelve?" Hale scratched his head frantically. "With their lies, secrets, and killings? We keep wondering that and not getting any answers. I mean, shit, I haven't heard from them since Rete's death. Have you?"

They all shook their heads.

There were so many questions. So much to decide and then live with. It made Eleksander nauseous with nerves.

Avelynne clasped her hands tight. "Also, if the king finds out that we were working with them, we know what he'll do to us and that is a choice we are free to take. However, there's also what he'll do to our friends and family..." She let the sentence fall heavy on the floor between them.

"He might torture or kill our loved ones, and us, if we come back without finding new land too, though," Eleksander said. "The only way we can keep us and them unscathed is if we either manage to hide our plans from him, or if we do what he says. The latter we can't do and when it comes to the first... I don't like our odds, Lothiam has eyes and ears everywhere."

Sabina stood, brushing herself off. "We will find the first wave, and perhaps new land while we're out there. While we do that, we'll come up with a plan to reveal the king's behaviour to his people, one that also safeguards us and our loved ones."

"You really think so?" Eleksander asked, not wanting to say how unlikely he found that idea. What brilliant plan could they devise out on the dangerous seas that they couldn't concoct here in the comfort of a safe, quiet bedchamber?

Sabina's eyes were unblinking with no hint of that violet that Avelynne always enthused about, they were pure metal-blue determination now. "Aye. We'll find a way to make him reveal who he really is. People won't listen to us? Then we'll find a way to show them."

Avelynne chewed her lower lip. "I'm sure we will. Nonetheless, I'm wondering if it might not be a good idea to share some of what we uncovered during the first term and this one with others? In case we don't survive."

"Who would we tell?" Hale said.

Avelynne kept worrying at her lip. "I think I shall write a letter to my family. Little as they like me, they dislike the king more. At least sometimes. They complain bitterly about him and his high tithes, then it's like they forget when something else to complain about arises." She paused. "Anyway, whether or not they believe me or act on the information, at least I'll know I tried telling someone. The secret won't die with me."

"I suppose I could tell my uncle and my parents," Sabina said. "Although, they aren't usually interested in what I do or think. Still, as you say, Avelynne, even if they don't believe me, I'll have tried."

Eleksander wrapped his arms around himself, willing himself to tell them. "My parents do care. However, they're very busy and often think I overexaggerate. I'll send them a letter, though. My father is a successful and trusted merchant and my mother a rather famous musician. If I can get them to believe me, they'd be people that Lakelanders would listen to. It's just..."

Avelynne tilted her head. "What?"

Dread tingled through Eleksander. "I don't think they will. Look, don't be angry at me but during the

Winter Solstice I hinted at a few of the events and facts to my older sister." He kept his arms wrapped around himself as he hurled out the rest of his tale far too fast. "Since she was a servant here when it happened, Ellenaria believed me and was spitting venom at what Tutor Rete did and the king's true nature. But, the next day, it was like she had forgotten it all."

Avelynne shot him a reassuring smile. "We're not going to be angry that you told her. We all know Ellenaria is reliable."

"Aye. Moreover, you're not the only one who blabbed. I had to tell my uncle about Rete's death," Sabina said, then jerked her head back as if remembering something. "And you know what, any involvement of the king did seem to be swept under the rug. I didn't think about it then. Huh. That's odd."

"No one wants to speak ill of our beloved king, I guess." Hale went to spit on the ground but stopped in the last moment, probably remembering that he was in a bedchamber. "Anyway, I've no one to tell but Ghar. He doesn't listen to anything that doesn't concern nature, fighting, sex, or food." He scratched the back of his neck. "But I can send a note to the Warden of the Woodlands. She answers all letters, I hear. Even if just to tell the writer that they're a maggot-brain."

Sabina frowned at him. "Write to the leader of

the Woodlands? You sure that's a good idea? She might tell King Lothiam."

"No, she doesn't talk to anyone else in power unless absolutely necessary. Besides, we might as well take some risks since we're likely to end up like the first wave. Missing or dead."

The silence filled every corner of the room, pressing against the walls, making Eleksander's stomach sour and clench.

Sabina sat back down and called Kall to her, using him as a shield of fur and feline muscle. Avelynne fretted with her necklace again and Eleksander himself... Well, he kept looking to Hale.

No clue why. Hale's not usually the one with the answers, he mused.

Nevertheless, there was a comforting quality to Hale Hawthorn. His steady strength. His honesty. His stubborn way of getting through anything with the force of his iron body as well as his iron will. He was the only one of them who didn't overthink things and Eleksander would've given anything to halt his own overthinking right now.

His stomach pain worsened until he felt as though his bowels were full of poisonous adders, biting at his insides incessantly. He sat down next to Avelynne on her bed, clutching his middle. She put her hand over his, like she was helping him hold his innards inside him. Her hand was so small, pale, and fragile. Not the hand of someone who could survive the mission awaiting them.

The only sound in the room was Kall washing his paws with that massive tongue of his.

"Stand up," Hale barked.

"Oh, not now," Sabina said quietly.

Eleksander understood what she meant. As usual, Hale was about to tell everyone to get their act together and stop being so sensitive and worried all the time. No one wanted to hear that right now.

"No, listen, I want you all to come see something. We can write our farewell letters with all the fact-spilling after we've done this."

Avelynne hesitantly stood. "Done what?"

"Snuck into the armoury," Hale said with a wide grin. "I was told that on the morning of their first long sail, the first wave got to go into the armoury and choose a weapon. Not the blunt sparring swords and such, but real weapons." No one answered so he took a step closer to them and added, "We should go check it out beforehand. We don't want to make a bad last-minute decision. Shitting silver beasts, we can have *our pick of the lot!*"

Eleksander tried to ignore his stomach pain, immersing himself in the joy on Hale's face instead. Sneaking into the armoury was such a Hale thing to be excited about, and yet there was something fun about choosing which of the academy's many weapons he would pick. More than that, it was nice to think that he was allowed to choose something in this powerless situation and a certain safety in that he could pick out something he could use to defend the other three, their sailors, and himself with. Even if he had to do so because power-crazed adults were sending him unprepared into the maw of sea monsters, cold seas, unknown storms, and the hands of possible enemies. All for their own land grabbing greed or, in the case of the Twelve, their so far ineffectual rebellion. He got up too, forcing a smile in Hale's direction.

All eyes went to Sabina. Who sighed, like a tired mother with silly children, and stood as well.

Hale pumped a fist into the air before leading the way out. By the light of the stars and torchlight, they crept out across the quiet courtyard, avoiding the guards over by the gate.

It had the same sort of forbidden thrill as when they snuck out for secret swims last term and Eleksander, remembering the sight of Hale splashing in inky waters with his soaked tunic clinging to his body, looked to the lad in question.

He was skulking along the walls with unexpected, quiet grace, like a Woodlander jaguar hunting its prey, until he stopped by the doors to the armoury, quickly picked the lock, and opened them.

The four students sidled past the sparring

weapons and into where the much smaller collection of sharpened, usable weapons hung on the walls or stood in stands.

Sabina, a lover of fighting with axes and broadswords, dithered between the two-handers and the vast array of axes. Then she picked up a hefty axe with a small snowflake carved into the white-grey steel of its head. A proper Northern war axe with letters on the hilt.

With reverence, she ran her fingers over the hilt's carved word and whispered, "Grimfrost."

Named weapons were rare anywhere outside the North.

Eleksander was happy to see her infatuation, she so rarely allowed herself something that wasn't merely practical or necessary. This axe may be useful, but it was also pretty and a reminder of home. Sentimental, that was what Sabina would normally call it. Now, however, she picked up a harness for the axe and strapped it onto her back with an expression that seemed to wonder if she was allowed such a treasure.

She had her weapon. *Great*, Eleksander thought with fondness. *Now, what about the rest of us?*

As a Lakelander, Eleksander knew he'd be most comfortable and skilled with a longbow. And he had spent so much time and coin being taught how to make his own arrows if he ran out. Yes, a bow was the natural choice.

He picked out a beautiful yew bow which looked freshly strung. It wasn't as lavishly decorated as the ones he was used to, but it was large enough for his frame and to comfortably strap onto his back when not in use. He picked the quiver that held the most arrows and fastened it across his back, his heart thumping when he thought of how important this weapon would be.

Avelynne was over by the polearms, looking through them with careful hands.

"Are you searching for anything in particular?" Sabina asked her.

"I am and I found it!" Triumphantly, Avelynne grabbed a war scythe. Its long pole was almost as tall as her, and the curved blade gleamed lethal in the torch light.

Eleksander hummed, worry returning to his stomach. "Those are not very practical to carry around, Ave. Too heavy. Also, they are mainly used for battles against enemies on horseback?"

"I know," Avelynne said. "But I have worked on my strength since our first term. I'm much stronger now. Its weight matters not."

"And the fact that a sword, axe, dagger, or any other smaller weapon for melee might be a better choice?" Eleksander said, making his voice kind instead of lecturing.

She shrugged. "We might be fighting large beasts from the seas. Not to mention regular sharks and whales. A war scythe allows me to not only fight big creatures, but to fight from a distance. That may come in handy."

"Aha," Sabina said suddenly. She walked over and touched the war scythe. "I know where I've seen this before!"

Even in the dim light, Eleksander could see Avelynne blush but Sabina kept talking, "This is the weapon that Tutor Rogan said was too large for you. That day when we sparred with sharpened weapons, you know, when Hale forgave you for keeping your secret?"

Avelynne still blushed and fidgeted self-consciously but held on to her scythe as if someone was trying to take it away from her. "Rogan was wrong. Both about my lack of skills and that I couldn't fight with such a large weapon." She turned the polearm so the blade caught the light. "I will make this war scythe a symbol for that. When I find my confidence falling, I'll remember how I've mastered this weapon."

Now it made sense. Eleksander couldn't help but be proud of her. "Well, you *will* look exceedingly fearsome with that strapped to your back," he said.

Sabina ran her fingers down the scythe's handle. "Aye, and when we get back inside, I'll help you trim and sand down the handle to make it lighter and to fit you perfectly."

"That would mean the world to me," Avelynne whispered with reverence. "Thank you."

They shared a long look, one so intimate that Eleksander was about to turn away when Sabina said, "That leaves only our excited Woodlands warrior. Where is he?"

Eleksander couldn't see where Hale was, he must've climbed into the very back of the armoury, searching no doubt for the deadliest thing available.

"Anyone want to wager that Hale Hawthorn comes out of there with a trebuchet or some sort of battering ram?" he said, hearing how affectionate his voice sounded. Much akin to when his mother spoke of her "cute wittle housey kitten" who was a beast of a cat and the main predator of their town.

"Hm. No. He'd be annoyed by having to carry it," Avelynne answered, with similar affection. "You know what he's like, he'll want something that doesn't take up too much room or bother him when he's not using it."

Sabina shook her head and waded further into the armoury while calling, "Hale, pick something and let's go before we're caught."

A moment later, she came back out, dragging

Hale by the sleeve as he fiddled with a dusky-metalled weapon. As they got closer, Eleksander saw that it was a crossbow.

"Look at this sexy beast!" Hale said. "It's black for stealth, has a quick trigger, is light to carry, and ask me about its bolts!"

Avelynne scrunched her nose up. "All right. What part of it is the bolt?"

"They're the arrows of a crossbow," Eleksander answered.

Hale frowned. "Obviously. Have you not been listening in Rogan's projectiles lessons, Ave? Anyway, that's not what you were meant to ask!"

Avelynne stifled a smile. "My apologies. Tell me, Hale. What are its bolts like?"

"They have tips that spring out into thistles when inside your enemy. It also had the biggest, most well-filled quiver of them all!"

"Is that it?" Sabina said as she let him go. "It doesn't sing a song when you hit your target, too?"

"No," he said, missing the sarcasm and beaming like a proud new father, "but it does have a leather strap attached to both quiver and the bow, so you can wear it like a knapsack and have your hands free for using magic. Or punching."

Eleksander could feel just how high his eyebrows had risen. "Huh. I was so sure you'd pick a hand weapon to use in close combat. Don't you always say that staying back to fight is a Lakelander's tactic?"

"I do. And it is. That's why I also got these!" He preceded to show hidden blades in sheathes attached with straps around his ankles, inside his sleeves, and two small throwing knives along his lower back. All in all, making for six concealed knives and daggers of different sizes.

"You can't do that!" Sabina exclaimed. "We're allowed to take one weapon, no more."

"Yes, and doesn't that seem odd to you?" Hale said. "Why would they ask us to do something this dangerous without arming us to the teeth?"

Avelynne looked uncertain. "They want to keep the weight of the ship down, right? Besides, all the sailors will have a short sword each and we shouldn't need too much weaponry considering our mission is to find the first wave and then explore peacefully." She frowned. "No wait, Lothiam wants us to fight and conquer any people we meet."

Hale pointed to her. "Exactly! Also, a few knives and lighter weapons wouldn't weigh the ship down much. If we're meant to fight, why not arm us more?"

Even more questions. Eleksander was still painfully without answers.

Hale spoke on: "Is it because they think we're all going to die? And they don't want to waste the weapons? Huh?" No one answered. "Because that's how it feels to me. The king might want us to conquer for him, but he won't educate or arm us. Why? Because we're disposable."

"But there's no third wave to take our place if we die," Sabina said.

Hale scoffed. "Not yet. I bet our worm of a king has a plan for changing how the recruits are trained. Or which ones are picked. He no longer cares about hiding his plans. The shithead's getting bolder."

"Or more desperate," Eleksander interjected. Because there was something frantic about all of this. Something not properly thought through.

"Anyway," Hale said, patting his hidden knives. "I've not taken more than I can easily strap to myself and still move jump and swim unrestrictedly, you know I wouldn't do that."

"No. True. Well, fine, bring them," Sabina said. "But don't be surprised if Rogan notices, confiscates them all, and chops off your fingers for your insolence."

"Ha! He could try!" Hale cracked his knuckles. "Right, we should all go in and write some letters and then get some sleep."

A new worry popped up in Eleksander's mind. "About the letters... We might not want to trust this information about what the king actually wants, and about the Twelve, to the Hall of Explorers' letter ravens."

"No, I suppose not," Sabina muttered. "They stand out. And might be intercepted before they leave the Centre."

Eleksander nodded. "We don't want to give Ellenaria all the letters either, in case something happens to her." He swallowed hard at the thought. "Basically, we can't put all our valuables in one purse."

"Right," Sabina said. "I suggest you give your sister your letter, Sander. Hale hand-delivers his to Ghar to give to the Warden when we've sailed and he's returned to the Woodlands. And you leave your letter with Myllie, Avelynne." She motioned towards the servant's quarters where Myllie was probably asleep. Avelynne's maid had been planning on going back to Ironhold castle but new excuses to stay on a while longer kept popping up.

Eleksander had theories regarding the reasons for that.

Because the long journey back bored Myllie - Quite likely.

The climate being warmer and drier here - Somewhat likely.

The Hall of Explorers nearness to the beefy king's guards that she liked to flirt with - Extraordinarily likely.

"All right," Avelynne replied. "What about your letter?"

"Oh. Um. I didn't think of myself."

You never do, Eleksander thought. He did have a solution, though. "Sabina, perhaps you want to give your letter to Ellenaria, too? She can send it via a standard raven when her carriage stops at an inn for food and fresh horses?"

"Aye, I'll write it tonight and pop down to the servants' quarters before breakfast and give her the letter."

They said their goodnights and parted.

When Eleksander was back in their bedchamber and washing in front of their small mirror, Hale threw himself onto his bed and asked, "Do you think they'll let us come back here? After we've sailed and found new lands, I mean."

Eleksander rubbed the soapy cloth under his arms with vigour. "What for?"

Hale yawned and mumbled, "I don't know. More training?"

"I'm not sure they'll see a point in that. If they find we can explore, make maps, and captain a ship full of soldiers... They'll expect us to simply carry on doing the job."

Captain a ship full of sailors. His hand stilled. That responsibility was so much more real now. They hadn't even met the sailors; well, except for Ivar and Taferia. What if they all hated the spoiled, inse-cure, merchant's son? What if all his decisions were wrong and he did more harm than good? Thank goodness he had the other three to captain with him.

He was about to say something about that when he spotted Hale in the mirror's reflection. He was asleep. Of course he was. Eleksander went over and pulled the covers over the softly snoring Woodlander.

When he returned to the wash basin, he looked at his own reflection. Frown lines, worried eyes, and stubble on his usually so perfectly shaven chin. Unlike Hale, he wouldn't get much sleep tonight.

Chapter Seven

THE TIME HAS COME

Sabina leaned up on her elbows in bed, knocking over a book on longship schematics, and glanced over at the opposite bed. Avelynne was awake, too, clearly roused by the sounds of tutors and servants bustling about, preparing for the new day.

This wasn't just any day, though. Not for the second wave. It was sailing day.

Avelynne sat up, her nightdress having fallen off her left shoulder and her hair a sleep-mussed mess. Her beauty left an ache in Sabina.

Kall came over to greet her and Avelynne scratched his cheeks before kissing his wide head. She doted on the snowtiger in a way that Sabina had been told not to do since childhood up in the North. A companion was a respected counterpart to its human, functional and for protection, not a pet. You could show it some affection, but not spoil it. Much like her parents had raised Sabina and made her raise her siblings in turn.

Nevertheless, Sabina's heart soared every time she saw Avelynne lavish love and affection on the tiger. Kall and herself were as one and they both loved the young woman currently stretching and standing.

"Good morning, snowdrop. How did you sleep?"

Sabina had to yank herself out of her thoughts when she realised Avelynne was talking to her. "As well as can be expected considering what today is. What about you?"

"Same," she said, padding over to the wash basin and mirror.

She poured water from the jug into the basin. There was an unspoken deal between them, that Sabina turned her back as Avelynne made her ablutions. They had done so all last term and every morning of this one.

Now, however, Avelynne gave her a mischievous smile and said, "I suppose, since we will be doing everything in sight of each other on the ship, that you may as well watch this time?"

Sabina couldn't help it, she laughed. With joy as much as with excitement. It bubbled up from inside her and filled her entire tired body, and she knew she must be grinning like a mad person.

Avelynne's flirting could resolve so much tension and dread.

"Well now, is that appropriate, Countess?"

"I'm not a countess anymore. And it is not appropriate at all." Colour rose high on Avelynne's cheeks. "But it's what I'm in the mood for. It would take both our minds off the sailing, the fate of the first wave, the conspiracy, The Twelve, the king... all of it."

"Aye. That it would."

Sabina stood as well and closed the distance between them. Avelynne's nightdress was still adrift along her shoulder, and Sabina was starting to wonder if it was intentional since she hadn't pulled it back up.

That expanse of sweet skin, a forbidden glimpse, an illicit treat to touch.

"What," Sabina whispered, "if I want to do more than watch?"

"You know how attracted I am to you," Avelynne breathed. "How attracted I've been to you for months. You know I want you to do more than watch."

"You said that the four of us shouldn't complicate things with romance."

"I'm not talking about romance, snowdrop. I'm talking about knowing what your touch feels like before we head for what might be our death."

Sabina was barely breathing, her pulse pounding

in her fingertips as she reached out to touch Avelynne's slender, bared shoulder. Was it her imagination or did she see a little more muscle there now?

The skin was creamy, both in colour and in softness, smooth and inviting.

Sabina hesitated.

She had been in a relationship before she was accepted to the Hall of Explorers. Back when she was young enough to mistake admiration for love, she thought she had met the love of her life, until she got to know the girl and found out that not only was she vain and cruel, she was also betrothed to some lad from a less poor family.

They had never done more than fumbled under each other's clothes and kissed. The touches had been a teenager's excited fumbling, hot and fast.

This... This was different.

This simple touch of a shoulder was more intimate and meaningful than all the kisses and groping touches of her past combined.

She knew from anecdotal mentions in letters and conversations that Avelynne wasn't a virgin. In fact, she had plenty of experience.

Another impressive thing about her, Sabina admitted to herself as she stared at that beautiful shoulder.

She hadn't given Avelynne any clues about her own experience, only saying that she had a girlfriend once. Still, she was sure Avelynne knew. She always knew everything. As if to prove that, she seemed to know now that she'd have to take the first step. She placed her hand on Sabina's and laid it on her own naked shoulder. Sabina caressed along it and up the curve of her neck, fingertips grazing the silver chain of her necklace.

Avelynne hummed with pleasure, soft and quiet, and grasped Sabina's hips. Slow enough that she could ask her to stop, she tugged Sabina towards her. She got a whiff of the sweet smell of Avelynne's hair and then, before she knew what to do or say, they were kissing. First, their lips were only locked in the sweetest and gentlest of embraces, it was teasing in a way that made Sabina dizzy as much from arousal as the sheer fun of it. Then Avelynne moved her mouth to intensify the kiss and when Sabina felt the tip of a tongue between her lips, she opened them with a muffled moan and let Avelynne all the way in. Her heart pounded manically and her whole body pulsed with heat. That feeling of fun was changing, because this meant too much to just be exciting for her. She had wanted to be kissed by Avelynne for so long.

This moment was the core of her world now.

The kiss grew frenzied and soon they tumbled into bed, Avelynne laying perfectly on top of Sabina, her nightdress hiked up. One of Avelynne's legs slid between her own, the connecting touch making Sabina gasp into the open-mouthed kiss.

Her hands slid down Avelynne's back, only that thin nightdress separating their skin. Her heart was beating out of her chest.

She'd always thought Avelynne would be an excellent first lover. Knowledgeable, understanding, passionate, patient, and she loved Sabina. She wasn't in love with Sabina. But she loved her.

Sabina froze.

No. Not in love. That shouldn't matter. Especially not this morning. They were young, free, they wanted each other, they might die soon! Of course, it shouldn't matter.

But it did.

And Sabina hated that. If she hadn't been in love, if she, like Avelynne, had been driven by desire only, she would be tearing both their nightdresses off right now. However, she was in love with this woman and the knowledge that Avelynne would just as happily be in bed with Hale doing this? That sliced into her heart like an icy knife.

She put her hands on Avelynne's shoulders and lifted the smaller woman up, making their mouths part. "I can't."

Avelynne's eyes went wide with worry. "Oh dearest, why not? Is something wrong? Did you not like it? If you're not ready for something more advanced, we can just keep kissing?"

"No, it's not that. Sure, you would be my first, but I'm ready for that. What I am not ready for is being this intimate with you without knowing where we stand."

"I thought we had talked about that?" Avelynne said softly. "I thought that last term, and in my letters, I made myself clear that I am not... relationship material and don't quite grasp romantic relationships. That while you are an absolute catch, I'm not in the catching business."

Sabina did know that. She remembered all too well last term when she and Hale had made fools of themselves chasing the alluring countess, while Avelynne herself was busy dealing with her parents' vice grip on her, wondering how to keep her big secret, and trying to figure out the conspiracy they were all mired in. She had told them all then, in no uncertain terms, what she wanted in life. Or rather, what she didn't want.

"We got as far as that you are not interested in relationships but that I am. Now, I know you cannot make yourself be in love with me, nor am I asking that you pretend to be. I don't want to change you or make you live a lie." She lowered Avelynne's body back down, her arms getting tired from holding

Avelynne away from her and her heart missing the feeling of Avelynne's beating next to it. "What I would like to ask is that you try to have some sort of special connection with me. Not a full relationship where you're tied to me, but that I am, well, your first pick?"

Avelynne's smile looked sad but understanding. "You want me to choose you over others—perhaps Hale in particular? — and to promise that you and I have something special?"

"Yes. Even if it just means that I am the only friend you have s-sex with." She couldn't believe she had stuttered on the word sex. Although, it was the first time she could remember saying that word out loud so perhaps it wasn't strange.

Silence crowded their small bedchamber. Had she asked for too much? Was it too much like a relationship?

Then Avelynne gave a small nod. "I suppose I can do that. I will not flirt with, or bed, anyone else. More than that, I will have to think about how my, or rather our, future might look. When we're out of danger, we can discuss this again."

Sabina smiled, saying nothing. Not only did she worry their future would keep on providing danger, she also worried Avelynne wouldn't be able to keep to one lover without feeling hemmed in. Although, she did hope she was wrong on both counts.

The weight of her body was slight on Sabina's, yet somehow so comforting.

Sabina took a steadying breath, getting a nose full of the scent of sleep on her own sheets mixed with arousal and, of course, the sweet smell of Avelynne. "Are you... going to tell Hale about our arrangement?"

"Yes. It isn't the best timing considering he, like us, has a lot on his mind today but I suppose the four of us should have no secrets, or anything unsaid, before we sail."

"I think that's a good idea. We should be open and honest with each other, considering no one else is."

"True." Avelynne gave her a quick kiss on the nose and began to climb out of bed.

Sabina pulled her back. "Whoa, whoa, not so fast. First of all, it's pointless telling Hale anything before he has eaten. He won't listen properly and he certainly won't take any bad news well on an empty stomach. Secondly, I'd like to give you a reward for, well, picking me."

"A reward? Snowdrop, you don't need to give me anything for that."

"No, but I *want* to."

Something in her voice clearly made Avelynne understand what she meant as her confused look morphed into a flirtatious one. "Oh, well, I never wish to stand between you and what you want, my sweet."

Sabina didn't answer, but simply rolled them over so Avelynne was on her back and began tugging up Avelynne's nightdress over those short but oh, so beautiful, legs. Every uncovered expanse was more beautiful than the last and Sabina had to remind herself to go slow and savour it.

She had a vague idea of what she was going to do with her mouth on what was between Avelynne's thighs and was trying to remember every daydream about it she'd had during the winter break, mainly for ideas.

Right as she leaned down towards the mass of dark curls, she was stopped by a knock on the door and Eleksander's soft voice saying, "Avelynne? Sabina? Are you awake? Time for breakfast. Today of all days, we cannot be late."

"Shit, shit, shit," Sabina hissed.

"I second that," Avelynne whimpered. She sat up and called, "We'll be right there, Sander."

She took a gentle grip of Sabina's chin and brought her face up to hers for a kiss. "I suppose this will have to wait."

"For when? It is not like we will have our own chamber on the ship. It's only one big open deck where everyone can see everyone."

"I know." Avelynne sighed. "I suppose we'll pick up here when we come back?"

"Or maybe when we make camp somewhere during the journey and there are bushes?"

"Why, Sabina Rosenmarck," Avelynne said with mocked reproach. Then she smiled. "I love the way you think."

"Glad to hear it."

Avelynne gave her another peck, this time on the lips. "I will speak to Hale after breakfast and then we can start afresh the way we should, just you and me, everything out in the open and the both of us knowing where we stand." She kissed Sabina again. Longer and deeper. "You are so very special and you mean so much to me, I want to make this right for you. And I want our first time to be perfect. I'm willing to wait for that."

Sabina swallowed away her impatience and her lingering fear that they might not get another chance. "So am I. I have to admit though, I'm happy that I don't have to wait for breakfast. I'm starving!"

Avelynne laughed as they got out of bed and began quickly washing and dressing.

Sabina took the opportunity to watch her get ready, memorising every part of Avelynne's body, from birthmarks to stray hairs to all the skin that she was going to kiss and caress.

If they both lived and she got the chance.

Chapter Eight

ONE FINAL PIECE

Eleksander sipped at a glass of milk. They were all equally sombre and bleary-eyed during this final breakfast at the Hall of Explorers and ate with barely a word spoken.

Avelynne put her fork down. "Hale. After breakfast, I need to have a quick talk with you."

"Sure," he said, bent over his plate and tucking into the last of his eggs.

Sabina and Avelynne shared a glance over his head, one that took Eleksander out of his thoughts about them setting sail today. Something even more immediate was going on here.

He kept drinking his milk while trying to guess what, but his tired mind failed.

When they were all done, Avelynne and Hale hurried ahead towards the corridor with the bedchambers while Sabina kept him back to tell him what Avelynne was about to say.

Eleksander couldn't help it. He was pleased. Sure, this didn't stop Hale from being in love with Avelynne, but at least it meant that Eleksander wouldn't have to watch them have a relationship, maybe even wed and have children one day. He was safe from that torment at least.

They walked past Avelynne and Hale standing in an alcove. Hale had his arms crossed over his chest in a protective manner and was scowling like a wronged child. Eleksander's relief mixed with pity. He shouldn't be happy because of something that would hurt Hale. Ugh, why did emotions have to be so complicated? And why had he been born with all of them jumbled up?

Uncomfortable, he poured all his attention into listening to Sabina talking of her worries about having her monthly bleed at sea and the inconvenience of that since she was apparently a heavy bleeder. He offered genuine sympathy but admitted he had no tips and tricks to suggest. He was so out of his element when it came to this, never having even dated someone who bled.

"I don't want tips and tricks," Sabina growled. "I want to pause my womb until we get back from our journey. Or possibly longer since I don't plan to ever have children."

Eleksander thought hard. "You know, my sister said something similar to me once when we were sparring and she had to stop due to cramps. She's older than us, she might have some practical advice?"

"I suppose she might, I'll speak to her about it when I stop by to give her my letter."

"Do that; I hope she can help. See you later," Eleksander said as they reached his door.

Sabina waved at him and walked on.

Eleksander went inside the quiet bedchamber. He should enjoy this silence, soon there'd be very little of that. He shivered. He wasn't ready to sail. He supposed none of them were, not even the level-headed Sabina. As soon as Eleksander's gaze fell on what was on his bed, his shivers were for a different reason. He rushed after his Northern friend, barely knocking before entering her bedchamber.

"By all the waters! Have you seen it?" he said, pointing to Sabina's bed.

Chapter Nine

TO SAIL

Sabina had gone straight to the window to get some fresh air, not paying attention to anything else in the room, so when Eleksander came in babbling about something on top of her bedding, she thought he was raving. She looked at the bed, which she had made perfectly before she went to breakfast, despite that being the servants' job.

There was a high but neat pile of clothes.

Sabina stared at it. Their final uniform. They weren't meant to get this armour until they'd finished their education and were going to sail. Well, one out of two would have to do, she supposed.

Cautiously, Sabina unfolded each item of clothing.

It was so different from their plain, student's uniform. Every piece was in the colours of Hall of

Explorers, khaki and black with emerald green details. That green dye must've cost a fortune, clearly this had been ordered and made before Lothiam started cutting down on costs and making everything his garish red and gold. Other than the underthings and a thin, short tunic, the uniform was all in leather. Well, except the chain mail vest which obviously was in fine-meshed wrought iron.

"It looks practical but still handsome, doesn't it?" Eleksander said.

Sabina could only nod, awed as she was.

Most of the uniform was indeed practical but when it came to the outmost piece of the ensemble, it was nothing like the sensible but dull fur coats of Sabina's home. It was a hooded greatcoat, the leather dyed black, with khaki buttons and embossed patterns in emerald green swirling across it. It had all the pockets they'd been promised, to fit their compass, an astrolabe, star charts, and materials for mapmaking.

Sabina lifted the coat carefully, wondering if she might not fit some extra weapons in those pockets, too.

Avelynne entered the room, fretting with her necklace, proving that her chat had not been a pleasant one. Soon, the sullen footsteps of Hale followed her. When inside, he mumbled, "Why's everyone in the world in here?"

"We've received our uniforms," Eleksander answered, sounding unsure of how to address the Woodlander. "Yours is on your bed."

Sabina was still admiring the greatcoat in her hands. She'd never had expensive clothes, there was no coin for such things in a large family from a fishing village in the snowiest North. This greatcoat was opulent and, looking closer at it, had been tailored for *her*. So many clothes weren't made for her body type, too much muscle and too many curves, so she had to make do with what hand-me-downs her parents gave her. This coat, though... It was made for her. And it was practical, armouring, and even suited for colder weather if you wore extra tunics underneath.

More than that, it was beautiful. And, somehow, it was hers to keep.

She didn't dare to put it on.

"Did you know that the leather has been imbued with certain oils, to make magic attacks glance off more easily?" Avelynne said as she stroked the leather trousers.

"No, I had no idea," Eleksander said.

Sabina watched Avelynne fold up the leather trousers again, gently and neatly.

Eleksander chuckled. "How do you always know things that no one else does? It can't simply be that you keep your nose buried in books all day, Sabina and I do that, too."

"I don't know," Avelynne replied with a hint of embarrassment. "That particular detail was in the information pack we got when we were accepted to the Hall of Explorers." She hummed. "Although, I did once overhear the first wave say the oils aren't as effective as we've been told. Still, it makes the leather hardier and easier to move in, so it will do some good either way."

"Come on," Hale said, still with a face like thunder. "Let's go pick up the weapons we chose last night."

They did and then the four of them stood squinting through the cloud-greyed light, first at the academy they were leaving with Ghar and Ellenaria waving from the door to the servants' quarters, and then to the awaiting carriage with its horses neighing dolefully in the quiet morning.

She remembered that the first wave had ridden to the coast, all proud and eager, with their doting Head Tutor escorting them and the rest of the academy staff cheering them as they went.

What a difference time and circumstances could make.

"It's time," Sabina said before calling Kall to her side.

As one, the second wave marched to their carriage and their fate.

After some time in the silent carriage, they arrived at the coast, all displaying the same tense body language, Eleksander most of all. He kept fiddling with his tight-curled braids, finally tying them up into a ponytail.

To the sound of seagulls and the bustling of the harbour, they checked over the Wolfsclaw. She looked impressive, solid and beautifully crafted. Although, Sabina had to admit that she didn't really know what to look for. They were meant to have lessons regarding longship schematics next week.

"It's strange seeing her in the water and not in the dockyard, isn't it?" Sabina said to Hale, hoping to take his mind off Avelynne.

She needn't have bothered, to her surprise Hale was fully enrapt by the ship and his surroundings, his eyes as full of glee as when he was picking out weapons.

"I suppose it sort of is," he granted. "But she's where she's meant to be. The really strange thing is that it's where *we're* meant to be now, too."

He wasn't wrong.

Watching the ship as well was a long-limbed man with round spectacles and ashen skin. His eyes, as grey-blue and cold as the air, swept to them, taking in their faces one by one. "I suppose you are the... captains I shall be travelling with?" He didn't wait for an answer. "Your young age is a benefit, not a hindrance, I'm told. I'd hardly credit that unless it came from our beloved and sagacious king. I'm Physician Faville."

Sabina had wondered if this medical man had a first name, but after hearing him speak of King Lothiam with such an admiring expression and seeing the way he now glared in disgust at Kall, she didn't want to be on a first name basis with him.

"A pleasure to make your acquaintance," Avelynne and Eleksander said in unison, almost drowning out Kall's growling.

"Likewise, I'm sure. I shall see you onboard later as I have a final task to attend to before we sail," he said before striding off.

Hale was still regarding the Wolfsclaw. "Weren't there meant to be two, small rowing vessels attached to the longship? In case something happens and we need to abandon ship?"

"Not anymore," Taferia grumbled as she stopped in the middle of loading the last crates and barrels of supplies. "For haste and ease in preparing the ship, and to aid the ship's buoyancy since a heavy ship might've been what got the first wave into trouble, we've been ordered to cut down on everything. Including the number of sailors."

There it was again. King Lothiam was desperate for them to find new lands for him fast, but also unwilling to give them the tools needed to succeed. Unless the buoyancy thing was true. Still, what was the point in a light ship if you didn't have the resources you needed?

Sabina couldn't decide if the king was short-sighted and stupid in not realising how the two things were not compatible, or simply assumed the second wave could do the job with only the bare minimum.

The grandfatherly Ivar and his icewolf joined them but received distracted greetings as they were all busy with their conversation.

Avelynne's face was still showing confusion at Taferia's words. "How many sailors will we command then?"

"The schematics changed during the Winter Solstice, now allowing for ten rowing benches, which fits twenty sailors," Taferia said. She had stopped and was now wiping her brow. "I figured they'd cut down to only one captain as well, but I suppose they must have one from each region to appease all four counties. Didn't they tell you any of this?"

"No. We've been short on actual education and

information lately. It's mainly been sparring and bucketloads of propaganda," Hale grumbled.

"Hale!" Sabina said. He couldn't say things like that, not with others around.

"It's all right. I... understand what you mean," Taferia said.

Ivar on the other hand looked confused. "Aye, it'll be twenty sailors. We won't have any Northern sailors but us, I'm afraid," Ivar said to Sabina. "It was assumed that Northerners would all want to bring animal companions, which would get heavy. It's thought we need this ship as light as possible."

Sabina patted Kall, partly out of joy that he was coming along and partly to keep him from bothering Ivar's icewolf. Although, it would probably be the other way around as the icewolf seemed as cheerful but as clueless as its master.

"Thought? You're not sure?" Eleksander said.

Ivar shrugged. "Since no one has travelled more than a few days off our coastline and come back to tell the tale, we have little idea of what a ship should be like to survive out there."

"Well, that's encouraging," Hale muttered.

"What we *do* know is out there, right off the coast to be exact, is a tiny excuse for an island," Ivar said. "But it can contain a camp. The fishermen who've dared venture the furthest out have stayed there."

"Kohland?" Avelynne asked.

Sabina recognised the name. Thank the ice there were some things they had covered in their lessons.

"Aye, it's from these fishermen we have most of the stories of creatures lurking in the sea and waves with a mind of their own," the old man answered.

Hale clapped his hands together. "All right. We'll make camp there for the first night. Nice to have *something* settled."

He was right. Everything looming ahead of them worried and terrified Sabina, some of it would probably try to eat her. Knowing where they'd sleep for the first night was at least something.

The Wolfsclaw sat sturdy in her berth but the water around her was churning. A shadow passed by her keel. Probably just a small shark, she'd heard that they ventured close to the coastline when they were starving.

Sabina squinted at it. It didn't look like a shark. She shut her eyes. There was enough to worry about without seeing monsters everywhere before they had even set sail.

Chapter Ten

STEADY AS SHE GOES

Eleksander had been the last of the second wave to board the Wolfsclaw. He could smell hints of spring in the air, soil finally warmed by the sun and fresh grass. He'd said farewell to the scent of Cavarra and hurried aboard, facing the sea ahead instead of turning around to see the familiar land he had to leave.

The sea was quieter today with only a breeze to send them off, not nearly as intimidating as when the waves crashed during their first visit to the shipyard. Still, Eleksander couldn't shake a preference for the lakes he had grown up with. They had gone to the sea sometimes, swam in it, too, but it had been the inlet close to their city. A tamed, warm little slice of the ocean sheltered by chalk white cliffs and framed by fine sand.

Here, the sea was a landscape onto itself. A world onto itself. There was nothing tamed about it. Who would even know where to start taming an ocean like this? Somehow, this sea felt endless and older. More passionate. More deadly.

Before he knew it, they were moving. He heard Hale call, "Starboard five."

"Starboard five," Sabina moved the steering oar accordingly.

"Great!" Hale consulted his compass. "Now, steady as she goes."

Sabina checked her own compass and adjusted so that the ship would stay on the exact course that the compass was on when Hale gave the order.

This was no easy feat. Still, it made sense that two captains steered together and kept each other accountable. That way, there'd be no mistakes in keeping the ship on the exact route the first wave was meant to take. Unless they had veered off course for some reason. Then all bets were off and Eleksander had no idea how they were supposed to find them.

A chill wind came in from the west and Hale visibly shivered. No wonder, since he was wearing only a tunic. He had been so proud of his unform, but, as always when it was on, he found it too confining. Woodlanders slept under the stars in the most comfortable clothes. Confinement was their pet peeve.

Eleksander was about to offer to retrieve Hale's greatcoat when he found himself staring at the new tattoos peeking out of the tunic's unlaced neckline. He had seen them before of course, when Hale showed them off at start of term and whenever he worked out shirtless in their bedchamber, which was a near death experience of desire for Eleksander.

Nevertheless, he couldn't help but look again now. Amongst the crisscrossing of scars and scant curls of hair, was a likeness of their copper compasses. The ones they got for practical use but also to identify them as students of the Hall of Explorers. Under the compass was the headline THE SECOND WAVE and underneath that:

Hale

Avelynne

Sabina

Eleksander

There were no surnames, and the four names were not alphabetically arranged, but in that seemingly random order. Eleksander swallowed, trying once more to pretend to himself that it didn't hurt that his name was last.

He knew why Hale had gotten that tattoo and what it meant. Why it was so important to Hale to prove he had attended the Hall of Explorers. That he belonged to a tightknit, caring group.

A constantly disregarded orphan — who had tried incredibly hard to prove himself worthy of love, admiration, and people's time all of his life — would treasure the proof of his attendance at the academy of Cavarra's saviours and the fact that he'd made three friends who found him more than worthy of their time, love, and admiration.

It was sad. But sweet.

Eleksander wondered how much their childhoods had shaped them, how those formative years had brought all four of them to the Hall of Explorers.

Hale, currently scratching at the stubble he was growing out to a beard to look older, had grown up being passed from adult to adult, depending on who had a spare moment to teach him to hunt or how to read. There'd never been a stable family for Hale Hawthorn.

Sabina, who stood in the middle of the ship and re-braided her long, white mane of hair? Well, she had too much family. Always having to be a parent to her many siblings as her parents worked themselves to death in a land of near perpetual winter. Never having time for herself, having to study when she should be sleeping. Sparring with blunt old axes with her siblings to keep warm.

Then there was Avelynne, who right now listened to a sailor talk at length from his rowing bench. Her parents had cheated to get her accepted into the academy, officially to stop a civil war, unofficially due to ambition, but she had also wanted to come. To stop being the child who was never good enough and to escape the confines of the castle that served more as a prison to her than a home.

Himself? A foundling. Taken in by a rich merchant, spoiled and loved beyond all compare by his family. He'd lived the best and easiest life of them all. And yet, he knew he was the one hardest on himself. He gave himself the hard time his parents never had, making himself be the best at everything to be good enough to earn the love his family gave him.

He fished deeper. What else lurked in his own childhood that might've brought him this mad mission? Well, of course, like all adopted children he'd ever heard of, he obsessed over where he came from. Why his biological parents had abandoned him, naked and helpless, on a road close to the border between the Centre and the Lakelands.

He watched the sea, wishing for the millionth time he could remember anything about them or his life before the Aetholo family adopted him. Wishing he didn't have this conviction that his parents hadn't cared about him and sold him off for coin or booze. Was that conviction connected to real memory or was it yet another way for his self-loathing mind to torture him? Perhaps it was because the many posters the Aetholos spread across the town asking for his family, or the constant enquiries they made through the years, all went unanswered. No one missed five-year-old Eleksander, despite him being found with manicured nails and perfectly treated hair. He had been cared for at one point. Then thrown away. Why? Was it something he'd done? He'd give anything to remember!

Either way, all four mapmakers-to-be had devoted themselves to studying, practising their magic, and honing their fighting techniques. Anything to escape into the academy. To get to make a name for themselves. To be free. To be themselves.

His gaze went back to Hale, who still shivered but did nothing to fix the problem.

Eleksander picked up the greatcoat which lay draped carelessly over a barrel and brought it to its owner. As he pulled it over Hale's shoulders, he couldn't help it, he let his fingers graze Hale's muscle-corded neck. His breathing hitched with the fear that Hale would flinch back from the touch. He didn't, so Eleksander prolonged the caress, making it an obvious show of affection.

Hale still didn't flinch, instead he nodded in thanks and recognition of... what? Their friendship? The kindness Eleksander had showed him? The possible enjoyment of the touch?

Either way, Hale was happy with what had just happened, making Eleksander's breathing return to normal with a deep sense of relief and secret joy filling his chest.

"You all right there, Lakelander?"

"I'm fine. Especially now that I know you won't freeze to death," Eleksander said, stepping back while feeling a smile start to tug at his cheeks.

"Course I won't. Not with you around," Hale said.

They smiled at each other and, suddenly, Eleksander was more focused on that his name was on this man's chest than it what position it was in. Or their pasts and futures.

He planted his feet, feeling steadier than before.

Chapter Eleven

GAZE ON THE HORIZON

That afternoon, Sabina had some time to eat and drink with Hale, since Avelynne was at the steering oar with Eleksander on compass duty.

Knowing Hale, he'd probably go relieve one of the rowing sailors later. Sabina would join him, she could use the movement for her stale muscles and, besides, just standing about made her feel useless. She'd rather be working.

She sniffed the air. The wind was harsher now, bringing new scents. There was a hint of something flowery mingling with the normal fragrance of seawater and the wood of the ship. Oh, and unwashed sailors. Some of them had smelled bad even before they departed, and the rowing wasn't helping. The idea was that they should all wash off with saltwater from buckets frequently, but a number of sailors had replied that the salt itched and dried their skin. Eleksander, a Lakelander so thereby obsessed with hygiene, had asked Ivar if they as captains could order the sailors to wash. The matter had been tabled for when they were further into the trip.

Sabina threw a morsel of salted pork to Kall, mindful that she'd have to make sure he didn't get used to the human's food. He and Ivar's wolf would have to live off the fresh fish they caught every morning.

Hale swallowed a mouthful of apple beer and bent to scratch Kall behind the ear. "When do you think we'll find them? The first wave?"

Sabina shrugged. "Who can say? I'm more worried about what stopped them from coming back."

"Ugh. I'm tired to shit of never having answers," Hale said, eating his last bit of salted pork. "Let's go do some rowing, keep our muscles and stamina up to scratch."

"I thought you'd never ask, little brother."

The afternoon changed into evening and it was time for a shift change. To Sabina's annoyance, the ship began rolling and pitching, making it harder to enjoy the sunset painting the open sky in oranges, pinks, and reds. Sabina and Hale had just arrived by the steering oar to start their shift, when Avelynne moaned and covered her eyes. "I feel... strange."

"Strange how?" Sabina asked.

"I don't know. Nauseous? I'm lightheaded too, and my temples throb."

She grabbed Sabina's arm to steady herself. Her face was blanching.

Physician Faville was only steps away but ignored all else to carry on making notes in a small grey notebook, the content of which he kept out of view from everyone.

Instead, it was Ivar who rushed to Avelynne's side. "Sounds like seasickness. Let's get you to the middle of the ship, lassie. It's the part of the ship that's the most balanced."

Sabina followed them, curious to what the ship's balance had to do with anything. When they stood dead centre on the ship, in a line so as not to interfere with the rowers on either side, he instructed Avelynne to breathe slowly and keep her gaze on the horizon. "Your eyes are telling you that everything is unmoving here on deck, but your balance says that you're moving. Watching the still horizon can settle you."

Sabina saw her chest expand fully and her eyes fix on the horizon. After a while, normal colour returned to her cheeks.

Ivar placed one of his massive, grizzled hands on her shoulder. "Better, lassie?"

"Much, thank you! My stomach is settling and the dizziness fading. The headache is still hovering but I'm prone to headaches so that's nothing new."

That was certainly true. Avelynne had an entire term of headaches back when she was keeping her secret.

Ivar beamed. "Excellent! I'll be over there, seeing to your Woodlander, he's looking a wee bit unsteady as well. Thank the ice we have your sea-legged Lakelander to keep the steering oar."

Avelynne squeezed her eyes shut and gave a small grunt.

Sabina touched her hand. "What's wrong?"

"I have fought so hard to make myself stronger, heartier, and better than I was. All to match up with you three. Still, here I am. Weak and still a drain on the team."

"Look at Hale over there, his skin is greener than grass! He's not a drain on the team and neither are you."

"I am." Avelynne opened her eyes. "You know, I don't understand why the Twelve let me sail."

"The Twelve?" Sabina checked that no one was

listening to them and lowered her voice. "What do they have to do with anything?"

"Tutor Rete was aware that I got in because my parents cheated, he said that the Twelve all knew. Why didn't they speak up and have me thrown out? Why did they let me carry on with my studies and then sail?"

"I don't know. Maybe it wasn't seen as important in the scheme of things? The Twelve have bigger things to worry about. I assume. I mean, we haven't heard from them so they could all be dead for all we know."

"It doesn't make sense," Avelynne said, rubbing her forehead. "None of this makes sense. There is something bigger at stake here, Sabina. I just can't figure out what!"

"I think you're seeing shadows where there are none. We have enough to worry about."

As she said that, there was the disgusting sound of Hale throwing up across the stern. Physician Faville joined him, retching even louder. Hale screeched that he had been poisoned, making Faville snip that Hale had less brains than a dead dung beetle.

"See, they are worse off than you and not at all worried about being a drain," Sabina said with a laugh.

Avelynne wasn't cheered, or even distracted. She

stepped forward into Sabina's space. As usual, Sabina wrapped her arms around her and nuzzled into her hair, not caring if anyone saw. The sailors might've gotten used to that their four captains were particularly close, but this was clearly more than friendly to anyone watching. Who cared?

Avelynne fit herself perfectly into the embrace as always, burrowing her face into the crook of Sabina's neck. They stood like that, in the dimming of twilight, for a moment before Sabina prepared to ask if she was feeling better and if there was anything she could do to help.

Avelynne beat her to speech, whispering, "I wish *it* was this easy."

"Huh?" Sabina replied, eloquent as always.

"Being physical with you is so easy and natural, be that in a friendly or sexual context. It's easy with anyone I'm attracted to, but especially with you."

"I'm glad to hear it."

"I wish I felt the same about being in a relationship with you. I wish it was as easy to be what you need as a life partner."

"You shouldn't have to adapt. I will." She kissed the top of Avelynne's head, sneaking glances at the sailors to make sure no one was overhearing. "I can make this work; I'll take whatever you can give me and I'll make this work. For the both of us."

"You shouldn't have to fix this. You're forever taking on every problem as your burden and breaking your own back for a solution." Avelynne thumped her forehead against Sabina's shoulder. "Argh. Why can't I be like everyone else? I want to give you what you want."

"You do," Sabina said, "You give me your friendship and affection and the physical stuff. Just without the settling down, getting married, and being monogamous, spending most of our time together, and you know... all that stuff."

As she listed those things, she realised how much she wanted them. She kissed Avelynne's head again to hide her heartbreak from anyone watching. Maybe even from the twilit sky itself where stars had come out to spy on them.

"Land to port!" one of the sailors shouted.

Sabina spotted the small Kohland island, all grey sand and weeds, in the middle distance.

"That's where we'll disembark and set up camp for the night," Hale shouted, suddenly seeming less seasick now he had a task to do.

"We'll finish this conversation another time," Sabina said, kissing the top of Avelynne's head one last time.

They began preparing for the disembarkation procedure as the Wolfsclaw made for Kohland.

Having made land right as darkness fell, everyone but Sabina had left the ship to set up camp. Using their magic, Hale, Eleksander, and Avelynne had detached the massive square sail from the ship and were now, with the manual help of the sailors, putting it up as a canopy for them all to sleep under. The silvery light of their magic lit up the makeshift camp with an eerie but beautiful glow.

Sabina had told them to go ahead while she stayed on board. A lantern with a flickering candle was her only light, if one didn't count the moon and stars. The sea was so smooth with the lack of wind that it resembled a massive black mirror for the stars and the moon, while the moonlight painted a line across that mirror in a way Sabina had never seen. Or even imagined.

She had laid out the maps and star charts they'd been given on one of the rowing benches and now she bent over their most detailed map, touching the large white area where they would have to fill out what they found. She was squinting at it in the dim light when she heard someone clear their throat for attention.

Physician Faville was standing beside her, the differing sources of dim light painting shadows across his hawkish face. "You appear to be always working, Ms Rosenmarck. I'm relieved to see someone is taking the role of captain seriously. Your little friends appear to think the work ends when they disembark the ship."

Sabina gave him her best scowl. "The others take it seriously, too. They simply know the merit of resting after a hard day's work."

"And you do not?"

She had no answer for that, no way of saying that she couldn't relax until she was certain she'd done everything to ensure they were safe, to ensure that she didn't make another fatal mistake. To ensure that no more blood ended up on her hands.

She busied herself with folding up a map and picking up a star chart instead. "I'll be done soon and head for my bed. Why don't you go rest, Physician? We need you at your full capacity."

He didn't take the hint. Instead, he stood there, staring at her with his strangely pale eyes framed by those spectacles. He shifted so the light reflected in their glass, shielding his eyes as he said, "I shall tell you something I would not tell the other three." He took one measured step closer. "When I return, I will tell King Lothiam what I have seen and heard on our venture. I shall tell him of your diligence but also of your rudeness, Ms Rosenmarck. Think carefully about how you would like me to portray you."

Sabina sat back, trying hard to see his eyes. His

words had been said with enough emphasis that she understood that he was warning her. She could leave it there. She could simply nod and watch him leave.

But that wasn't her style.

"Huh. So, you're basically telling me that you're here to spy on us for the king and that if I treat you well, you'll report that to the king?"

He sniffed. "You have no appreciation for subtleties, do you?"

"No. I like plain, clear truths. Maybe it's the Northerner in me? Maybe it's coming from my village's warrior family?" She tilted her head. "Or maybe I just don't like lies, veiled threats, and pretences."

The light still glinted off his eyeglasses as he gave the briefest, coldest of smiles and said, "Neither I nor the king have any use for plain, clear truths. We do, however, need warriors to do the violence part. You, and your Northern muscles, may serve the king well if we find inhabitants of lands that we want."

He didn't wait for a reply but turned and walked the gangplank onto dry land.

When she was sure he had gone, Sabina blew out a long, tired sigh. Yet another thing they had to deal with. Perhaps they shouldn't have sailed after all? Perhaps she should've stayed on Cavarra and instead plunged a knife into the scheming king's heart.

Plunge a knife in.

Sabina shuddered. The way it had felt when the dagger was thrust into Tutor Rete's chest came back in a flash of terror. The look in his eyes, as it morphed from homicidal rage into the realisation that the life ending would be his own.

Warriors to do the violence part.

She trembled more aggressively, shaking her head back and forth. She couldn't kill again. Couldn't even finish the thought of killing.

With her heart hammering, she returned to the drawn constellations on the star charts. She had to calm down before she went into the sort of frenzied fits she'd suffered in the nights following the attack, the ones that she still had sometimes, the ones she couldn't have in front of all these people. They needed her to be strong and reliable. Not broken.

She needed to focus on the star charts, their quiet practicality was calming. More than that, they were beautiful. They should be, Avelynne drew them. When was that? Start of term... Wait, was that really only a couple of months ago?

She heard the others settling in for the night.

Avelynne called her name and she replied, "I'll be there soon."

She folded up the charts and maps without really focusing on the task. She was busy gazing at the endless midnight sea. Tomorrow, they'd go beyond what was mapped. The maps she had seen, that anyone had seen, had all been blank after this point.

Her stomach turned. It was all so real now. She had to keep them safe, she had to get all of this right.

Chapter Twelve

GRIMFROST AND DELICATE LADS

The next morning, they'd all eaten, packed up, and returned to the Wolfsclaw bright and early. To his surprise, Eleksander was well-rested and ready to go.

By now, they'd sailed for hours and were well on their way into unknown waters, but no one seemed afraid. The sailors were singing and chatting as they rowed, while Hale and Avelynne, currently on captaining duty, were playfighting over the steering oar.

Everything, despite their worrying mission, was as good as he could ever hope.

The sea, unexpectedly free of seaweed and cloudiness out here, was like deep blue glass so you could spot the ocean floor below as well as the many fish, some of which they'd already caught, thereby securing lunch for themselves plus a certain snowtiger and icewolf. The breeze was in their favour, too, billowing the sail just enough to push them along at a safe and manoeuvrable speed.

All that *and* the sun beamed down on them, the sky without a single cloud. The only grey cloud in sight was the one metaphorically looming over Sabina as she approached with heavy steps. She didn't merely look like someone had banned her from sunshine for life, she looked weighed down, in more ways than one. Eleksander decided to start with the physical one.

"Sab. You do know that you don't have to carry that on your back all the time?" He tugged at a leather strap across her shoulder. "None of the rest of us walk around with our weapons, you can put that big axe—"

"Not 'that big axe.' It has a name, remember? Grimfrost."

He made sure he didn't smile. There were only two things which threw Sabina's sensible ways out the window, that axe and Avelynne Ironhold. "Yes, of course. My point still stands."

"I know. I just feel safer having it close by. Like I can protect you all easier."

"You sound like Hale. You know, I think he still has knives strapped to his legs. Thank the waters you both have the blades of your weapons sheathed or you'd cut yourselves to ribbons."

"We both know about weapons safety and maintenance. Don't worry, pure heart."

Now he smiled. He liked "pure heart" better than when Hale called him "soft heart" to mean overly sensitive or sentimental. "That's a new nickname, isn't it? I like it. Anyway, other than your axe—"

"Grimfrost."

"Fine. Other than *Grimfrost*, what else is weighing on you? Let me guess, is it Physician Faville and what we're going to do about his spying?"

At first light this morning, Sabina had taken the second wave aside and told them all about her conversation with the king's spy. Said spy was now standing at the stern, scribbling in his notebook, and throwing dour glances their way. Eleksander's mood lifted as he saw Taferia Palm walk past the physician and bump his shoulder, in mock accident, so he dropped the notebook.

"No," Sabina said, frowning at the man who was blowing imagined dust off his notebook. "Faville does not deserve a spot in my mind."

"All right. Is it the Twelve, then? Or the king? Our mission?"

"No," Sabina said. "Although, all that needs brooding over, too. Especially as Avelynne has a paranoid idea that there's something going on in regard to why she was allowed to stay in the second wave even though Rete and Santorine knew her secret."

Eleksander rubbed his jaw, tingling with the dryness of having washed with saltwater. "Oh? Well, at this point, nothing would surprise me. We're always the last to know things." He sighed. "Isn't it funny that our age apparently makes us perfect to captain a ship and save Cavarra, but it means they won't tell us silly little youths anything of importance?"

"Mm." Sabina's gaze was glued to Avelynne, who was tying up her hair with a strip of leather, the sun really bringing out the scarlet tones of her red-black hair. Although, Sabina probably wasn't objectively considering the play of colours like he was.

Eleksander cleared his throat. "Speaking of Avelynne, are you aware that you've been staring at her ever since yesterday?"

"I have?"

"Mm-hm. What's going on with you two?"

Sabina rubbed her eyes, making Eleksander notice the dark circles underneath them. "The usual. Avelynne adores me, you, and Hale and wants to bed us all, particularly me, of course, but..."

"But doesn't want a relationship, even with you,

whom she chose over Hale. I know all of this," Eleksander said, watching Avelynne double check her compass and say something to Hale, who held the steering oar.

Eleksander took Sabina's hand. "I'm with you so far, but it can't be only that, considering that situation has been going on since our first weeks at the Hall of Explorers. What's different now?"

"I guess what's different is that I keep seeing Avelynne hurting and feeling bad for not being able to give me what I want, for feeling that she's not enough."

"Well, Avelynne always feels she's not enough. It's a trait she shares with me."

He offered a smile but she gave none in return. Instead, she scowled out at the open sea.

"I wonder if that's all it is. She promised to pick me over others and that's great, but I worry she regrets it. That she feels trapped."

Eleksander pondered that. "No, I'd say she's all right with what you've compromised on, as long as it's always up for re-evaluation. I think you were right when you said her sadness is due to her guilt that she can't give you more, can't commit to a relationship with you."

"I suppose so. I merely wish she'd tell me what's bothering her and what I can do to fix it, even if it hurts me. You know how she wants to help and please everyone." Sabina scowled even deeper. "And how she'll sacrifice her own happiness and comfort to do it."

Eleksander's heart bled for them both. "Mm. To be honest, you're lucky that she didn't pretend she was all right with being in a relationship with you and forced herself to commit. I think the anxious, people-pleasing countess we met at our first day at the academy might've done that."

Sabina turned to him. "You think so? That would be awful. I can't have her sacrificing anything for me. I love her and I want what's best for her. I don't want her to feel bad anymore, but just saying that the way we are now is fine? That isn't working."

"And is it? Fine, I mean?" He hesitated. "Correct me if I'm wrong, but while you're clearly struggling, you don't seem as heartbroken around her as you were at the start of term."

"I'm not. I mean, she gave me as much of a commitment as she can, and I appreciate that so much." Sabina went quiet, then huffed out a mirthless little laugh. "More than that, though, I think I'm getting better at dealing with the disappointment."

"How so?"

"It's like, I don't know, I suppose I've gotten a confirmation of what I always suspected—that I can't have the life I dreamed of with her—and I'm learning to live with it?"

Eleksander's gaze was drawn to Hale and Avelynne who were standing face to face, that handsome night-eyed lad laughing at something Avelynne had said. "Well, Ave did warn you and Hale from the start, Sab. She told you that she didn't do romance."

"Aye. Maybe my heart, while still falling for her, did keep that advice and shielded itself a little."

Eleksander snuck another look at Hale, noting that the piercing sunshine didn't feel as cheering anymore. "Mm. Shame that Hale's heart didn't do the same."

"I don't know about that," Sabina said, sounding more logical and less emotional now. "I don't believe he's as in love with her as he thinks. Infatuated, yes. But I think she's more a symbol for him."

"A symbol?"

Sabina pensively played with her braid. "Yes. Of the sort of woman he thinks he can't have."

"What do you mean 'sort of woman?' Aristocrats? Intellectuals? Beauties?"

"Sure, that too. But I suppose I mainly meant ladylike, graceful, overly kind, and... delicate. He's used to tougher lasses, like me, being the only ones willing to put up with him."

"What about lads?" Eleksander said softly, barely

able to get the words out. "Do you think he likes delicate lads?"

He worried what Sabina might answer. While she straddled the line, she was more the rough warrior type like Hale than the overthinking, sensitive type like him and Avelynne. Sometimes her answers were a little too honest.

Sabina wrapped an arm around his waist, though it didn't reach all the way. "He should. All those nice things we just said about Avelynne? They apply to you, too, minus the aristocratic title." She did a double take. "I mean, as long as you don't take 'ladylike' as an insult?"

"Only when *you* use it for people who squeal when they get their boots muddied."

She finally cracked a smile. "No, I mean it in the way of being stylish, sweet, and well-mannered, even when you get mud on your boots. The bottom line is that you're a catch, my pure hearted friend."

Eleksander scoffed. "Hardly. Besides, even if Hale did like lads, he'd probably want them as pretty and dainty in size like Avelynne. I think he likes the idea of being the big man who protects."

"You may be more broad-shouldered and taller than him, but he's more muscular and better at fighting, right?"

Eleksander chewed his lip. "Yes."

"Well, then, he'd still be your strong protector.

Besides, who cares about size? You've got a sweet, delicate, dainty, noble spirit and a pretty face. Just like Avelynne. You should be his type."

Shrugging, he looked down at his boots. Sabina tightened her hold on him.

One of the sailors behind them stopped rowing with a loud groan.

"Ah, looks like Jero pulled that muscle in his back again," Sabina said, nodding to a Lakelander sailor. "Mind if I go take his place so he can rest?"

"No, go ahead."

Eleksander, tired of wallowing, approached Avelynne to see if he could help with anything. She was talking to Ivar about trimming the sail as the wind was changing.

Midsentence, she fell silent and the colour on her cheeks drained. Eleksander stopped dead, followed her gaze, and realised what she'd seen.

A spider of fear skittered up his spine at the sight of something huge breaching the water. Not in the way animals of the ocean did, not like a fish, not a shark or whale, nothing like anything he'd ever seen or heard of. This chilled the air, bubbled the water, and rushed the subsequent waves with tendrils of black, making a sound like an enormous pot of water boiling over. The wind hadn't changed due to the weather, whatever was coming out from the depth had created these winds, as well as these waves, in the blink of an eye.

The creature came into view, enough of it above the rushing waves it made for them to see four massive white eyes against pitch-black and tentacles thicker than a man's thigh and longer than the ship.

One of them swung right towards the Wolfsclaw.

Chapter Thirteen

ATTACK

Sabina dropped the oar as she stared at the creature now looming over their ship. A tentacle swung for them and ripped the sail before retracting, drawing screams from everyone on board.

She stood on wobbling legs, trying to judge their foe and figure out what in the name of all ice they should start with. What technique fought off something like this?

The monster's head resembled a massive replica of the dragon figurehead from the first wave's ship, while the upper body looked more like the front half of a caterpillar. Its bottom part was all oversized octopus, though, giving its long torso six short arms and its lower body multiple tentacles. They were constantly moving under the water it had inked up, so Sabina couldn't count their numbers. It was too many for her taste, though.

The creature's skin looked hard, black, and rough as coal, something which was confirmed when one of the tentacles got close to her as it swiped down to smack a nearby sailor unconscious.

Sabina shot a volley of magic at the tentacle. It made the monster move the limb but didn't seem to cause any harm. On a human, a blast like that would've tossed the target back, caused bruising and intense pain, probably knocking them out. The monster barely seemed to have noticed, though, it kept roiling the sea and swinging its tentacles.

"Shitloads of arms *and* tentacles? Did that thing go to some sort of market sale on limbs?" Hale screamed as he picked up that complex crossbow of his, nocked a bolt, and aimed at a nearby tentacle.

He stopped his war cry as the shot hit home. By the strange sound from the impact, Sabina guessed the bolt's thistle-like head did spread out while inside its target as it should. However, instead of pulling the injured tentacle back, the sea monster flicked it at Hale. The blow tossed him through the air so he landed on his back with an "oof" and his crossbow flew overboard.

That blow could've been harder or made to throw Hale overboard too. Was the beast toying with them? Or did it have bad aim?

Eleksander went to check on Hale, who luckily seemed unscathed. The Woodlander was even getting back on his feet while cursing about a bruised rump and his lost crossbow.

Sabina wondered if the other two regretted not carrying their weapons with them, having to admit to some smugness as well as the burden of being right about keeping Grimfrost weighing on her back and tearing at her shoulders every day.

She pulled it out of its straps now and quickly removed the blade's sheath. Its weight in her hands felt right as she swung it at a passing tentacle and sliced a coal-like tip off.

The creature screeched in pain and Sabina answered with a roar of triumph.

"Good work, lass!" Ivar called, waving a short sword in a way that showed his lack of experience with weapons. He and his icewolf chased after a tentacle that had narrowly missed Avelynne.

Sabina cast a glance at Avelynne who nodded her head in silent confirmation that she was fine.

Quick as lightning, a tentacle swiped down, clearing quite a few of the rowing benches. With a start, Sabina noticed that it came perilously close to one that Kall was under.

Why was the silly snowtiger sitting under there? He loved a fight!

Sabina squinted under the bench while trying to

keep one eye on the monster, which was currently being pelted by Eleksander and Avelynne's magic plus the weaker magic of some of the sailors. Oh, and by Hale, who was throwing anything not nailed down at it. Including the crates of food, she realised with a wince.

Nothing did much damage.

When Sabina was closer to her companion, she understood why Kall wasn't moving: his long tail was stuck under one of the collapsed benches. With a gasp she rushed to him, calling his name.

Her cries caught the attention of Ivar's wolf and then of its owner. They were closer to Kall and so ran to free him as well.

Sabina's panic hit a new high as she saw one of the monster's tentacles swipe down on that part of the ship again. Following the trajectory of the appendage, it would hit right where Kall was trapped!

She ran faster than she had ever done in her life, images of Kall as a cub, Kall letting her cry into his fur, Kall saving her life, all moving through her mind.

The tentacle was almost upon the snowtiger, when Ivar stabbed his sword at the appendage, only glancing off it but still getting the sea monster's attention.

It moved to strike Ivar instead.

Sabina called a warning but was too late. The tentacle didn't hit him, though, it grabbed him instead and brought him up to its gaping maw.

Sabina's heart stopped beating.

In an instant, the fiend had devoured the sweet old man, despite all the magic that every sailor and every member of the second wave threw at it.

The icewolf howled for its master. As enraged as it was confused, it leapt at the monster to the sound of everyone's screams to stop. The poor thing didn't listen to them, it only wanted its master. A tentacle grabbed the wolf and, in a blink of an eye, the loyal animal was with its master deep in the belly of the beast.

Sabina's heart was beating again, pounding out her rage, grief, and disappointment in herself. She quickly went to release Kall from where he was stuck and then slumped to her knees on the deck, staring at the monster's still open mouth.

Ivar. Why hadn't she saved him? Or his icewolf? With shame, she realised that she didn't even know the animal's name. Why had she never asked?

Everyone but the sea monster was quiet. Then there was a stifled sob from a sailor, followed by a whimper from another.

"Of all the people, why him?" Avelynne said quietly, giving voice to what they all thought.

Guilt now pounded in Sabina's chest like a second heart. This was her fault.

The monster screeched and swung a tentacle over them.

"We grieve later. Now we save everyone else. How do we kill this shitty thing?" Hale bellowed.

He was breaking oars in half to use as throwing spears and Sabina was about to ask him to throw something they wouldn't need. But, then, if they all ended up eaten by this thing, what did it matter?

"Look at its eyes," Avelynne called over the din of anguish and disbelief.

The dragon-like head had four large milk-white eyes wide open, only obscured when the creature's blue tongue—at least she assumed that's what it was —came out to lick across them.

Sabina stared at the white orbs. There were what looked like deep cuts across all four of them.

"Its eyes are scarred over, I don't think it can see us very well, especially not when we move. Keep moving!" Avelynne added.

That would explain why the tentacles weren't aimed very well. The fiend could have smashed the ship to firewood and grabbed them all for snacks by now.

Unless it couldn't see them.

It attacked again and Sabina jabbed, then ducked, then swiped with Grimfrost. The axe struck true, cutting off yet another part of a tentacle. Avelynne had been right, moving fast was the only way to touch this thing.

None of them stood still anymore, attacking with weapons and magic, some sailors even smashing oars into the tentacles.

Few got close to the face or the caterpillar-esque body of the beast, though, and even when the tentacles were cut and bloody, it stubbornly kept attacking.

"Magic doesn't work. Has anyone seen my bow and quiver?" Eleksander shouted.

"I think it's tucked behind the crates and barrels over at the stern, like my war scythe," Avelynne whinged with frustration.

They both headed for the stern while everyone else continued trying to fight off the monster. It began wrapping one of its tentacles around the ship —whether to drown it or to bring it closer, who knew —but with great effort the sailors managed to slash the gripping tentacle to shreds.

Hale roared with frustration. "I can't believe I spent all that time picking the perfect weapon, one that we could really use right now, and this cursed fiend made me lose it!"

Sabina was about to shout back that this was no time to fret over lost crossbows when she saw the sea monster grab Taferia. Before it could bring her to its mouth, Sabina lunged and chopped that tentacle off.

Taferia stepped out of the dead appendage's tight grip with a, "Thank you," and rushed to grab her sword.

All the tentacles were either cut short or injured now, but this monstrosity kept on attacking with them anyway.

"Someone needs to get closer to the body! We need to stab it in the face," Sabina called to anyone who would listen.

"Don't you think I've tried shoving a dagger into its face? Whenever I get close enough, a tentacle comes out and smashes me aside," Hale said.

The other two came back looking crestfallen. "Our weapons aren't there. Neither are the crates they were with, they must've all been knocked off the ship by those wretched tentacles," Eleksander said.

Avelynne pulled at her hair. "This was exactly the sort of thing my war scythe was made for. I cannot believe it now rusts at the bottom of this infuriating ocean!"

Sabina let them lament while she considered ways to get close to the monster's body. Commotion surrounded her, the sailors were fighting tentacles with short swords and oars, Hale was cutting tentacles to ribbons with his daggers, Avelynne had picked up Ivar's sword and was taking aim to throw it at the beast's face, and Eleksander seemed to be… kicking the nearest tentacle? Which, considering the size of his legs, did quite some damage.

And then there was Kall, batting a cut off tentacle tip which squirmed along the deck as if trying to get back to the sea. His big paw landed on it and, to Sabina's disgust, he ate the writhing appendage.

Taferia stood next to Eleksander, who looked out of breath and dejected, and shouted something to him. Sabina strained to hear what she was saying but only caught the last few words: "And we have put too much effort into getting you four to where you are now for you to be eaten by some monster!"

Hale and his trusty daggers, one in each hand, was closer to her now. He was aiming them at the abomination's face, about to throw them like Avelynne had done with the sword. Hopefully, he wouldn't miss like she did.

A half-cut tentacle came for him and Sabina jumped to the side to cleave it off.

"Thanks," he said, still aiming while saying, "I wish I had a great big polearm."

"Like a war scythe?" Avelynne murmured.

Hale's daggers both glanced off, whether that was because of its rough skin, the fact the beast kept moving, or Avelynne's utterance distracting him, Sabina didn't know.

"Oh, forget about your shitty scythe," he barked.

Then he hung his head, groaning. Hopefully recalling how he himself had whinged about his lost crossbow. "Sorry. I'm not angry at you, Ave. Only at the shit-for-heart monster who ate Ivar."

The sea creature was backing away but taking the Wolfsclaw with them as it did so. They all lurched with the movement and looked at each other. What was this thing doing? Either way, the urgency to put a stop to it only grew with each moment.

Sabina turned to the biggest person around. "Sander, can you throw me at that thing? Then I'd be close enough to stab it in its ugly, half-blind eyes?"

Eleksander scrunched up his face. "No. If I do that, it'll eat you. Or grab you with those many arms. I think we need to attack from a distance again but together this time. Maybe if we pool our magic attacks, it'll be strong enough to affect the fiend?"

Hale had just used his magic to retrieve one of his tossed daggers but stopped himself right before he threw the blade again. "Huh? Worth a try, I suppose."

"I think it sounds exceedingly sensible," Avelynne said. "I'll start."

She launched a volley, the silver magic striking the creature like a stream of rushing water. It hit right in the eyes. Her aim with magic was clearly better than her aim with swords.

This time the sea monster did scream when

struck, perhaps because it was blinded by the light or because Avelynne had actually managed to hurt it.

Hale and Sabina nodded at each other before sheathing their weapons to instead use their hands to also shoot magic. Sabina shaped hers as a cage to keep the beast still, while Hale fired his jet right into the two top eyes, since Avelynne's stream was hitting the two lower ones. Another magic cage laid itself on top of Sabina's, strengthening the hold on the monster, Eleksander must've joined in.

Then, the silver magic flashed, and changed.

Sabina blinked over and over, not trusting her eyes.

As their four streams of magic hit the creature and touched each other, they changed from the normal brightness and colour: the silver that had made the silver beasts and had been such an everyday sight to any Cavarrian.

Their streams of magic turned the colour of gold.

Not only that, it shone much stronger. Not the usual ethereal wisps but so dense it looked almost tangible. Like paint or liquid gold. The golden magic drizzled down the creature's coal body and poured over the water around it, even surrounding their longship, spreading out across the waves like oil on water, until the sea appeared golden.

Sabina heard the others give shouts and gasps of surprise. She watched her own hands, then the others. How were they doing this? What even was *this*?

The monster bellowed from its spot in the now golden sea and several tentacles snapped towards them.

They could worry about what was happening to their magic later, right now they had to protect their sailors and stay alive. Annoyingly, their magic wasn't knocking their foe over the way a volley of silver magic would.

Another tentacle swung above their heads.

From the corner of her eye, Sabina saw Hale staring at the magic streaming from his hands and bellow, "How does this stuff work?"

She had no answer for him. She tried to focus and to steer the magic to do something, like shape back into the cage she had made from the start. But it wouldn't. It shot in a stream towards the monstrosity and then gushed down to coat the waves. She concentrated harder but, just like when they steered the Wolfsclaw, this magic seemed slow and sluggish, any adjustment taking ages to actually come into action. Perhaps if the others worked with her?

"Try to subdue the tentacles," she shouted, before realising that the clamour of battle had quieted, all the sailors standing around gaping, so she could speak normally now.

"I'm trying," Hale grunted. "But it's not like normal magic, is it?"

"No, it cannot be controlled in the same way," Avelynne said through gritted teeth.

"Wait, are we all aiming to do the same thing?" Eleksander panted. "I was focusing on shooting at the body, which seems to be doing nothing."

Sabina tried to look over at him without taking her focus off her task. "We all were, but the tentacles keep swinging for us so we must contain them!"

"Yes," he answered calmly. "But containing the tentacles is a little vague? Are we trying to hit them with volleys of magic, cut them off with blades of magic, or enclosing them with caging magic streams?"

And perhaps that was the problem? If four people were trying to do the same thing with the same matter but in different ways, what would happen?

Sabina was about to suggest they all clamp their magic around the tentacles, when she heard Hale say, "Cut the shitty things!"

It all became a moot point. The golden magic stopped dribbling down into the water, instead encasing the sea monster. The tentacles were drawn into the body as though they were glued in place by the thick magic. Soon, the monster was a shining metallic blob, like an apple dipped in hardening caramel but with liquid gold.

The creature was clearly subdued. However, its massive eyes still moved.

Sabina had no doubt that it was still alive and ready to attack at the earliest possible moment. She heard some sailors whisper to each other behind her, but otherwise it was eerily quiet. Especially now since the beast wasn't flailing in the water.

"All right, it's immobile, but who knows for how long?" Eleksander said, still sounding calm.

"Is it suffocating in there?" Avelynne asked.

Sabina stared at it. The golden cocoon appeared to move as if the monster was breathing. "I don't think so," she answered.

"What do we do now, then?" Hale said.

No one answered for a long time. They'd not been trained for this. Magic didn't behave this way; it was a substance that your mind shaped and used. This golden-hued stuff was odd, stronger and almost seeming to have a mind of its own. Even the fact that they hadn't tired was strange since silver magic drained you fast. They had been streaming magic for a long time now and she didn't feel exhausted.

Be that as it may, she was done with this confusing fight and done with the fiend who had eaten Ivar and his wolf.

"Imagine squeezing the monster," she said. "Perhaps we can somehow strangle it."

She heard Hale say, "Now you're talking."

He made a squeezing gesture with his hands. Gestures helped with visualisation when you used magic, so Sabina tried that too. When the others followed suit and she saw their faces scrunch up in concentration.

The beast howled in pain from within the gold, like an icewolf in labour. It did seem to be getting thinner too, as if squeezed by giant invisible fists.

Then the creature gave an ear-bursting groan and sank below the surface.

Sabina waited, heart in her throat, but the monster didn't resurface. Instead, black and blood-thick liquid spread across the waves, tarnishing the gold coating.

Eleksander lowered his hands with a look of horror.

Sabina followed suit and staggered. The moment their magic wasn't in the mix, it turned back to two normal silver streams.

"Are you all right?" Avelynne asked, lowering her hands too.

"Aye," she mumbled.

And physically she was, the golden magic hadn't drained her and she wasn't injured. It was the panic that had been driving her throughout this, its power was waning.

"I'm tired too," Eleksander said, reading her mind.

There was a rushing in the air, Sabina put it down to some sort of after-effect of the monster's death. She was busy trying to regain her balance and reliving Ivar's death in her mind. Then the rushing noise picked up and now buzzed in her ears, making the little hairs on her neck stand up.

What *was* that?

Sabina turned around and forgot everything else in the blink of an eye. Ahead of them were two tiny islands, one containing only a tree and the other made up of three spikey cliffs. In the space between them was what had caused the noise - a waterfall of great proportions. That wretched sea monster had led them right to a waterfall!

Sabina turned to the steering oar but knew it would be no use to try getting away, they were being pulled in by the merciless power of the water. Neither rowing, their poor torn sail, or that steering oar was going to be any help. Maybe they could jump ship and swim to one of the islands? No, the waterfall was too strong. Besides, those chunks of land were too small to fit them all anyway.

Sabina searched wildly for something to save them. Prepared to try anything, she threw her magic

—the normal silver now—like a lasso at the tree. It stopped their journey towards the fall for all of a heartbeat before the tree tore in half.

Next to her, some sailors were dropping the anchor. While that was to no avail, it did give her an idea to make an anchor of magic. Maybe if the four of them pooled their magic and tried to make one out of gold, it would be strong enough to fight this powerhouse of a waterfall. Eleksander and Hale were doing something with magic, so she headed for them, calling their names.

That was when the world began to tilt.

Chapter Fourteen

UNFORESEEN ALIGHTING

Eleksander's gaze travelled the deck, trying to find the other three. Avelynne had rushed over to help Physician Faville with the sailors who were injured or killed by the sea monster's attack, but she now sat gaping in shock at the waterfall while holding a hand against a gushing wound on a sailor's chest.

Sabina had just sent a lasso of magic around a tree, one which Eleksander didn't think could take the strain.

And Hale was coming toward him, shouting, "We're going over!"

He shouted back, "I know, we have to do something!"

Hale's eyes were wild and unblinking as he looked around. He pointed to a spikey bit of cliff on the island next to them but instead of explaining what he was going to do, he made his magic into a rope and threw it like a lasso as he'd seen Sabina do. The cliff would no doubt be sturdier than her tree had been. However, Eleksander knew there was no way it could save them. Hale's magic would never be enough to hold the ship against a waterfall of this magnitude. He hesitated, then closed the distance between them. Maybe they could make the more powerful gold magic with just the two of them? He threw his magic onto Hale's. It wrapped around the jagged rock and, yes, it slowed their pull towards the fall, but stayed silver.

Then the pull got harder. Eleksander and Hale held on, but it wouldn't be long until they couldn't anymore. Eleksander's arms were already shaking from muscle fatigue as well as the draining use of normal magic.

He opened his strain-closed eyes to search for Sabina and Avelynne in the throng of panicked people. Perhaps it needed all four of them to make the golden magic, and maybe *that* would be strong enough to keep the ship from going over?

No, they'd never make it on time. They were almost over the falls!

Eleksander had to find a way to save them, this very instant. If not all of them, then at least as many as he could. This was what he did best, calmly think of solutions when everyone else was lost in emotion. He had to think!

As he did, he watched their magic still shaped in a rope, lassoed over the cliff point to little use.

Rope.

Eleksander fetched an actual rope and began tying himself to the figurehead, which Ivar had boasted was fastened with iron to the sturdiest parts of the ship's hull, and then shouted to the sailors around him do the same with other pieces of rope and to tie the knots around the wolf's open mouth. He wasn't sure how many heard him, but he had no time to stop and check. He had to get Hale.

He moved as close to the Woodlander as the rope would allow and secured Hale around the waist with a relieved sigh. Hale's magic still had that anchoring grip on the rock, but the sweat poured off him. He'd have to let go soon.

Sabina was calling his name and running to him. Eleksander held out a hand to her and she reached for it.

That was when the ship began going over.

Sabina was lost to the air and water as the Wolfsclaw's world became a tumbling, terrifying blur.

When the fall was over, Eleksander realised he hadn't trusted the hold of the rope, he had also clung to the bow for all he was worth.

All six of them had. There were the two sailors, a man and a woman that he couldn't remember the names of since they'd only met two days ago, Taferia Palm, Physician Faville, him, and Hale. They had been lucky that the figurehead and bow held through the fall, and that it had kept floating when they landed. Now, however, the bow was taking on water and sinking fast. They all untied themselves and got ready to swim.

Between long, measured strokes, Eleksander took in their newfound land. This certainly wasn't what he'd been trained to locate. Cavarra expected him to find a new continent that was large, lush, and full of natural resources. This, well, this looked like a barren, wind-torn island with nothing but a small mountain and, next to it, a grouping of slender trees. Sure, there might be something behind the mountain, but he doubted it. This isle was about the size of the Hall of Explorers courtyard.

When their feet were on land, Hale coughed up some water—he'd never admit it, but he wasn't the strongest swimmer—and stared out at sea. "I can't see the others! Does anyone know what happened to them?"

One of the sailors, the female one, answered, "As

far as I saw, only we stayed on a surviving part of the Wolfsclaw. The others were thrown off the ship and into the water when we went over the waterfall."

"I didn't see any of them after the fall, did you?" Eleksander asked her, blinking through the increasing wind at the waves.

"I saw some bobbing heads, Captain Rosenmarck's snowtiger being one of them, but I cannot say where they all ended up."

Kall. Did that mean Sabina was all right? Was she with Avelynne? They *had* to be all right.

The other sailor pointed to the small mountain. "I could climb a bit up that and see if I can spot anyone out there?"

"Yes! Good thinking, man," Hale said.

The sailor began climbing while Hale and Taferia paced their little beach, checking out the island as much as keeping an eye out for survivors, Eleksander assumed. He was too tired to ask.

Eleksander and the remaining sailor went to the aid of the yowling Physician Faville.

"Are you all right?" Eleksander asked.

"Of course not, you silly brat!" Faville said, holding his leg. "My shin collided with something hard when we hit the water."

Eleksander eyed the leg. "Oh, is it broken?"

"No, but there is severe damage," he snipped, as if Eleksander had questioned whether it was injured at all. "Not at all improved by having to swim, like some common fisherman."

Eleksander hid his anger, wondering if this callous man cared at all that people who were under his medical care had died or were missing. He and the sailor helped Faville to stand, then they all tried to shake off the worst of the water and get their breath back.

"I can't see any survivors," the climbing sailor shouted, the wind nearly whipping his words away. "Oh, and there's nothing but a sheer drop into the water from the backside of this mountain. What you see is all the island has to offer."

"Agreed," Hale said, returning from his perimeter check. "There's an opening into that mountain, though. Could be a cave where we can rest away from this wind and make our plans."

They made their way towards where Hale had indicated. The sailor up the mountain, a Woodlander by his accent, shouted that he was going to stay and look for survivors.

"Fine. I'll come up and relieve you soon," Hale promised.

They got inside and found that the cave was more of a tunnel, heading all the way into the mountain but with little height, meaning they had to crawl in and not even the shortest of them could stand up.

"Let's not go any further in," Eleksander said. "I think we should stay where the daylight reaches us."

No one argued, so they all settled down, trying to sit comfortably despite all their bruises and scrapes.

Eleksander was still so exhausted from the ordeal and how much magic he'd used. He couldn't imagine how Hale was feeling since he used his magic for much longer. Still, glancing over at his handsome friend, he only found him peering out at the grouping of trees.

He pointed a mud-and-blood-spattered finger at them. "Those are korkorand trees."

Taferia followed Hale's pointing with wide eyes. "Grand, we'll have some source of hydration!"

"Those trees will give us something to drink?" Eleksander asked.

"We have those trees in the colder parts of the Woodlands," Taferia explained. "They grow what looks like a bigger acorn, but which is full of thick, clear liquid that's drinkable."

"Yes, not unlike the coconuts from the palms of the warmer parts of the Woodlands." Hale rubbed his face and offhandedly added, "But the korkorand acorns are obviously smaller, with thicker milk, and sadly without the meat. Still, the juice is nutrient-packed."

Good," Eleksander said, relieved there was some good news, however slight. "If we catch some fish, that and the juice may sustain us and any other members of our crew that find this island. Until we find out how to leave, I mean."

One thing at a time, he reminded himself.

He hoped that the sailor out there was spotting the others, especially Sabina and Avelynne. He had no idea how he would survive losing them.

The wind howled outside, blowing gusts into their little cave.

"Thank you for saving us," the female sailor said.

Eleksander wished he could think of a way to ask her name without sounding like it hadn't mattered to him before. Why hadn't he spent time memorising everyone names on the first day?

He held his hands up. "No need to mention it. It was my job as captain. In fact, I should've saved more. If only I'd thought of the ropes earlier!"

"Never mind," Taferia said. "You saved as many as you could and we're grateful for it."

Eleksander watched Taferia, a memory flaring. "What did you mean when you said the four of us had been placed in our positions?"

She blinked. "What?"

"When we were fighting the monster. You said too much effort had gone into placing us in these positions for us to die at the hands of a sea beast."

"Shh," Hale said. "What's that noise?"

"What noise?" Eleksander asked before he heard

it too. It wasn't the wind howling, it was a buzzing coming from the trees. And it was growing louder.

Then the male sailor, who Eleksander had thought was still up the mountain, came running in, followed by a swarm of bright orange little insects.

His face, earlier so pale, was covered with red welts and he was screaming as he flailed his arms to get the bugs off him.

They all backed further into the cave, because where else could they go? The entrance was now filled with the insects and the sailor they kept stinging. Eleksander wailed, unable to think of a single way to help him! The poor man collapsed to the ground and the female sailor made a run for it, trying to jump over his body. Faville followed suit. Eleksander pulled at the sleeve of the physician's surcoat but he stared back at Eleksander with wild eyes, screaming, "Unhand me, brat. I must get out of here!"

"Yes, we all do, but running towards the bugs is senseless! We need to stop and think."

The female sailor was now the main target of the insects. She screeched as they stung her, attaching themselves to any bared skin and covering her with red bumps. The academic part of Eleksander's mind briefly wondered if they were drinking blood or just stinging.

Hale picked up a fist-sized rock and went to run

to her aid, mumbling something about wishing he had some fire to burn the very hearts out of those shitty bugs.

Eleksander wrapped an arm around his waist and pulled him back. He wanted to help the sailor too, but a rock wasn't going to do anything against that massive swarm. Grabbing Hale meant he had to let go of Faville, who right away limped towards freedom. Naturally, the bugs pursued him. He had taken the precaution of covering himself with his large coat as a blanket, so the insects took longer to get to his skin. It didn't help for long, though, as the insects soon flew in under the coat. Still, he managed to run out of the cave and towards the trees before they overcame him. Eleksander considered their options. How could they get the bugs away from him without drawing them to the three people still alive?

"We can't just stand here and watch it happen," Hale said, fighting out of Eleksander's grip but not leaving the cave.

"What else can we do?" Taferia asked, shifting her weight.

They swarmed on Faville until the wind picked up even further, creaking the trees until they bent perilously. To Eleksander's great relief, that drove the pests away. They flew off the island and out to sea.

No. Not all of them. One of the orange insects was still in the cave, right in front of him. Up close, it resembled a bee but orange with white stripes instead of black and yellow. It was right at arm's length, staring at him and hovering. Should he move? If these creatures were only stinging out of fear and defence, like bees, the best thing to do would be to stand still. If you ran or flailed, they saw you as a threat and stung. However, if they wanted to sting for blood, there was precious little he could do but duck or run and, of course, cover his skin. Which was the right choice?

It flew right for his face, only to be thwarted in the last moment by Hale throwing himself into its path. The bug stung the exposed skin on Hale's hands as he tried to kill it by smacking it between his palms.

Eleksander hurried to him at the exact moment he saw Taferia run towards the two sailors at the cave opening to check the damage done.

"Are you all right?" Eleksander said, holding Hale's hands to examine the stings. He had never seen stings or bites that infected and swelled so fast.

"It itches and burns like you would not shitting believe," Hale said through gritted teeth.

"They're both dead, I'm afraid," Taferia shouted over. "I'll go check on Faville, but I think he got stung even worse. Whatever those things are, they work fast and – Ow!"

Eleksander turned at her scream. "What happened?"

She hissed, holding her forearm. "There was one insect trapped underneath the sailor. It was squashed but managed to sting my arm a few times," she said with a grunt.

"How many are a few?" Eleksander asked, mentally calculating how many stings it took before the sailors and Faville went from screaming to collapsing.

"I don't know. Three, maybe four?" She checked her arm. "I have four welts."

"You win, then. I only have two," Hale said. He was grinning his usual swaggering smile, but it soon faltered.

Eleksander took his uninjured arm. "What's wrong? Is it the pain?"

"No. I'm... not feeling right."

There was a thump as Taferia sat down. Or rather *collapsed* down. "Neither am I. Dizzy. Nauseous. Hot."

Hale groaned. "It's like the seasickness but much worse."

Taferia leaned her head back against the wall of the cave. Eleksander went to ease her down into a lying position before rushing over to do the same with Hale.

Eleksander pulled at his braids. "What do I do? Should I be keeping you both awake? Or let you sleep? Why did the cursed physician have to get himself killed?"

"You don't have much choice. I'm sleeping, no matter what," Hale slurred, every word like that of a child about to fall asleep. "Check our wounds. If there's a stinging tail in there, take it out. Try to keep the stings clean."

"I will. What else?" Eleksander said, hoping for more information from either of the Woodlanders, who were used to surviving in the wild. His own experience was of market towns, which had posh apothecaries and multitudes of physicians to handle everything. Useless.

Taferia was already out for the count, her breathing fast but steady.

Meanwhile, Hale was fading fast, his eyes barely open. "Keep our temperature normal... give liquids... ah, shit... I'm sorry, love."

Or was that last word not connected to the apology? Was he about to say something else about love?

Perhaps Eleksander had misheard it completely. It did sound too good to be true.

Hale's eyelids fluttered closed. His breathing was as quick as Taferia's and sweat pearled on his scarred brow, despite the mild temperature in the cave.

I can't lose him.

An overwhelming sense of misery and exhaustion made him sit down. He was so tired but reminded himself that now was no time to rest. He needed to get the dead sailors out of the cave, maybe even bury them and Faville somehow. But, before then, he needed to take care of the two unconscious Woodlanders. He dragged himself over to Taferia and was relieved to find that there were no stingers left behind.

He moved on to his next patient. When Hale's wounds were also seen to, Eleksander watched the other lad's tanned, oh, so familiar face, letting his gaze trace the scar across the left cheekbone and then the smaller one through Hale's right eyebrow. He wanted to touch them. He often did. Instead, he used his sleeve to wipe away the perspiration and seawater still dripping from Hale's hair onto his brow.

Eleksander was so heartsore he worried his heart might never recover.

"Don't leave me," he whispered.

Chapter Fifteen

BREAKING THE SURFACE

Sabina's descent through the waterfall felt like it lasted a lifetime and a blink of an eye all at once. Confusion and panic filled every part of her as her limbs flailed, trying to find something to hold on to or to land on. Her throat burned from screaming.

Then, what she had thought impossible happened, things got more confusing. Her body hit what must be the water with a painful smash and everything was dark and tugging at her and everything hurt. Her clothes were so heavy, the straps that kept Grimfrost on her back cut into her shoulders, the axe and her clothes all conspiring to pull her down. Water rushed and rubbed against her skin. With great effort, she made herself stop screaming so she could preserve air and not inhale seawater.

She opened her eyes and saw only water. Under,

next to, and worst of all... above. Wait, was that above? Shit, which way was up?! Her lungs ached, half with panic and half with the length of time since her last breath.

The water to her left looked brighter. That had to be the surface. Unless her eyesight was failing due to lack of air or because she'd hit her head somewhere? She had to take the gamble, knowing full well that if she went in the wrong direction, she wouldn't get a chance to try again. She flipped herself around and headed for the lighter water, begging for air. Only a few strokes in did she realise that her begging was aimed at her mother, begging her to help, saying how frightened she was, how she wasn't ready to die.

Turning back into a child during the last moments of her life was absurd and went against everything she had been taught. So was thinking anyone or anything would help her. She was the one who gave help, not the one who received it.

She considered trying to remove her greatcoat and mail vest, aware that she would have been twice the swimmer and only half as fatigued without them. But the tight straps holding Grimfrost would make undressing nigh impossible under water. She would have to swim with the weight of her armour.

The water was murky, making it hard to see anything, especially colours matching those of her own clothing: brown, black, and green. However, dark red stood out in her periphery. Scarlet tinges in hair floating around a pale face like seaweed with a silver necklace caressing the dead-looking skin. Avelynne. She wasn't moving, only floating like driftwood. It wouldn't be long until she sank, though, weighted down by her wet clothes.

Sabina grabbed her and kept swimming towards the lighter waters. Her lungs ached worse and worse and she had to use every ounce of her strength to propel them both. It didn't matter, she couldn't stop. Fuelled by panic and the will for them both to live, she kept swimming with her grip on Avelynne vice-tight, kicking her legs so hard her muscles burned and were near to cramping.

Still begging. Now for the both of them.

The light above them was getting brighter! It was either the surface or the after world, where her ancestors would welcome her home and she would see her grandparents again. She swam with the last of her energy because, yes, it was the sun up there, piercing through the murky water. More than that, she saw the white fur of Kall where he paddled in circles, probably searching for her.

She pushed herself even harder, screaming in her mind since she was out of air and unable to do it with her throat, until she finally broke the surface with Avelynne in tow.

She gasped in breath after breath, accidentally

swallowing seawater as she did, then realised Avelynne wasn't breathing. Tugging at her, she whimpered, "Wake up."

It didn't work, but the tug on Avelynne's middle had another effect. Water trickled out of her mouth. Sabina repeated the gesture and more water came out, then, mercifully Avelynne gasped in a breath. However, her eyes didn't open. Sabina kept treading water, her muscles aching, keeping both their heads above the surface and calling Avelynne's name to no avail. Kall swam next to her, trying to get her attention but she had none to spare.

"Are you all right, Captain Rosenmarck?"

Sabina blinked saltwater out of her eyes. One of the sailors, Jero, was swimming towards her. Behind him swam another sailor, one whose face was so covered in blood that their identity was unclear.

"I think so. Avelynne won't wake up, though."

"Perhaps she hit her head during the fall," Jero said. "Is she breathing?"

"Aye."

"Then she'll surely wake up soon." He peered at the lifeless Peakdweller in Sabina's arms. "Her coat has ripped. Perhaps you want to leave that heavy thing here in the water, Captain. It'll make her easier to transport and give her more room to breathe."

Sabina looked at the torn, soaked greatcoat. Their uniform had meant so much to them all. And who knew if it would get cold and Avelynne might need the coat?

Then I'll give her mine, Sabina decided. The decision was easy, despite what her greatcoat had meant to her.

"Good idea. Help me take it off," she said. "The mail vest is connected with fiddly clasps, so, sadly, it'll have to stay on."

While she and Jero tugged the coat off, Sabina nodded to the bloodied sailor treading water next to them and asked, "How are you two faring?"

Jero slowed his gasping. "Alive, which after the mass of shattered and submerged bodies I saw back there, is saying a lot."

Sabina scanned the sea, finding only debris and, when she squinted, faraway bodies that were indeed mainly under water and dyeing the sea red with blood. She was too exhausted to swim all the way over there and check all the broken bodies. She could barely tread water. "Any other survivors?"

The bloodied sailor was too busy trying to stay afloat to answer.

Jero shook his head. "Not that I've seen. Every person I came across was dead. I did spot some land, though." He extended a helping hand to his fellow sailor and, with the other one, pointed to their right. "It's over there. We need to get to shore."

"Aye, that we do," Sabina said, longingly eyeing the landmass Jero had found.

She considered dropping the heavy axe from her back but knew that whatever awaited them in the future, she'd need something that could work as both weapon and survival tool.

Jero took one of Avelynne's arms and together they swam with her to shore. Kall arrived first, shaking himself to clear the water out of his fur. Vexingly, he appeared almost unaffected by the disaster. Snowtigers were built to last. Luckily for Sabina, as she had no idea what she would have done if Kall was missing or dead.

When the humans had dragged themselves after him onto the rocky shore, Sabina panted, "When you saw all those dead bodies... you didn't see Eleksander and Hale, did you?" to Jero.

The bloodied sailor answered instead, croaking, "I did. The other two captains and a few sailors were on the bow of the ship, which was still floating, and heading away from me."

Good, Eleksander and Hale were probably alive.

Annoyingly, the image of their magic turning golden was at the back of Sabina's mind. Why? She had more pressing things to worry about. She couldn't control her mind, though. She was so tired she felt feverish. Her thoughts rushed all over the place while her body sagged down, beyond exhaustion. The battle, the drain of magic use, the panic inducing fall, the near drowning, the pain in injured body parts, the swim ashore... not to mention all her worrying about Avelynne, Hale, Eleksander, and the crew of the Wolfsclaw. It all spun in her mind, making her dizzy.

As she lay there on the rocks, the sun peeking out of the clouds and the wind brushing her hair and face across her face, she closed her eyes. Only to rest for a moment.

Chapter Sixteen

BODY WARMTH

Darkness was falling outside the cave, leaving the skies the blue and purple of bruises. Eleksander had dragged the three deceased bodies out and covered them, as respectfully as he could, with rocks, sand, and the large leaves of the korkorand trees.

Now he closed Hale's greatcoat with the idea of buttoning Taferia's sailor jacket next to keep them warm, but he noticed their body temperature was higher than his own. A fever perhaps? He loosened their clothing instead but buttoned his own greatcoat. This island would surely be lovely in summer, but now, while warmer than it had been on Cavarra when they left, it was still chillier than he would've liked.

He missed open fires, blankets, and spiced tea served steaming hot.

He shook off his self-pity and went outside to the korkorand trees. Their nuts or seeds, or whatever one should categorize them as, really did resemble oversized acorns.

He tried climbing the trees but struggled, especially as it was dark. Instead, he tried shaking them and found that a better method. Next came the riddle of how to open these things, luckily bashing them against the cave wall worked.

Squinting in the dim light, he opened Taferia's mouth and let the thick acorn juice dribble slowly into it, one drop at a time, carefully so she wouldn't choke.

Then he repeated the process with Hale.

It was painstakingly slow, and he found his eyelids drooping more than once. After he had made sure they had two acorns full of liquid in their bellies, he opened up a few for himself. This day had left him famished. He drank down the thick liquid, which, despite being clear as water, tasted like a mix of cream and tree sap. It wasn't the spiced tea he had dreamt of, but it didn't taste bad. Most of all, it was filling. He had as many acorns as he could before his hands, cut and bruised, couldn't open any more of them.

Then he leaned back against the cave wall and rested.

When he next opened his eyes, night had fully

fallen. Through the cave opening, he could see the moon and, beyond it, the Utter Northern Star twinkling. He was glad the moon was full, illuminating this dark night as much as it could. It made him feel a little less lonely.

He blinked at the stalwart, cream-white moon. Were any of his shipmates out there somewhere, watching it too? They couldn't all be dead. He wondered if, on some level, he would know if Sabina and Avelynne were dead but discounted the notion. They were a close-knit group but not twins or soulmates or something of that ilk.

He thought back to when the four of them had combined their magic and, strangely, unnaturally, it had turned golden and so much more powerful. No, they weren't connected in any way he had ever heard of, yet the four of them did share something mystical.

Taking out his compass—which was drenched with seawater in his greatcoat pocket but undamaged—he touched the engraving on the back; his name and the words "The Second Wave."

He tried to remember if their magic had ever touched before. He knew the four of them had teamed up to beat the silver beasts kept at the academy for target practice, but he couldn't remember their streams of magic ever connecting. Certainly not all four of them.

His tired gaze fell on Taferia, bathed in moonlight and still breathing fast in her sleep. What had she meant when she said the four of them were chosen? Did that have anything to do with the golden magic?

So many questions. Was life always going to be a slew of questions?

He scrambled to sit up straight and yawned, his tense jaw clicking.

Next to him, Hale stirred at the noises. Eleksander touched his forehead; it wasn't fever hot anymore. He went to check on Taferia and she was back to normal body temperature as well. He was so relieved that their fever had gone so fast that he could've cried.

Taferia was sound asleep, her breaths deep and calm. Hale, on the other hand, was still stirring and now making little groaning noises, as if in pain and about to wake up. To make sure that Taferia didn't wake from the noise, Eleksander used magic to move Hale further into the cave and away from the sleeping sailor.

He wiped some dried blood from a cut on Hale's neck and settled them both comfortably.

The bitter wind of the night had picked up and was spreading through the cave. Hale was shivering a little, whether that was from the fever breaking or the cold air, Eleksander wasn't sure. Either way, he watched the person he loved shudder with chill and couldn't stop himself from helping.

He laid down behind Hale, hesitating for a moment, but then spooning the shivering young man to give him as much body warmth as possible.

Hale not only stopped shivering, but also ceased his groaning and stirring. His breathing calmed and his muscled, lithe frame relaxed in Eleksander's arms. The usual peppery scent of his skin was mixed with the salt of the sea and a hint of sweat and blood. Eleksander didn't mean to fall asleep. He was only going to warm Hale for a while and then get up and check on Taferia again. But he was exhausted, and this was so nice that he couldn't stop his eyelids from closing.

A ray of sunlight brave enough to venture into the cave woke Eleksander, shining red through his closed eyes.

He must have slept through the night. Correction, *they* must have slept through the night, considering that Hale was still cuddled up to him. However, they were not in the position they were when he fell asleep. Instead, he was on his back and Hale lay next to him with his head on Eleksander's shoulder and his arm draped down over Eleksander's body with a hand on his leg.

Eleksander was just considering if he should move, or wake Hale, when the man in question awoke by himself and blinked up at Eleksander.

"Hey. Ugh, I feel like death. And why did a cat piss in my mouth?"

Eleksander laughed. "Vulgar as always, but I get your drift. You've been ill from the stings, remember? So has Taferia."

Hale looked around so Eleksander explained, "She's closer to the cave entrance, you were making noise and I didn't want you to wake her. And, before you ask, I'm afraid the other sailors and the physician didn't make it. I gave them a makeshift burial."

"Thanks," Hale mumbled hoarsely. "Any sighting of Ave? Or Sabina?"

"I'm afraid not. None of the rest of the crew either, or natives of any sort. It's just us."

He was shocked and surprised that Hale didn't move from their intimate position, not even removing that hand on Eleksander's leg. Had he not noticed how their bodies were arranged? Eleksander's heartbeat picked up, the way it always did when they touched. This time even more, though, because they had slept in each other's arms and now, when both awake, they were still so entangled.

Hale closed his eyes again. "I'm too tired to get up. Can we sleep another month or so?"

He yawned adorably and rubbed his sleepy, beard-scratchy face into Eleksander's shoulder, trying to wake up. Why did he have to be this cute? Why did his rough voice have to be so sexy?

His hand was still on Eleksander's thigh and the thing that couldn't happen, did. Eleksander hardened enough to strain against the fabric of the trousers, right above where Hale's hand was.

Hale stared at it, suddenly wide awake. "Oh."

"Shit! Sorry!"

Hale sniggered. "Don't worry about it, these things happen in the morning."

"No, I'm really sorry. I mean I know you don't like me in that way..." He trailed off, panic making him tongue-tied.

"Relax, soft heart. It's fine. I know the feeling. It's been a long time since I was with a lass too."

It was time. He had to say it now.

"Hale. I've never been with a woman. Nor do I want to. I prefer men."

"Oh," Hale croaked.

"I know that's not common in the Woodlands, or in my Lakelands. Which has always made me wish I was born in one of the other two counties," Eleksander spluttered, too fast, too eager to explain, too worried about what Hale might answer. "But here we are. I'm attracted to my own gender."

"Like Sabina is," Hale said, sounding as though he was working through this new concept. "But not attracted to all genders like Avelynne?"

"No, I only fall for men."

A beat of silence, then understanding dawned on Hale's face. It was soon joined by something harder to place. "Sander, this may be me being conceited as usual and I don't want to assume stuff."

"But?"

"But all those times when I've caught you looking at me and when you've complimented me. Was that..."

There was a sensation of wanting to sink through the earth, or run away, but Eleksander fought it. "It takes a lot for me to be attracted to someone. However, yes, you caught my interest from the moment we met." He tried to smile. "I have to say, both Ave and Sabina thought you were rather slow-witted not to notice that I, well, *care* about you much more than friends do."

Hale rubbed his face, like he was trying to force it to wake up. "Why didn't anyone tell me?"

"I asked them not to. I wanted you to figure it out yourself. Just so that if you didn't feel the same way I do, things wouldn't be strange between us. Our friendship means the world to me."

Hale looked as puzzled as if someone told him that the sky was made of egg.

Eleksander's heart pounded out the passing moments painfully.

Hale cleared his throat. "It..."

Eleksander's heart picked up further.

"It means a lot to me, too. Or, like, you mean a lot to me. Or I mean I—" Hale cut off and rubbed his knuckles into his eyes. "Shit, I don't know what I mean."

Neither did Eleksander, but he knew one thing: Hale seemed neither repulsed nor angry. In fact, he was showing that he still liked him. That was all he needed for now. He shook off as much of the tension that had crept into his very bones as he could and tried to slow his drumming heart.

A cough was heard, then Taferia calling out a hoarse, "Hello?"

Eleksander got up. "You think about what you mean and take a moment to come back to life. I'll go see to her."

"All right."

Eleksander ducked through the low-ceilinged tunnel towards her. Her eyes were still closed, fluttering open only on occasion, and she was pulling at the high-collared tunic, trying to open it at the neck, so he helped her. That was when he saw it.

Silver tattoos.

He was immediately brought back to the day of Tutor Rete's death. Taferia wasn't covered in the tattoos, like Rete had been. Nor did she have as many as Tutor Santorine, but there were enough for Eleksander to know what organisation she must belong to.

"You're one of the Twelve," he whispered.

Her eyes flew open and she stared around. Seeing that it was only him, her, and Hale in the cave she looked calmer.

She blew out a long breath. "This wasn't how I wanted you to find out."

Eleksander chewed the inside of his cheek. They had been so upset with Faville being a spy, an upset which was pointless since he didn't even survive to divulge his information. And now to find out that there had been another spy among them. One much better at hiding. One who might survive this whole thing to report back.

Could she be trusted?

Hale had clambered up and come over. "What in the name of the shitting silver beasts is going on?"

"She's a spy for the Twelve," Eleksander said.

"Not a spy." Taferia wiped a lock of matted hair out of her eyes. "I was sent by the Twelve to protect you and to make sure that you hadn't fallen victim to the king's propaganda. To make sure that you still remembered your mission to peacefully find new lands."

Hale scoffed. "You mean to find new land *for the Twelve* to set up your rebel base on, and then help you plot your uprising against the king?"

"No," she said, her voice still raspy. "All you needed to do was find new land in an ethical manner and make the maps to show us where it was on your return." She coughed and leaned up on her elbows. "We would do everything else."

"How generous of you," Eleksander mumbled. "And nice that you sent us a minder so we wouldn't stumble into being violent colonisers."

"I'm sorry that we didn't trust you. Or told you who I am," Taferia said. "But King Lothiam gets to everyone. Somehow. Even good people are swayed. So, we had to send someone along with you. Although, as I say, it was mainly to protect and help you."

While Hale was ranting at her about sneaking onto the ship and asking about how many of their sailors were actually working for the Twelve, Eleksander thought back to what Taferia had said before.

"Tell me what you meant back when you said something like 'we've put too much work into getting you four to where you are now' during the fight with the sea monster."

Taferia sighed. "You remembered that, huh? I

should not have spoken out of turn, I panicked, and the words flew out."

"What. Did. It. Mean?" Eleksander bit out.

"You better answer him. He's losing patience, which is a rare occurrence and never ends well," Hale said.

That was an obvious lie, but maybe Taferia didn't know that.

"All right, keep your boots on, I'll tell you." She held her hands up. "You may know that the king was deeply involved with the first wave right from the start. In their acceptance to the academy, their training, even what they did for recreation. The second wave, you were meant to be ours. The class that we could get through to."

"You mean use?" Eleksander asked, more tired than angry.

Her face fell. "No, Eleksander! I mean the ones we could make understand. That was why Rete and Santorine made such a point of keeping the king away from you and your lesson plans." Her tone softened. "I understand that you must feel like all adults are lying to you and keeping secrets, but the Twelve truly do want to save Cavarra and defeat the king. Before his silver beasts kill us all."

Hale surged forward. "*His* silver beasts?"

"Ah," Taferia said on a dejected sigh. "I suppose I

might as well tell you all of it. After all, unless someone comes for us, we will all die on this island."

"So tell us," Eleksander said.

She nodded while trying to wet her dry lips.

"But first," he said reluctantly, "let me go get you both some more korkorand acorns, to get your strength up and quench your thirst."

He crawled out of the cave and shook the trees, trying not to think of the fact that there were only a handful of acorns left.

Chapter Seventeen

HETHKLISH

When Sabina's eyes flew open, it was dark. Kall was by her side, tiredly licking her face. Ignoring that moving hurt, she bumped her head against his in the feline way of appreciation and he returned the gesture before laying down next to her. How long had she been asleep? She tried to tell Kall he was a good boy, but her mouth was drier than parchment and had the tang of saltwater.

She checked on Avelynne. Still breathing, but not conscious.

Jero was a few steps away, shaking the bloodied sailor before croaking, "He's dead."

Sabina was about to answer when she remembered that she hadn't come to on her own. Kall's warning growl had woken her, and most likely Jero, up.

And now the snowtiger stood and growled again.

She put her hand back on Grimfrost's handle and stared around her. She couldn't see anything in the moonlight, but thought she heard distant footsteps. After a while she was sure. Those were steps in the sand. She hissed a warning to Jero and pulled Avelynne to her, looking around for places to hide. There were none.

She drew Grimfrost and stood, far too fast, and fell down again. She hadn't even pulled the sheath off the axe blade. She was weak as a new-born, not thinking clearly, and thirstier than she had ever been.

People approached; her tired eyes made out about five of them, maybe six. They stopped and, to her befuddlement, some of them ran off. To get reinforcements, perhaps? What for? She, Avelynne, Jero, and Kall were helpless as baby mice.

The remaining two walked towards her, slow and cautious, not running to attack. Also, she couldn't see any weapons.

After a spell, one of them, a woman probably about her own age, kneeled in front of Sabina.

She and her taller companion looked like humans but had slimmer faces and builds. The woman clasped her hands in her lap, she had an upturned little nose and a sweet mouth locked in a friendly smile. She couldn't have looked more nonthreatening if she tried.

Sabina, with great effort, sheathed Grimfrost to show that she meant no harm either.

When she turned back to the stranger, she saw that she had pointed ears which were lighter skinned then the rest of her, meaning they stood out even in the light by the moon. Her companion had them too.

The woman must've been studying her too because she blurted, "Your hair is white! Is that common where you're from? Where *are* you from? What's your name?"

Sabina tried to wet her lips enough to speak. "Water."

The woman tilted her head fast, giving her a bird-like expression. "Your name is Water? Or are you saying you're from the water? Wait.... why do you speak our language?"

"No. Need water. To drink," Sabina panted, at this point not giving a toss why or how they spoke the same language.

The man handed the kneeling woman an opened flask and she gave it to Sabina. "Right, sorry. I get distracted. Here's some water. Let me know if you need help drinking."

Sabina sniffed it. She was about to ask if her rescuers could have some first to prove it wasn't laced with something, but dehydration was stronger than her distrust, and she took a couple of deep gulps before handing the flask to Jero.

"Thank you," she said, feeling better now that her tongue wasn't dried to the roof of her mouth.

The woman inclined her head. "Sorry again about my misunderstanding. I get carried away. I'm Aurea, second in command of the grand ship Qetesh and its sister vessel, the Parataxia." She pointed to the man behind her. "And this is the grand old man in charge, Captain Naseer. We're Hethklish. From Hethekla, that is. Where are you from?"

"Cavarra. We came in a ship that was thrown down a waterfall and sunk with many casualties. My name is Captain Sabina Rosenmarck, second wave of the mapmakers from the Hall of Explorers. This is one of my skilled sailors, Jero."

Jero bowed to them, still drinking from the flask.

Sabina was about to introduce Avelynne and explain that she was alive but not waking, when this Captain Naseer crouched and said, "Welcome to this island, which is as yet unnamed. We can't all agree on a name, even after having stopped here for near a week."

Kall had been lurking in the shadows, ready to pounce despite how exhausted he must be. Now, he crept forward, no longer in fight mode since his mistress had calmed.

Sabina petted him and promised him some water soon.

Aurea's eyes went wide, more with thrill than fear. "Whoa! What is that?"

"This is Kall, he's my animal companion. Where I'm from we keep an animal as help with hunting and protection, but also as company. He's a snowtiger and quite safe, as long as I don't command him otherwise," Sabina explained. It couldn't hurt to point out that while they were helpless and at these strangers' mercy, Kall was not.

"He's magnificent," Aurea breathed. "Those turquoise eyes. That thick fur. The size and musculature of him! The cute nose!"

"Um, yes. You should see the teeth," Sabina said, secretly proud to have fascinated this stranger with her companion. Kall seemed to like it, too, preening as he paced around her.

She noticed that Captain Naseer's gaze had fallen to Avelynne where she lay in Sabina's arms.

"This is my... friend and fellow captain, Avelynne. She hasn't woken up since we went over the waterfall. I fear she might have hit her head or something. She's breathing and I can't see any injuries, unless they're hidden by her hair."

Captain Naseer winced. "Ah, well when someone is knocked out like that, it's best to move them very carefully in case they do have an injury inside the skull."

"Poor thing. Hm, she's not big. We can carry her," Aurea said.

Sabina sat straighter. "Carry her? Where are you taking us?"

"Only to our camp so you can rest, eat, and drink while you tell us your tale." Aurea smiled. "I don't know if you've noticed, but I'm dying to learn more about you! We sent the others back for reinforcements, but we'll catch them up and tell them there's no need."

"Where's your camp, if I may ask?" Jero asked, sounding both shy and hoarse from their ordeal.

Aurea pointed back to where they had come from. "Over there. This is a quite large island, our ships and the temporary camp we've set up are on the other side. You know, we might not have seen you unless we were patrolling the island for sea serpents."

"Sea serpents?" Sabina queried.

"Oh, not to worry, we haven't seen any in quite a while. You'll be safe."

Sabina decided they had no other choice than to trust these people. Left on this beach, they'd soon die of exposure or starvation. Or these sea serpents. She gave the ocean one last examination, trying to see any Wolfsclaw crewmembers swimming or floating towards them. Her heart begging especially for a glimpse of Eleksander's braids or Hale's splashing style of swimming.

Nothing.

The Hethklish carried Avelynne and, while Jero, Kall, and Sabina stumbled behind them, Aurea explained that they were a seafaring folk and had made port on this island for a rest during their exploration.

She finished with, "We've sailed far and wide, but not ventured much in this direction."

Sabina had just enough time to explain that Cavarrians had recently begun exploring the seas, about the sea monster, and then the waterfall, and that she didn't knew where the rest of their crew was, when they arrived at a camp.

A linen awning was connected high between tall trees, creating a sizeable area covered from wind and rain, including two of the sides. Inside there were hammocks hung between shorter trees, stones arranged to make a fire pit, intricate lanterns hung from branches, and crates set up as tables and seats.

It made the Cavarrian camp on Kohland look like a child's picnic.

What really made Sabina's jaw drop, though, were the ships. There were two of them, with several sails of different sizes connected with intricate rigging, and they stood proud above the waves, high enough to be two storeys.

They made the Wolfsclaw look like an overgrown fishing boat, which, on closer thought, was exactly what it was.

"I shall find a bed for your friend to rest in," Naseer said, smoothing down his thinning, wheat-blond hair.

"I'd... like her to not be out of my sight," Sabina said.

"She'll be right there." He nodded towards the nearest empty hammock.

Sabina watched them gently place Avelynne in the hammock and check that she was comfortable and could breathe freely.

Then she and Jero sat down on a crate each and were given more water by some sailors. Two bowls of purple, dried things were placed on the table before them, some sort of fruit if its sweet smell was to be believed.

"This is dried canefruit," Naseer said, taking a bite from Sabina's bowl. "Very nutritious. Good for recovery."

Jero tucked into his bowl and Sabina followed suit, only pausing to give Kall a piece of the fruit and ask for some water for him.

"Yes!" Aurea went off, to soon return with a big

bowl of water and a chunk of some sort of uncooked meat.

"Will he eat raw weasel flesh?" she asked as he sat on his hindlegs, making him as tall as Aurea, and nibbled at the meat in her hand.

"Oh. He's so gentle even when so hungry. What a sweetheart," Aurea said, dropping the meat so he could gobble it up.

"He's well-trained," Sabina said around a mouth full of fruit. "Thank you for feeding him. And us."

"You're welcome. The sea is cruel, so we who travel it must be all the kinder to one another."

The respite and food were more needed than Sabina had thought.

Mid-bite, she heard Jero tell Captain Naseer about the deceased sailor on the shore and ask about burials. As they all decided to see to it when the Cavarrians had rested, Sabina found her gaze magnetically pulled to the massive ships anchored by the shore again.

"Those are magnificent," she said to Aurea.

"They are certainly easy to manoeuvre and built for speed. Not magnificent by our measure as we have much bigger and more advanced ships," Aurea sighed happily, "but I do love them both after all the storms I've weathered on them. The larger one is the Qetesh and the small one is called the Parataxia."

"And you're the second in command of both of them?" Sabina asked.

"Right now, yes. I grew up on ships so I'm a natural sailor. Last year, though, I quit to become a printer." Aurea ruffled her short hair into an attractive mess. "However, when my old mentor Naseer wanted to journey in this direction, he knew it was the only part of the world I hadn't explored. So, he asked me to take a few months' leave and come. Did you know that Hethklish sailors favour going west because they have a superstition about going east?"

"No. I didn't." Sabina was getting a feeling that you had to pull this woman back to a certain topic you wanted to discuss, otherwise she'd launch into four new subjects one after another and you'd forget your question. "Can we get back to your occupation? A... printer?"

Aurea looked at her blankly. "Yes, I'm a printer."

"Aye," Sabina said, trying to be patient despite her fatigue. "What does one of those do?"

"I print books. Oh, and advertisements, pamphlets, public notices, and all that sort of stuff."

"You do what to books? Wait, do you mean you copy them out? We have scholars who do that."

Aurea frowned. "Copy? Like copying texts for hand?"

"Aye, onto new parchment and then binding them all together in a book."

"Oh! I get it now; you haven't invented something like the printing press. I'm sorry. We've only come up with it in the last decade ourselves. All right, how to explain this? Hm."

Sabina kept eating, watching Jero's head loll back as he went to sleep.

Aurea tapped a finger against her chin. "I suppose I should start with that Hethklish put a lot of stock into the written word, mainly to describe everything we've explored and learned. Copying texts out by hand took too long and we find inventing things to speed up slow processes are important. It saves time as well as resources in the long run. Do Cavarrians love books?"

Sabina thought about that. How did you measure what was love and what was merely needing something? "Um, we like them and use them. But reading isn't prevalent everywhere and most people only read factual things, they find stories a waste of time."

Aurea's eyes widened. "How can they resist the pull?"

"The pull?"

"The draw of telling and hearing stories? I mean, there are fragments of stories in the air all around us."

"There's what now?" Sabina asked, aware that her role in this conversation was the confused sceptic. As well as that, she was probably too tired for this chat.

Aurea's expression became self-conscious. "With so many people, all thinking, experiencing, and feeling? Living their own stories and daydreaming and *actually dreaming*, the air must be filled with fragments of stories." She waved a graceful hand between them, as if wafting forth a bit of story. "So, we believe that some people, the ones who know how to listen, or perhaps can't help but listen, try to catch the fragments and write them down. Or, at least analyse and explain them."

Sabina thought about that as she chewed her last piece of canefruit. "Cavarrians... Well, we tend to tell our stories in speech, and we value drawing very highly. I guess if there are story fragments in the air, we paint them instead of writing them?"

"Ah, I see. That's wonderful! Are you any good at that?"

"Pretty good. To be chosen to be a Hall of Explorers mapmaker, you have to be able to draw well. Otherwise, no one would understand your maps." Sabina swallowed the fruit. "Well, geography and calculating distances goes into mapmaking as well, of course, but drawing matters a lot."

Aurea gave a sly smile. "So, when you say 'pretty good,' you mean you are brilliant enough to have been chosen to be a mapmaker extraordinaire?"

Sabina's cheeks heated up. "I'm quite proficient. Not as good as Avelynne, though." She glanced over at the sleeping form in the hammock, her sweet countess looked so small. "She could've been an extraordinary artist. If her parents hadn't decided that she had to get into the Hall of Explorers."

"Interesting! I'm terrible at drawing," Aurea said with a smile. "Luckily, we have lots of maps, so I don't need to worry about that. Besides, I have other talents that society needs, I don't need to be creative."

Sabina watched her, at first unsure what about this conversation was making her uncomfortable. Then it dawned on her. Aurea's humble confidence felt... healthier than the pressure to excel at everything that Sabina was used to.

"Anyway, tell me more about this printing business," Sabina said. "It sounds like something Cavarra needs."

Aurea lit up and, once more, the words poured out of her like the wild babbling of a brook. "We make little metal squares, each containing a raised letter. We place the letters in a large press to form words. Then we spread ink onto the metal pieces to print word after word onto the book. When you have done that on one page, you can just take another piece of paper in and do it again."

Sabina tilted her head. "Paper? Is that like parchment?"

"Yes, but instead of making it from animal hide, it's created from bark or cotton broken down in water. Long process, actually. Anyway, it's easier and cheaper to make and use than parchment."

"I see."

Sabina wished she hadn't asked about this. There was so much to take in. So many new things when her mind was already filled with all that had happened, and the worry for those still missing. And guilt over all those she'd lost.

Aurea watched her with concern. "Would you like more to eat and drink?"

"Actually, yes," Sabina admitted, anything to try to get some energy back.

Aurea strode off and soon came back with a plate of hard tack, while a burly sailor brought two tin tankards filled with something white. His arrival woke Jero up.

"Here's some oaty crisp bread and goats' milk," Aurea explained. "We go nowhere without goats. They bring luck. And food and drink, of course."

Jero tucked into the milk while Sabina had some hard tack. She could taste the oats and tried to remember the last time she'd eaten them. Silver beasts had gobbled up the oats first, until it was a rare luxury saved only for Cavarra's rich.

She was about to ask Aurea about if they had

silver beasts too but found herself too shattered for more conversation.

"Doldrums, I'm so sorry for standing there rambling on when you clearly needed more rest and sustenance," Aurea said.

Sabina had her mouth full so Jero replied. "That's fine! We are so grateful for any help." He hesitated. "Sorry. I, um, didn't understand the first word you said? It began with a D?"

"Doldrums," Aurea said.

They stared back at her, waiting for her to explain.

She sat back. "Huh, so while we do speak the same language, not everything is the same. Interesting. Anyway, we say doldrums to indicate something that's...well, bad. It can be used as a mild curse word as well." She looked pensive. "I suppose its equivalent is when we use another sailor's term, tailwinds – often shortened to tails, when something is good or when we celebrate something."

Jero swallowed a mouthful of milk. "And those are sailors' terms?"

"Yes. You don't have them?"

"Not as far as I know," Sabina said. "Only fishermen sail where we come from and I've never heard them use those words."

"Doldrums is when you're becalmed, meaning

the sea is still and there's no wind in your sails. Our ships can be stuck out at sea for long periods during doldrums. At best, it means delays. At worst, it means running out of food, and, you know, dying a lot," Aurea said in her quick, energetic chatter. "Tailwinds means when the wind is in your sails, increasing your speed and leading you where you wanted to go."

"I see," Sabina said.

Burping quietly, Jero stood and said, "Thank you so much for the food." He bowed to Aurea then turned to Sabina. "Would it be all right if I lie down to rest, Captain Rosenmarck?"

"Of course," Sabina said, embarrassed that he had to ask. Were you still a captain if your ship was gone and most of your crew dead or missing?

"There are hammocks everywhere," Aurea said. "We sleep in shifts here so there are always a few free ones. Go ahead and grab one; we'll wake you if there is any news."

Jero bowed again. "Thank you so much. For everything." Aurea smiled at him and he went off towards the hammocks, passing the one that Avelynne slept in. A thought hammered in Sabina's mind: *She has to wake up. The world needs someone like her awake and working for its improvement.*

Captain Naseer returned and asked, "How is our shipwrecked survivor? Fed and comfortable?"

"Aye, many thanks." She cast a glance over to

Avelynne, laying so strangely still. "I'm fine, just worried about Avelynne. She hasn't had anything to drink or eat."

Naseer rubbed his chin. "Well, we do have a method for carefully dripping a little goats' milk down the throats of unconscious people without drowning them. Should we try that?"

"If you wouldn't mind," Sabina said, embarrassed at how her small her voice sounded.

"I'll get started right away."

Sabina nodded, gaze still on Avelynne.

Aurea touched the back of her hand, brief and light as the flitter of a butterfly wing. "She'll be fine, I'm sure."

By the light from the camp's lanterns, Sabina realised that Aurea had copper-coloured hair, which matched her warmly toned skin and amber eyes. More interesting, there were raised lines along her cheekbones.

Aurea caught her staring. "Looking at my aging scars? I did notice that none of you have them. My people burn them into our skins when we come of age. It's a ritual to teach us to tolerate pain and to mark that we are adults. No Cavarrians have them?"

"No. Some of us do imprint ink into our skin with needles, though. We call them tattoos."

She thought about Hale and his tattoo. Where

was he now? Was he alive? Was Eleksander? They had to be!

"Fascinating! There are so many things I want to ask you," Aurea said. "But you must be tired."

Tired was an understatement. Nevertheless, Aurea's enthusiasm and curiosity were not only sweet but strangely invigorating. Besides, if she kept talking to this woman about the differences between their homes, she didn't have to think about how she was going to have to explain everything about the king's true nature and about the Twelve to Jero.

Or, more crucially, all the dead sailors whose lost lives were her responsibility.

At that thought, the infectious nature of Aurea's bright-eyed joy lost its power.

Sabina looked to the sea. So many sailors gone. Including the one they would bury later. She didn't even know his name. Without that, how would she honour him at his makeshift burial? If she ever got back to Cavarra, how could she look his family in the eye?

Her guilt over killing Rete came back for some reason, hitting her straight in the chest, soon joined by the memory of Ivar and his icewolf being devoured by that monster.

How much more death was she responsible for now?

Chapter Eighteen

SOLSTICE BORN

The cave was lighter now, the morning well on its way. The mood was still dark, though, Eleksander thought. All the unanswered questions and mistrust overcrowding the small space. He and Hale watched Taferia search for words. Or perhaps stall.

Taferia scratched at the tight, coiled curls at the back of her neck before saying, "Where to begin? Well, the year you four were born had a peculiar summer. To be exact, it had a peculiar month around the scorching summer solstice."

"Please tell me we're not going to discuss weather," Hale snarled.

She gave a mirthless chuckle. "In a way, we are. At the summer solstice of that year, we had what at first looked like a simple heatwave. The high temperatures, and the lack of clouds or rain, wasn't all that happened, though."

Hale rolled his eyes. "Let me guess, there was also no wind."

Eleksander wished Hale would calm down and be quiet but he knew him well enough to recognise this behaviour as his way of coping with stress.

It didn't matter as Taferia ignored him. "The sun didn't just shine all the time; it darkened to a golden hue. The nights were shorter than at a normal summer solstice, too."

"Wait, I was born during the summer solstice," Hale said.

"Exactly," Taferia said giving him a meaning look. "All four of you were. That summer solstice the animals had larger litters with healthier young. The crops, which should've died without rain, grew more bountiful. The air was heavy with heat and magic. Everyone waited, sensing something significant was happening."

Hale opened his mouth to say something. Considering the grin on his face, Eleksander was pretty sure he was going to say that his birth was the significant thing. Luckily — for Eleksander wanted to know more since he'd never known his exact birth date, always celebrating his birthday on the day when the Aetholos took him in — Taferia spoke over him.

"What did happen was the children born around the summer solstice had strong magic right from birth. They floated toys into their cots and slept with swirls of magic emanating from their tiny baby fingers. Or, should I say, *you* did."

Eleksander was about to ask follow-up questions when Taferia added, "We all thought that those of you born during that solstice would be the strongest magicians of our age. But, as you grew, your magic settled back into the normal amount of any child. So, we thought whatever strangeness had happened that solstice ended when the summer did. Most people forgot all about it."

"I guess the Twelve didn't forget? You seem to know a shitload about this," Hale said, arms crossed.

"We do. One of our scholars specialised in the research of that summer solstice. In fact, you know her. Tutor Atha Santorine."

Both lads reacted with noises of surprise and contempt, making Taferia hold her hands up. "I know, I know, you've had negative experiences with her. Nevertheless, you will recall that she never tried to hurt you and that she had a brilliant mind." Taferia's face took on a wretched and somehow also hero-worshipping expression. "Well, she still has. And she continues to study best she can, considering where she is."

"The dungeons, where she belongs," Hale said.

That did not need saying; Hale was only trying to hurt Taferia because he felt hurt and confused. Unless, Eleksander was misinterpreting, which was unlikely. Hale might not be able to understand his own emotions, but to Eleksander they were as clear as the sea that morning they left Kohland.

Taferia didn't take the bait. "Back when Atha had access to a lab and library, she kept animals who were born during that summer solstice. Most of them turtles, due to their long lifespans. They—"

"What did she do to them?" Eleksander interrupted, anger surfacing at the concern that these turtles may have been experimented upon.

"She only watched them in different situations. She always argued that those animals were more unique than we thought. On the outside they look like normal animals, but, when those solstice-born animals are placed together, they behave differently."

"Differently how?" Hale said.

"They show more defensive and offensive skills as well as a higher social cohesion, working as a team even when they were normally solitary animals. When her studies showed this and the next batch of Hall of Explorers candidates were from that year, we helped you four solstice-born get your places."

Sunrays pierced deeper into the cave, showing how grimy, wearied, and tattered they all were. Eleksander could hear Hale's stomach growling too. Still, none of them moved. Not to eat. Not to wash. Not to empty their bladders. This was too important.

Hale narrowed his eyes at her. "If you hand-picked us for when we were born, does that mean we weren't the ones most successful at our tests?" His hands clenched into fists in his lap. "I mean, I know Ave wasn't, but the other three of us thought we were the best from our counties? I sure as shit know I did brilliantly!"

Taferia sat up straighter, seeming to regret it when she sat back with a wince. "That was it. All four of you were the best in all your tests! Whether that was merely a fluke or because of when you were born, I do not know." She shifted her position and then picked back up. "The academy officials who tested Avelynne still claim she was the best in the Peaks, but too insecure to show her strengths and so holding back, convinced that she couldn't do as much as everyone else. That was the only reason others looked like they did better on the tests. In truth, she could've run rings around them."

So, she hadn't gotten in due to cheating! Eleksander had to tell her that.

If he ever saw her again.

"That was one of the things that supported the validity of Santorine's theory about the magic of those born during that summer solstice," Taferia said. "The fact that the four of you were all so easily better than the others, not only at magic but also your other subjects. It seems to me her theory that you'd be even better together is proven by that golden magic you produced."

Hale leaned back, breathing out a low, "Well, shit."

Eleksander took out his compass, flipping it over and back and then over again. Its weight and solidity were comforting. "How do you know when we were born when I have no idea? I only know when my adopted father found me walking the streets naked and alone." He sighed at that this stranger had to tell him his birthday and added a mumbled, "Yet another reason to hate my birth parents."

Taferia's face snapped up, appalled. "You shouldn't hate them, that's not fair! Your mother had no choice and your father never knew of you."

Eleksander nearly dropped the compass. "You... you know who my parents are?"

Taferia swore and then muttered, "I wasn't meant to tell you."

"Why not? Who are they?" Eleksander heard how high pitched his voice had become but did nothing to counteract it. He had a good reason to be upset, didn't he?

Taferia sat there, just looking at them.

"Tell him!" Hale snapped.

"Fine. I've exposed everything else, so why not?"

Taferia looked down at her clasped hands in her lap. "I suppose I should start with who they are, or, in the case of your mother, who she was."

"Was?" Eleksander whispered, already less sure he wanted to know.

Gaze still on her hands, Taferia said, "I'm afraid she's no longer with us. Not in physical form, but her spirit and legacy do live on. Not just in you, and your eyes and nose which are exactly like hers, but in our cause. In the very core of the Twelve."

She looked up at Eleksander as if this should explain everything to him. It didn't. "Who was she?"

"The Queen."

"What?" Eleksander croaked.

"Your mother was Queen Lea of Cavarra, formerly from the Peaks. I know everyone was told that the king beheaded her because of some clandestine dalliance with another man but—"

Hale interrupted, "That was a lie. Yes, we know. It was actually because she founded the Twelve, after finding out that her husband was bleeding his people dry in more ways than one."

Taferia nodded. "She found out many things. In fact, it's believed she uncovered some big secret of Lothiam's but died before she had time to pass it on to the rest of the Twelve." She appeared lost in thought for a moment. "However, she *did* have a hidden love affair. Not when she was married, though, but a few months before her official betrothal to Lothiam."

"Poor thing, having to marry that bag of worms," Hale said.

Taferia ignored that, busy with her tale. "Queen Lea was young and so was her lover. The affair ended when the Queen's parents decided to marry her off to the king when she came of age. But it turned out she was already with child, having hidden it with large gowns, as was the fashion then."

"Sounds like the point where nobles, especially from the Peaks, would try to make her lose the baby," Hale said, making Eleksander slap his leg. While Hale was right in what he said, there was no need to be so brutally blunt.

"She was too far gone for that. She had the baby in secret, then it was given to a wetnurse while they decided what was to be done. Our awful king would certainly not marry someone who'd borne someone else's child." Taferia sought Eleksander's gaze. "So, the Queen was promised that you were adopted out to a loving family. She missed you terribly but knew that if Lothiam found out about you, he'd not only shun her, but feel so duped he might have you killed."

"And that's how I ended up with the Aetholos?" He jerked his head back. "That doesn't make sense. I was about five years old when they found me, walking the roads between the Centre and the Lakelands."

"You were raised by that wetnurse for the first few years. The Queen's parents couldn't decide where to adopt you off to. Where would you be safe? But more importantly, where would *they* be safe from both the scandal and from your mother being shunned, or even killed, if the truth one day came out?"

"And?"

Taferia gave him a pitying look. "I'm afraid they couldn't think of a place. No adoptive family they trusted enough. When you were about five, they finally lost their nerve and made a decision they never informed the Queen of. The wetnurse was given orders to kill you."

"What?" Hale shouted.

Taferia kept her eye contact with Eleksander, though. "To drown you, to be exact. She went along with it at first, taking you out for a swim in a nearby, quiet lake. But as she saw you bathing and playing like any innocent five-year-old, she couldn't do it. After all she had raised you from a baby and cared for you."

"What did she do, then?" Eleksander whispered.

"She pulled you out of the water and told you to run before anyone saw you. That it was a game and that she'd catch up with you soon. You were always a good boy and did as you were told." Taferia's voice was thick with emotion. "She admitted this to the Twelve many years later, saying she felt that if she let you run away, it was up to nature and fate whether you lived or died, not her. She was nearly driven mad by the ordeal, quite frankly we're lucky that she didn't follow the orders."

"Lucky? What's lucky is that the Queen's parents are dead, it saves me the work of kicking the shit out of them," Hale said.

Eleksander sat quiet, trying to digest all of this. "Wait, what about my father? Where was he in all of this? Who was he?"

"Well, the reason the Queen's parents hid you and your wetnurse on the edge of the Lakelands was that there was at first a plan to tell your father about you and have him raise you. But his family was deemed untrustworthy, more interested in ambition than loyalty."

"My father was from the Lakelands?"

"More than that. He was, or rather is, the Duke of the Lakelands."

"The current duke?" Eleksander croaked.

"Yes. He still doesn't know about you. The Twelve were sworn to secrecy by the Queen. We keep our promises. Even after death, even when it means keeping a boy from his father."

Eleksander filed that away as something to be

royally furious about later, for now he had too many questions.

"Are you actually telling me my father is still alive? And doesn't know about me? He didn't abandon me?"

"No. And I'm sorry we couldn't tell you, but we knew you had a lovely family who raised you and loved you. One who would probably be a better option than the duke and his lot."

"Why?" Hale asked, rubbing his face.

He had dark circles under his eyes and so did Taferia. Eleksander should let them both rest and recuperate, but how could he when he was finally getting answers?

Taferia sucked her teeth. "They tend to be... vain and pompous as well as overly ambitious. Almost as cold as Avelynne's family, if not as strict."

Eleksander couldn't disagree with that. The Aetholos were all he could ever have asked for in a family. While they may be a little reserved and pushed their children hard to excel, they were kind, encouraging, intelligent, creative, and caring. Not to mention financially well-off, but not in the centre of societal attention like a noble family was. Being an Aetholo was much better than living with a doomed queen or a shallow duke would've been. But still, never having known. Never having been given the choice. Never getting answers. It wasn't fair.

A voice inside his mind reminded him that nothing that happened to Queen Lea, *his mother,* had been fair either. She had acted in his best interest even though it hurt her to be without him and she'd thought he was growing up in a good, loving home. Which, of course, he had done.

Poor Lea. How old had he been when she was beheaded? Thirteen? Fourteen? He had no idea that it was his birthmother's head that fell that day. Perhaps that was best.

He didn't know how to feel about having hated his parents for abandoning him all these years, about the certainty that his parents had been wastrels or criminals who left him by the roadside because he wasn't important to them. Had that sprung from his self-loathing? The Aetholos certainly hadn't said anything like that.

Eleksander was about to ask one of the other fifty questions growing in his mind when there was an ear-splitting screech from outside the cave. He forgot the cave's height and shot up, hitting his head. The screech was heard again, closer now. He cursed and ran outside. The footsteps of the other two, slow and hobbling, rang out behind him.

Outside, he squinted to see through the morning sunlight, which was turning the sea golden with its glare. That was when he spotted it, something coming out of the waves, flapping its tail so that water crashed onto their little island. It left the water and slithered onto the sand.

"I think it's some sort of serpent," Taferia said quietly behind him.

Eleksander agreed with her. Except that serpents weren't thick as his waist and the length of two of him. Nor did they exude some sort of smoke that trickled out from between its scales. It was coming towards them now.

Hale swore. "I'm too drained to use magic."

"Me, too," Taferia said.

Eleksander, exhausted as well but in better shape than the other two, gathered up his energy and threw magic towards the snake. The volley knocked it back into the sea and they watched the surface for movement.

Stay down, stay down, repeated in Eleksander's mind.

It didn't obey.

It came up from the waves again and, at great speed, slithered towards them on its belly. Its green opalescent scales glistened and so did its emotionless grey eyes. How could it be that quick?

The sea serpent gave them little time to prepare, certainly not enough time for Eleksander to aim with the magic he'd just conjured. Instead, it appeared next to him and flicked its massive tail. Eleksander tried to duck but the tail struck his side and he was flung back, losing the magic-summoning energy he had amassed and getting a face full of sand.

While he was trying to stand and get rid of the sand, the fiend went for the two Woodlanders. Hale drew the longest of his daggers while simultaneously kicking at the beast, his foot going high above his head and smacking into the body of the serpent.

The creature screeched again, backed away, and turned its attack on Taferia instead. She picked up a fallen branch from a korkorand tree and whacked at the swift creature with it. Meanwhile, Hale jumped and dodged both the serpent's head, with a set of impressively long fangs, and the swiping tail, trying to stab at its body as he did so.

Eleksander rushed the creature from behind, clambering up onto it and clutching the part below the head with his thighs, attempting to use his sizable legs to strangle it. Maybe magic wasn't strong enough to subdue this thing, but no one could function without breathing, right?

It didn't work. The monster swung its head back and forth, nearly shaking Eleksander off every time. If it managed it, who knew where he'd land or if he'd survive the fall?

The serpent's head dove, trying to sink its fangs into Taferia who had lost the branch in her last attack and lay unarmed on the sand.

Just as it opened its mouth, Hale pounced and

plunged the dagger into the maw of the creature. All the way up into its flat head. The dagger was too thin to have done much damage anywhere else, but pierced into the roof of the snake's mouth, it must have reached something crucial. The serpent gave a wail and then sagged into a heap, as thought it was made of cloth. No more smoke emanated from it.

Hale kicked the dead serpent with fatigued movements, and then with much effort yanked out the dagger. "See, I told you it was a good idea to strap all those blades to my body."

Eleksander couldn't help but laugh. How he wanted to kiss that boyish, self-assured grin off Hale's mouth. Instead, he braved going closer to the sea serpent, checking that it wasn't coming back or simply faking.

Hale wiped his dagger on the sand, then lumbered closer to Eleksander. It was obvious that he was back to utter exhaustion now that the heat of battle had left him. "Very dead. Very unable to use those fangs. Great." He rubbed his taut belly. "Shitting silver beasts, I am starving, do you think we can eat that thing if we cook it properly?"

Taferia joined them, wiping her face. "I doubt it. Snake meat is not the safest food, and we don't even know if this is a snake as we know it. Or if it contains magic." She peered over to the water's edge. "However, when it flapped its tail, I am pretty sure it brought up something grey, could have been rocks but I think it was fish." She went to check.

Meanwhile, Eleksander eyed Hale. "Are you all right?"

"You know me. I'm always fine. I mean, shit, I'm not the one who got my whole life story turned upside down in that cave. Tough stuff, that."

It was such a Hale way of expressing empathy that Eleksander felt a bit better.

Taferia came back a moment later with a massive, gasping fish. With much effort, she banged it against a rock to put it out of its misery and held it up. "A haddock! We'll be having more than just korkorand juice today."

Hale expertly filleted the fish, while Eleksander gathered branches for firewood, and Taferia prepared a spit.

Taferia started the fire, seeming happy to have something to do with her hands. "Why don't you go clean up and see to any calls of nature?"

Grudgingly they obeyed. After all, they were the captains, why was she making the decisions?

When they came back, the haddock was cooking on the spit. They sat down and Taferia slipped away to see to her own needs.

Hale took over cooking duties, mumbling that it was just like home. "Food tastes best when cooked over an open fire."

Eleksander watched him, happy to see colour on his cheeks and animation in his movements. Before he could stop himself, he blurted out, "You know, my birth parents and us being born during some odd, magical summer solstice wasn't all that came out in the cave."

"No," Hale agreed. "But I haven't had time to think about... that."

"But it doesn't change how you feel about me?"

"No. You're my closest friend, my co-captain, my teammate," he mumbled. "Nothing's changed. I still think you're a soft heart, who has no right being better at rowing than me."

"Or swimming. Or archery." Eleksander laughed at Hale's responding grimace and added, "I suppose that'll do for now."

If he pushed Hale, things would only get harder.

Taferia came back as the fish finished cooking. Hale split it into three pieces and they ate in silence, wolfing down the white meat. Eleksander didn't even mind the lack of seasoning.

Then the fish was gone and the air full of unsaid things again. Eleksander watched the sea, thoughts firing like arrows and impatience nagging at him. He knew he should give everyone time to recover from the fight and to digest, not to mention recover from whatever those stings did to Hale and Taferia. But he needed answers now. "Taferia, can we get back to—"

He stopped himself when he saw that both the Woodlanders were asleep. Taferia scrunched up against a tree and Hale on his back, splayed out in his normal sleeping position. Woodlanders, they really could sleep anywhere.

This time he did button Hale's coat, then sat back in his lonely vigil.

Everything unsaid would remain hanging in the air, like building tension. He wished he could talk to Avelynne or Sabina about it. Or his family. Were the Aetholos worried about him? Yes. They would be. Fair enough, he was worried about himself, too.

Eleksander closed his eyes, brooded for a while, and then plunged into dreams of lost mothers, sea serpents, young men with cocky grins, and golden magic spreading across the sea.

Chapter Nineteen

BOOKS AND DIPLOMACY

Two days passed. Or was it three? Sabina had lost track of time. That wasn't like her, she was more responsible than that. She had to try harder!

Avelynne was still unconscious and no other survivors, or remains, had reached their shores. Sabina was sure it was only a matter of time, though, and always kept one eye on the sea. Jero told her there was no point, that it was in the hands of fate now. She couldn't accept that. Nor could she accept the fact that she had failed to save the first wave.

Stuck here as she was, Sabina had spent the days mentally and physically recovering, usually with Aurea. Right now, she was about to follow the second-in-command onto one of the ships to inventory how many crates of hardtack were left. It surprised Sabina how well they were getting along. It was easy and natural. As if they'd known each other for years. And, yet, lurking beneath was the thrill of something new.

Setting foot on the Qetesh, Sabina once more gaped at the advancement and size of the Hethklish ships. Especially when they went below deck and, in the belly of the ship, saw where the sailors slept in hammocks, most of which had been moved on land now.

While Captain Naseer had a small cabin up on deck, Aurea lived down with the sailors, although slightly apart. She pointed to a corner where there was only a single hammock and a tiny wooden table ladened with books. "That's my domain. The others know not to bother me there unless it's an emergency. And to turn around when I'm getting changed, as a sign of respect for my position."

Sabina swallowed, trying very hard not to let her mind paint pictures of Aurea undressing. She made herself focus on Avelynne, still in the depths of unnatural sleep. Avelynne would be fascinated by the Hethklish ships when she woke up, even more so about the Hethklish themselves. If she woke up. No, *when* she woke up.

She would tell Avelynne about these ships. Like how they had different steering mechanisms called the ship's wheel. It was turned instead of a steering oar to change the ship's direction. She couldn't wait to show Avelynne that and let her try the ship's wheel, like Aurea had done with her.

They did the inventory and went back to shore. When they got there, they found Captain Naseer closing a thick book with a triumphant look.

"Tails! I think I've got it!"

"Got what? Print ink on your thumbs?" Aurea teased him.

"No, I figured out why we can understand the Cavarrians. This is a book of the early history of Hethekla."

Sabina eyed the salt-stained cover of a barely held-together tome. "You brought a history book?"

"We bring all sorts of books everywhere. They're our greatest treasure," he said, forehead furrowed in confusion at the question. "We did have *two* books on the history of Hethekla, but I couldn't find the other one."

"Hm. I haven't heard of any misplaced books," Aurea said. "Maybe it got waterlogged and had to be thrown away?"

"Perhaps. Anyway," he said, stabbing a finger onto the book's cover. "This one tells of where Hethklish came from. Many generations ago, a war broke out in our homeland. Our enemies were far superior when it came to quantities and brutality, but inferior when it came to intellect and ingenuity." He gave them a strange grimace.

"That is the book's attitude, not yours," Aurea said, deciphering his expression.

"Exactly! Anyway, the book describes that the Hethklish decided that the war would be hard for either side to win and would drag out until too many were dead. So, they took their chances with the sea instead, having already planned to explore the waters anyway."

"Smart," Aurea said.

Naseer didn't comment. "The Hethklish sailed from a port marked down in the book as being in 'the Lakelands.' Is that not where you said one of your missing co-captains came from, Sabina?"

"It is! The Lakelands is one of our four counties, the biggest one actually. It has a lot of sailing ports. That can't be a coincidence." She paused, a memory sparking. "There were tales of troublemakers that were driven out of Cavarra. They all drowned far out at sea beyond the Lakelands and their corpses were eaten by sea monsters. It was used as a warning for going to sea. I thought that was a fairy tale?"

She sifted through her memory to see if the troublemakers had been described as having slimmer faces and pointy ears but found nothing.

"I guess we have a likely explanation, then. The recounting of what happened long ago has been forgotten or twisted by those who told it for their own gain, and so our history together was erased. But we probably come from the same people, don't you think?" he asked with a smile.

"I do." It was nice to have an older person in power you felt you could trust to be honest and to listen to you, so Sabina smiled back.

"This could explain why Cavarrians avoided the sea for so long," Sabina said.

"Because all the curious people, those who would one day become us Hethklish, sailed away?" Aurea questioned.

"Maybe. But new adventurous people pop up in every generation. I meant more that Cavarrian authorities claimed sailing was dangerous so that there wouldn't be a drain of people following the Hethklish example, not wanting to live under..." Searching for the right words, Sabina thought of their history of monarchs treating their people any way they wished and somehow always getting away with it. "Violent, cruel, power-hungry leaders. Oh, and to save face. Their version of the tale made them come off much better than your book did."

"I'm sure our version of the events is skewed, as well. The larger numbers of Cavarrians compared to Hethklish was probably a big reason as to why our ancestors sailed instead of fought," Aurea said.

"Well, I wouldn't stay on a continent with lots of enemies who are known to be brutal but not intellectual, which might *not* be a skewed description of

Cavarrians on the whole," Sabina said, her defensive tone only scratching the surface of how she wanted to defend her home but couldn't think of a way right now. "I suppose our pathetic shipbuilding techniques proves that."

Naseer shook his head. "That's not fair. From what you've told us, it sounds like your ship was a lot like our battleships, the ones we have used during the two wars between Hethekla's three countries, what you call counties."

Sabina gaped at him. "You've only had two wars?"

"Yes?" Aurea answered with confusion. "I mean there have been skirmishes between groups, but we count wars as when countries officially declare their intent to fight and more than a hundred people die."

Sabina rubbed her forehead. "Our four counties have warred with each other so many times that I bet even the history books lost count. We've gone as far as colonising each other's land and taking slaves, killing large swathes of the population, and scorching the earth to keep anything from growing for our enemy."

When she said it out loud it sounded terrible and made her see why the history books of the Hethklish would see them as short-sighted, bloodthirsty brutes.

Aurea was the first to break the awkward silence. "All nations have their faults. It seems we Hethklish used to be quite judgemental and abandoned our neighbours. And, as you've gathered, we are curious beyond belief and have to discover and prod everything we see or hear of, even things we perhaps should leave alone."

Sabina regarded a group of sailors trying to build some sort of structure out of fallen korkorand trees without the use of precious nails. "It seems to me that wanting to explore, learn, and experiment is not such a fault."

"It can be if you sacrifice everything else to achieve it," Naseer said. "I'm ashamed to say there have been times when the governing elite prioritised exploring and inventing over caring for our poor or sick."

Sabina gave a hollow laugh. "I suppose one thing is the same for us then, our rulers let the people suffer."

"I know that wasn't the intent of some of ours, but yes," Aurea said.

Captain Naseer patted the history book with an air of hesitance.

Sabina tried to read his expression as Aurea had earlier. "Is there something else in there? Something you don't want to tell me?"

"It's not actually about not wanting to tell you; I have no reason not to. I merely worry about the validity of what I've read, considering we found that neither our history nor yours necessarily tells the objective truth but..."

"But what?"

"But the authors of this book make a big deal of a monster hiding beneath the castle at something it refers to as the Centre?"

Sabina jerked back. "That's where our king resides. And the academy where we were trained."

Naseer opened the book to a dog-eared page. "It says that your leaders, and ours, knew it was there but did not tell the population. It's probably propaganda against an enemy or fanciful embellishment." He put the book away and added, "Also, there were several mentions of how much more attractive we, especially our women, are. So once again, it may not be something you actually want to take very seriously."

He chuckled and Sabina wanted to laugh along, but her glance slid over to Avelynne and she found herself saying, "I can't imagine anyone being more beautiful than some of our women."

"Well, thank you very much," Aurea said, laughter in her voice.

"Oh, no, I didn't mean..." Sabina spluttered.

"I know you didn't," Aurea said. "I was joking."

Sabina watched her, the mirth crinkling her eyes and that pearly-toothed smile widening so it made her ageing scars move. She was stunning. In a very different way than the classic beauty of Avelynne's symmetrical features. Aurea had a more unique and vibrant attractiveness, one always in motion and drawing the eye. A picture of health, energy, and joy that left Sabina happy and a little breathless.

Sabina gathered her courage to say what she was thinking. "No, that book certainly doesn't know what it's talking about. Because it seems to me that the women from both our nations are equally magnificent."

Aurea, for once, appeared lost for words, only fidgeting with her hair, a shyer smile now playing at her lips.

Captain Naseer laughed. "She said humbly, being a woman herself. Kidding, kidding! Now, who wants a cup of ale?"

They were sipping away and discussing the contents of the history book when Sabina spotted a group of sailors fight off one of the frequent sea serpent attacks. Today there were two beasts, a large seafoam-coloured one and a smaller one in a deeper green.

The serpents attacked relentlessly. However, it was obvious that the sailors had experience with this, they all parried and ducked at the right time and soon had the upper hand. Their long spears, made in a strange blueish black metal that Sabina hadn't seen before, pierced the scales of the sea serpent and were long enough to stab even into the head.

"Shouldn't we help them?" Sabina asked.

"Oh, no need." Aurea said, regarding her sailors with pride. Or squinting at them with pride since it was hard to see them through the smoke the serpents secreted.

She was so calm. So able to let others take the reins. It was impressive. No. Annoying. No, both. Sabina didn't want to dig into why it annoyed her, she focused on watching instead.

One of the sailors used magic to knock the larger snake unconscious and then drove her spear into its head. She had the same coiled braids as Eleksander, making Sabina miss him so much it hurt. He would be so much better at dealing with these foreigners, he'd charm them with small talk and ask all the clever question in the politest way. He was a perfect diplomat. So was Avelynne, come to think of it. They should be here to handle this! But it fell to her, and she had to get it right.

Two other sailors killed the smaller serpent, cheering and firing off silver shoots of magic to the sky in celebration. It was amazing how strong and fast their magic was. And how they were not as drained by its use as Cavarrians.

Sabina put her ale down and voiced that thought.

"Well, every society has its strengths," Naseer

said, putting his tankard down. "We have found that during our travels."

Sabina sat forward. "I have to ask. With your stronger magic, have you defeated the silver beasts?"

They gave her blank looks, clearly at a loss to what she was talking about. She explained about the morphed insects that plagued her continent, eating the grains and parts of the cattle, and attacking humans. But mainly feeding on magic, being drawn to it.

They listened attentively before Naseer said, "No, we have nothing like that." He scratched his head. "It seems odd that only the insects mutated due to star-vation and human's magic overuse. Wouldn't other animals do the same? And humans?"

"Well, um, you know, insects are always a pest," Sabina answered, hearing how feeble that sounded.

He shrugged. "You'll have to excuse my probing; this is such new concept for me. If we assume it did hit insects because they are 'pests' then why didn't other things seen as pests like pigeons or rats or anything else that can breed fast and survive most things mutate? This seems almost targeted?"

Aurea nodded. "And why wouldn't we have some-thing similar considering we use so much more magic? From what you've told me of your nation, we're also more overpopulated than you are?"

Sabina sat back, questions whirring her mind.

Could they merely have been unlucky to get the silver beasts when the Hethklish hadn't?

"Hm. I shall have to speak to our trade and diplomacy department about this silver beast situation to see if they've heard about something similar in other places," Naseer said.

Aurea turned to him and said, "Oh, speaking of them, what about our chat yesterday about a trading partnership?"

He snapped his fingers. "Ah, yes, we wanted to speak to you about that, Sabina. I know it's early days and you have a lot on your mind, but we tend to quickly begin talks of trading deals with any people we find."

Nervousness made Sabina hot all over in an instant. "Yes. Of course. I should like to discuss that."

This was what she'd been trained for. Not fully, since her education had been cut short and altered to a more violent direction, but still.

Was she ready to manoeuvre such delicate diplomacy, though? Especially on her own? She had to be. There was no one else here to do it. These people, with their strong naval power, greater knowledge, and abundance of resources, were an important potential ally and that was one of the things she had sailed to find.

Besides, Sabina couldn't imagine a people so curious, so open, intelligent, and friendly to be anything other than a perfect partner for Cavarra. She doubted King Lothiam would think so since these people hated bloodshed and war, but neither he nor his spy were here to protest.

That reminded her of what she had yet to ask, a matter of ethics as well as of trusting this superior power. "One thing that's important to Cavarrians after our terrible history of enslaving each other, is that we aim to not conquer or exploit people. Where do the Hethklish stand on that?"

"We have never ventured as far as slavery. However, like you Cavarrians, we have had our experiences with exploitation and colonising in the distant past," Naseer said. "I believe it to be a common trap for populations to fall into, seeking someone to use and control for their own benefit." He drew his eyebrows together. "Doldrums, sometimes without even knowing they're doing it, believing themselves to be educating or caring for someone else. Not that this excuses anything."

Sabina peered at him. "What shape did these 'experiences' take?"

"After my people had settled on the uninhabited Hethekla, we sailed on. We conquered the next land we found," he said, his mouth downturned with as much disgust as sadness. "We compensated the indigenous people with barely enough for them to survive on, until they rose up against us. We've tried to atone for our crimes, but it is an unremovable taint on our nation that we can never forget, and they should not forgive."

Aurea took Sabina's hand, then let it go, as if worried she'd been too forward. "I can promise you that we have learnt from that inexcusable mistake and strive to never do anything like it again. Ever."

Sabina nodded, recognising that sentiment from her own people. Well, most common decent people anyway. In a way, she was glad to see the negative side of the Hethklish, they were starting to look too good to be true.

"Well, then," Sabina said, "I believe we should like to be your trade partner. Goodness knows we could learn a lot from you." She realised that this made the deal sound one-sided and quickly added, "And, as you yourself pointed out, we're fierce fighters and will defend you if you ask. And offer any of our natural resources or culture you might be interested in," she said, in a tone sounding more uncertain than it should. But what could they offer a more advanced people other than their ability to, well, brawl? If King Lothiam would even offer that. Yes. There was a point.

"I..." she started. "Must once again reiterate that our king is unpredictable, greedy, cruel, and selfish. I am at liberty to offer you a trade deal, but I cannot with good conscience lead you to believe our monarch will make for a good or reliable partner."

"We know," Aurea said. "We have partnered with civilisations that may not seem to have much to offer before. Nevertheless, they always do in the end, especially for a people with such curiosity as us. Cultural exchange is our main reason for trade and diplomacy." She gave Sabina a calming smile. "And if your king breaks any deals you made in good faith, we will hold him accountable, not all of Cavarra. And certainly not you."

"Furthermore," Naseer said with an excited expression, "I am very curious, as all of Hethekla will be, to see what happened to our old forgotten homeland after we left it behind."

Sabina worried they were about to be studied, like a new species of cute pets. Still, if that meant they got all the Hethklish advances, then why should they not be studied a bit? Everything had a price; Sabina knew that far too well by now.

"Excellent," she said, blowing out a long-held breath. She had completed her first negotiation with new people. There were no signed treaties, or leaders shaking hands, but it was a start. A first contact.

Sander will be proud, she thought.

If he ever heard of this. Was Eleksander even still alive? Was Hale? She hoped they were together, either way.

Chapter Twenty

YOU'LL BE MY FIRST

Eleksander heard Taferia clamber to her feet and stretch so every joint cracked, muttering, "Ugh, I'm really not nineteen anymore."

He was nineteen but was still stiff as a board. And he hadn't even been stung or unconscious. More than feeling tired and stiff, he also felt dirty. His Lakelander upbringing made him prickle at not having washed for days. Had it been days?

"I'm going to pick some acorns and eat them at the top of the mountain," Taferia said. "The air will be fresher up there and I'll get a view of the water around us, maybe I can spot survivors or any other landmasses they could've washed up upon."

"Good idea," Eleksander said, ashamed he hadn't thought of that himself.

Hale, busy yawning and rubbing at the healing

cut on his neck, said he'd come up and relieve her later.

"Fine. Take your time, though. I can use a moment to myself," she said. They heard her go shake the trees to get some acorns and then her heavy boots on the mountain above them.

Then all went far too quiet for far too long, the sort of quiet that came from a subject being avoided.

Eleksander couldn't face Hale. Was he thinking about their conversation about his attraction? Was he worried about how they had been in each other's arms last time they awoke? He couldn't stand the uncertainty. Or the dirt on his hands.

"I'm going to go out and wash up by the shore-front," Eleksander said as he stood.

"Good idea," Hale grunted and followed suit.

They both took off their boots and washed their feet, then undressed to only rolled up trousers before kneeling by the water's edge, waves coming to meet them.

As Eleksander scooped water into his cupped hands and poured it over himself, rubbing the salty water into his skin to scrub himself clean, he tried very hard not to sneak glances at Hale. He failed. When he did look, he was glad to see that Hale was watching him, too.

It couldn't be for the same reason, though. Could it?

Hale whipped his gaze away. He poured water over his head and rubbed it into his short hair, which had grown longer than its usual fuzz. The water dripped down his corded neck, over the cut, and all the pale and familiar scars.

Eleksander knew that next, water would rain down over those tanned shoulders, chest, and back. Over the tattoo and every defined muscle of his torso.

He scolded his reacting body, made himself breath deep and focus on washing.

Everything was different now that Hale knew about his attraction. A buzzing tension between them. It made it impossible to have the long conversation they both knew they needed to have.

He couldn't help it, he glanced over again. Once more, Hale caught him. But he didn't look away this time. Instead, he sat up, revealing far too much of his body, and smiled so wide that it dimpled his unshaven cheeks.

"Good, huh?" he said.

"What?" Eleksander sputtered, trying to rid all thoughts of Hale's body from his mind.

"It feels good to be clean?"

"Well, *cleaner* at least," Eleksander said, his face burning hot.

Hale chuckled and agreed.

They fetched some korkorand acorns and took them back into the cave.

When they were done with breakfast, Hale said, "Shitting silver beasts, I'm knackered."

"Of course you are. That sting was not to be trifled with, nor the sea serpent battle. Do you need to rest?"

"I don't want to. But I suppose I should," Hale grumbled before laying down.

"I'm just going to check that cut on your neck, then I'll leave you alone," Eleksander said.

"Oh yes? Not going to hold me this time?" Hale said, a wicked twinkle in his eyes.

"This isn't the time or place for your mocking."

"Hey! I never mock you, soft heart. I rib you at worst. Besides, the snuggle was nice. I remember freezing my balls off. Your body, I mean your *body heat*, helped. A lot."

"I'm glad."

"And it was... kind of nice, I suppose," Hale mumbled, looking down. "Being that physically close, I mean. It's, uh, been a while for me."

Eleksander didn't know what to say so he only nodded.

Hale smirked. "Judging by the state of you when we woke up, you really liked it, too."

"Don't," Eleksander said, making his voice as deep and forceful as he could.

Hale's smirk vanished. "Hey, it's all right. As I said, it's natural. I didn't mean to be an arsehole there. I don't know how to deal with these situations." He reached out and took Eleksander's hand, at first roughly but then his grip softened. "I mean, we all need to... let off steam. Most humans need touch." He began rubbing circles over the back of Eleksander's hand with his calloused thumb.

"I need *your* touch," Eleksander whispered.

"That's just it, pretty lad. I'm offering it," Hale said in a low voice, putting his other hand on Eleksander's thigh.

Their gazes locked, firm and unavoidable.

"Do you want it, Sander?"

Eleksander didn't know what was the most overwhelming. The fact that Hale used his nickname, and in that affectionate and aroused voice. Or that both Hale's hands were on him. Caressing him.

He croaked, "Yes."

Hale's hand caressed a little harder up his thigh. Eleksander swallowed, making himself say the words. "The thing is that I never had much time for love, always studying way too hard. And when I did like someone, he never liked me back."

Hale's expression grew puzzled. "Uh. Sorry to hear that?"

"I'm trying to say that... You'll be my first."

"Oh, that's all right. You'll be my first male lover," Hale said, unusually soft and gentle for him. "We'll do this the way we do everything; exploring and learning together."

"Yes. Yes please."

Hale cupped his face with his hands and leaned in for a kiss. The rasp of his beard scratched against Eleksander's stubble, but his lips were surprisingly soft. The kiss deepened and Eleksander felt the first tendrils of panic. He *had* to get this right.

Hale's hands were sure and comforting, though, manoeuvring Eleksander into the right positions without hesitation. Eleksander was safe in those calloused, scarred hands and the icy panic melted.

With smiles and kisses, Hale led him through every step. He even admitted, unusually humble, when he didn't know how male bodies best connected and decided they stick to the moves he knew from bedding women and from pleasuring himself.

Eleksander saw another tattoo, small text hiding in the trail of dark hair leading down from Hale's belly to his crotch. But in the cave's dim light, he couldn't decipher it, and didn't have time to stop and read things anyway.

Eleksander heard himself moan and sigh with every touch, every kiss.

Every moment was bliss.

Every moment was lightning coursing through his veins.

Every moment was sweetness on his tongue and brandy warming his limbs.

When they finally finished exploring and made one another come undone with their hands, Eleksander's world opened. Everything was brighter, everything was cleaner and shinier. He was so proud and happy that his heart spun somersaults in his chest.

Hale panted out the last of his pleasure and then pulled Eleksander to him, rough and possessive. Eleksander lay in his embrace, feeling their racing heartbeats pound against each other, trying not to think about the future.

Because Hale was happy to do this. Now. Here. But he liked women. He liked Avelynne. And Woodlanders did not court their own gender.

Eleksander shut his eyes tight. Why was he thinking about that now? He had gotten his wish, right here and right now. He had to enjoy it. He nuzzled into Hale's neck, breathing in the pink pepper of his skin, overlaid by the scent of seawater and lovemaking.

And he enjoyed it fully.

Chapter Twenty-One

HUNTING AND AWAKENING

Sabina laughed as Aurea showed how, as a child, she'd held her bow when she shot one for the first time. The mimic was hilarious, with fumbling grip, eyes crossed and tip of tongue peeking out between closed lips. Also, the bow was in the completely wrong position so the string could barely be drawn.

"But you figured it out?" Sabina said, trying to stifle her laughter long enough to get the question out.

"With much tutoring, yes," Aurea said with mirth.

"How old were you then?"

"Um. Well. It was last year."

"What?" Sabina sputtered.

"Well, my skills are more intellectual. I was never

great at fighting, or hunting, which is why I asked you along today."

Sabina regarded the three, keen-eyed sailors trailing behind them. Wouldn't they have been enough backup for Aurea's hunting party? Either way, Sabina was happy to be asked. The camp was running out of sources of protein and so, hunting and fishing were required, and Sabina was finally in her area of expertise.

There was no way she was letting her rescuers go hungry.

Kall must've been happy to hunt too, instead of only laying around and catching fist-sized spiders in the camp. It was clear that he was enjoying the chance to run ahead, sniff the terrain, then circle around to check on his mistress. This time when he returned, Aurea ruffled the fur on his head, and he took off again on those massive yet quiet toe-beaned paws.

Aurea sighed dreamily. "Goodness, but he is adorable."

Sabina tried to not roll her eyes. Who knew that the shortcut to every woman's heart would be her 350-kilogram, lethal animal companion? "So, what exactly is it we're hunting for? I'm not sure what lives on this island."

Aurea described, wordy as ever, what in summation sounded like a less well-insulated goose and finished with, "There's a lot of them hiding on this part of the island. They nest everywhere around here."

"Excellent." Sabina said, taking a firmer grip on the bow she'd borrowed from the Hethklish.

They moved on with careful footsteps. The ground was firmer than the beach which held the camp, but still had a sandy, dry soil that was as foreign to Sabina as everything else here.

"May I ask more questions?" Aurea said in muted tones, so as not to scare away any quarry.

Sabina quashed a smile. Aurea was always bubbling over with questions and it was growing on her. "Of course."

"Kall. We don't have animals like him." Aurea ducked to see the snowtiger as he sniffed the ground ahead. "The closest I can think of is what we call a lynx. But they're so much smaller and in duller colours. Kall, on the other hand, is huge! Like a mix between a pet and a war machine!"

Sabina tried not to laugh. "Was there a question in there?"

"Huh? Oh, yes, sorry. Where to start? Um, are all Northern companions snowtigers?"

"No. We also have iceboars, snowbears, and icewolves." She considered that for a moment. "I guess we're not very original when it comes to making up names. All these animals exist in non-northern areas of Cavarra. Just without the winter coats and colourings, and the ice and snow prefixes."

"Ice wolves? That sounds amazing. I've loved wolves ever since I read a book about them a few years back."

Sabina made a point to memorise that.

Aurea asked more questions about Kall, and Sabina answered best she could, often with a simple yes or no.

When the questions ran dry, Aurea petted Kall's head. "Ah, I'd do anything to see those animals. Especially when they're cubs! Kall must've been an adorable cub."

Sabina watched her companion, love filling her chest. "He was the quietest and proudest of his litter."

"No wonder you picked him then. Sounds just like you."

Sabina's cheeks burned. "Actually, he picked me. I was young and wanted a snowbear since they're the biggest companion pets. But Kall tottered right up to me and fell asleep on my skis."

"Then *he* made a good choice. Clever thing," Aurea said and scratched behind his ear.

She was silent for a while. A rare occurrence with her, but the silence was comfortable and easy-going, like Aurea herself.

The hunt continued, with all five of them, six if

you counted Kall, padding forward with arrows nocked and eyes peeled.

Then Aurea whispered, "Oh. I also wanted to ask, since you had so little room on your ship, where was the chronometer?"

Was this conversation ever going to end? Probably not. And strangely, Sabina was all right with that, even if it made hunting hard.

"Where was the what now?"

That look of intense fascination flashed over Aurea's face, animating it and sparkling her eyes. "The chronometer. To tell time. How else could you know what time of day it is?"

"At night, we use certain star constellations. In daytime, the sunlight. You know, using a sundial?" Sabina stopped, watching big but slender fowl in the distance. The birds flew off, but she set her course for their direction while adding quietly, "I know it's not exact and that you must have new-fangled inventions that work better. It's been enough for us, though. We only make simple fishing trips around Cavarra's coastline."

"You've stuck to the coastline?" Aurea asked in worried tones. "But that's rocky, making it easy to run aground."

"Aye, that's what many ships did," Sabina admitted. "Well, that and come back with tales of spotted sea monsters. So, we stayed even closer to the shoreline."

"But it's safer further out to sea? And most 'sea monsters' turn out to be large animals, no threat to humans." She grimaced. "But you didn't know that. Sorry, I'm sounding like such a know-it-all."

"It's all right."

And it was. Sabina detested talking to people. So why was it so easy to talk to Aurea, even when she felt embarrassed or didn't have answers? Maybe because she didn't have to do much of the work, she only had to answer questions.

They walked on, still hearing the cawing of the birds in the near distance. The three sailors were far behind them now, busy with their own conversations. The Hethklish sure were talkative.

Aurea tapped her fingers against her bow pensively. "I wonder what else is different in our societies. Hm. Do Cavarrians tend to be like you?"

"What do you mean? White-haired?"

"No, no. I understand that you don't all look alike, I mean, the three Cavarrians I've met had different colourings and features." She studied Sabina for a moment. "No, I meant the way you see the world. Are you all so... serious and hard on yourselves? So unable to relax and have fun?" Her eyes went wide. "Oh sorry, that sounded judgemental too. What is wrong with me? I'm *so* sorry! I meant it as a positive thing, that you are so intelligent and hardworking, not frivolous."

"It's fine," Sabina said, thinking it over. Was she more serious and accountable than others would be in her situation? "Not everyone is like me."

"Not just you. Jero seems to carry a heavy burden also. Although, I suppose you have just lived through a terrible trauma and will behave accordingly."

"Aye. Especially in Jero's case; he was much more carefree before the shipwreck. A typical calm and friendly Lakelander. Me... I've always been like this."

She explained about growing up in the village's warrior family and having to help her parents, who were often out defending or patrolling, raise her many younger siblings. She talked about how the harsh conditions of the North meant one didn't have much time to be carefree and fun-loving.

In general, she talked more than usual, saying things she'd only written to Avelynne in letters but never said out loud. It was easier to talk while they walked, Aurea wasn't pressuring her or even watching her. They both had their gazes set on the trees, their bodies in easy movement.

She heard herself say, "Coming from a warrior family, I should be able to handle having... killed a man to defend Avelynne. It is what warriors do. Fight to protect their own."

"But you're not handling it?"

"No. I keep thinking about it, dreaming about it, feeling terrible about it."

Aurea gave a pensive hum, then was quiet for a while before saying, "Perhaps it has more to do with your high expectations of yourself? Warrior or not, having taken a human life should always be traumatic. I wonder, though, if your anger at yourself for that death stems from feeling you should've found another way?"

"Another way?"

Aurea shrugged. "Maybe you think you could've subdued this man without killing him? Or foreseen his attack? I can't guess without having more background."

Sabina swallowed something jagged. It was as if Aurea had read those thoughts going through her mind when she awoke in cold sweats. And that was uncomfortable on the deepest of levels.

There only seemed to be one thing to do. Sabina told her the whole story of that night, explaining to them both that there was no other way out of that situation, no way for her to have known what would happen. Hearing the words out loud, so much clearer and blunt than she had explained it to anyone else, eased something that had been raw and bloody in her. Nothing was healed, but perhaps the blood flow was stemmed.

Aurea gave her a serious look. "There was

nothing else you could do, Sabina. You acted the correct way. The only way."

"Aye." She blew out a shaky, long breath. "I know. It doesn't make it all go away. But I do know that."

"Good."

Sabina was hot and cold. So many emotions, so much talking. She almost forgot that they were here to hunt. Almost forgot her duty.

Then their careful steps brought them to an area of tall grasses and there was a flock of the fowl. Just sitting there, cawing at each other over a collection of fish they'd clearly brought to eat and then regurgitate for their hatchlings.

Sabina stopped midsentence and held her hand up to stop Aurea, and the sailors, from speaking or in any way scaring the large birds. If she managed to shoot two or three, and the others managed to snag a few kills each, the whole camp could have at least a few bites and get some much-needed variety in their diets.

Sabina lifted her bow and stepped closer, silent as the approach of night. She calculated that if she re-nocked her arrows quickly enough, she could shoot the three nearest birds before they all took off. Especially as these birds seemed neither fast nor smart.

She had to show her worth. Had to feed her new friends.

She noticed her pulse quieting and her focus tightening. These were strange lands, foreign hunting fellows, and unknown prey. Nevertheless, every hunt from the age where she could first hold a spear or bow was stored as memories in her muscle and bone.

She took one more step forward, gaze on the bird nearest and... A loud snap! Her gaze flew to the ground. There was a branch under her foot! Shit! How had she not watched where she stepped, that was the first thing you learned!

The birds noticed them and scrambled to leave, even the hatchlings ran away, dropping plumes of downy feathers behind and squawking as if telling her off.

Kall and the three sailors followed the departing birds, trying to fell a couple of stragglers, which was what Sabina should be doing! She had much better aim and could've killed at least one bird as they flew off.

Except she'd been too shocked, angry, and disgusted by her mistake to even move.

What was wrong with her?

Aurea put a hand on Sabina's arm. "Let go."

"Of what?" She stared at the woman. "The bow?"

"No. Let it go. The mishap. You won't be any good to anyone if you just stand there blaming yourself. Move on."

"But those birds will be on their guard now, Aurea! There's no point in hunting them. I failed you. We needed that meat!"

"And we'll find some. Even if we don't, we won't starve. Just breathe and trust me."

She was so calm. How could she be so calm?

That hand on Sabina's arm squeezed. "You're not breathing and your muscles are tense as coils. It's all right. I promise we'll find food some other way."

"No. That shot was lined up perfectly, I shouldn't have messed it up by doing something as incredibly witless as *stepping on a branch*!"

Aurea shrugged. "These things happen. No problem. We'll find something else."

"Like what?" She heard the naked dismay and alarm in her own voice but didn't know how to mask it.

"Like catching some more fish. Or the little weasels that hide in the bushes sometimes."

"The sailors have fish all the time and those weasels have barely any meat. All of you will be disappointed. And hungry. Because of me." She hit a bush with her bow, immediately regretting it. She'd been raised not to show her temper or damage belongings. It was unwomanly. *Apparently.* "I can't handle more guilt and disappointment. I shouldn't have come with you."

There was no doubt that Sabina wouldn't have

voiced that out loud with anyone else, not even with Avelynne.

Aurea rubbed Sabina's arm, her smile warm enough to melt ice. "If the sailors complain, they're adults and can go get their own prey. You did your best. That's all you have to do." She stepped closer, filling all of Sabina's vision. She had freckles on her nose. How had Sabina never seen that? "I'm not disappointed, Sabina, and neither will any of the sailors be. I am however sorry to have made your problems with yourself, and your sense of guilt, worse. Try to let this go, and let's head back."

Sabina stared at her, ready to argue.

Then Aurea grabbed Sabina's bow and snatched it away, so quick that Sabina didn't have time to react.

"Cavarrian, that's it. I'm taking your bow and with it, all the pressure you put on yourself, and I'm leaving with it." She started running, calling back, "So you either stay here knitting those cute eyebrows, hating yourself. Or come get your bow back."

Aurea darted back to camp, waving the bow above her head.

Sabina couldn't help it, she laughed, called for Kall, and sprinted after Aurea. Faster and faster. Every step made her laugh harder and by the time they reached the camp, she was too distracted and tired to think about her failure.

At the edge of the camp, Naseer met them with a grin wide enough to split his weathered face.

"She's awake!" he boomed across the beach.

Sabina didn't need to ask who he meant. She ran towards Avelynne's improvised sickbed and, yes, she was sitting up! Well, mostly she was being propped up by a large bag of grain that Jero was putting behind her as a pillow, but she was awake and talking.

Kall got to her first, licking her hands and getting his head patted. Then Sabina arrived and threw her arms around Avelynne in the hammock, trying to be gentle but too relieved and thrilled to think her actions through. The hammock rocked and nearly toppled.

Avelynne laughed in a hoarse, unused voice and hugged back.

Holding her like this, it was obvious how much weight Avelynne had lost, she had been thin before but now she was nothing but bones. Sabina moved back to examine the patient. Her eyes were bright and alert, her lips had regained some colour. Her skin was dull and greyish, though.

"You're going to need a lot of feeding up, little countess."

Avelynne shook her head. "You're not meant to call me that anymore, remember?"

"You'll always be nobility to me," Sabina said, placing her forehead against Avelynne's. Not even caring that Avelynne's breath smelled like ground-up moths.

"How do you feel?"

"What? Oh. Better," Avelynne murmured. "Especially now that you're here, snowdrop."

Aurea softly cleared her throat and Sabina remembered her manners. She introduced Aurea, Captain Naseer, and the two Hethklish sailors who had spent most time feeding, watching over, and cleaning up Avelynne.

The pallid Peakdweller thanked them all while Naseer, having accepted his thanks graciously, pulled Sabina aside.

"Just because she's awake, doesn't mean she's perfectly well. She's still muddled and there might be lasting damage."

"What do you mean?"

He scratched one of those peculiarly pointy ears. "Head injuries, they can be more complicated than other wounds. You need to check how her thought processes and her memory is working."

"Well. She remembered me. And my nickname. And that her shitty parents informed her she wasn't a countess anymore, taking not only her title but her home. Sadly, she hasn't forgotten about that."

His expression went from worried to appalled.

"They're terrible," Sabina explained.

She regarded Avelynne, who kept chuckling at something Aurea said. "I will check on her mind. Surely that can wait until she's had something to drink and eat, though?"

"Of course." He patted her shoulder. "Now, if you excuse me, one of the sailors wanted to speak to me."

"Sure, Thank you. Again. For helping Avelynne, I mean."

"We only gave her goat's milk and kept her from laying in her own filth. She did the rest on her own."

"Hethklish are quite humble, aren't you?"

He grinned. "Not all Hethklish. Only us delightful and ruggedly handsome sea captains." He winked and walked off.

When Sabina, still chortling at that comment, looked back to Avelynne and Aurea, she found them still locked in conversation. She wasn't surprised, they would be excellent conversation partners.

Both were intelligent, sociable, and chatty. Avelynne had travelled all of Cavarra and Aurea had travelled every part of the world she could reach.

Aurea, with her openness, sense of humour, and charming curiosity.

Avelynne, with her patience, kindness, and love for satisfying curiosity.

Sabina gnawed on her lip when she realised that they were also very attractive. Both on their own, but even more so when sitting together like this. They would make a stunning couple. Avelynne laughed at something Aurea said, which made Aurea beam like the sun coming out on a cloudy day.

Sabina's stomach gave a pang.

Life surely couldn't be so cruel that, after all this, these two women would now prefer each other and leave her behind? Grow bored of her?

Sabina looked down at her own body, which was practical but had never felt attractive to her. Her personality was worse. She was uninteresting. Quiet. Solemn. Ordinary. The lass from a poor family who'd only ever left home to go to her academy.

Avelynne turned her head towards Sabina. "Snowdrop, come here. As soon as I awoke, Jero told me how you found me and swam ashore with me. I need to thank you as well."

Sabina shuffled over to the hammock, her stomach remaining a painful tangle of knots, and said, "You thank me by taking it easy and not talking too much. You need what little energy you have to recover."

"I know, but I still want to talk to you. To make

sure you've been all right while I have been taking this intense nap of mine."

Sabina laughed. "Is that what we're calling it?"

Avelynne shrugged with a weak smile and Sabina wanted to pick her up, hold her close to her chest, and never ever let her go. Never let anything hurt her again.

"Have you? Been all right?"

"Aye, I've been fine. Just enjoying my island holiday without a care in the world."

"Liar," Avelynne said, her unused voice still hoarse.

"Harsh!"

"True."

"Aye, true enough. I've been worrying a hole in my stomach. You're awake and healthy now, though, and that will help with nearly everything."

Avelynne took her hand and pulled her down to the hammock so she could place her lips against Sabina's cheek. The kiss was long, slow, and heartfelt.

Sabina didn't want it to stop and wondered how she could prolong it, when Avelynne moved to place a quick kiss on her lips as a finishing touch. It was much shorter than the one on her cheek but all the sweeter for its intimacy.

"Oh, I'm sorry. Do you two need to be alone?" Aurea said.

"No. I'm afraid Sabina is right. I need to rest,"

Avelynne said, blinking sluggishly and leaning back. "Look after my snowdrop until I wake again."

Aurea smiled over at Sabina. "I'll make sure she doesn't get into any trouble."

From behind them came the cheering and whooping of the three sailors from the hunting party. They had their arms full of freshly caught fowl.

Aurea raised an eyebrow at her, but mercifully didn't say *I told you so*.

Chapter Twenty-Two

BACK TO THE VITAL CONVERSATIONS

Eleksander woke up without having even realised that he'd fallen asleep, dazed and warm. There was a weight on top of him and it took him a while to figure out what it was. *Who* it was. His heart soared for an instant, leaping like a fawn in his ribcage. His chest had been an echoing, lonely, and aching space for so long.

Soon Hale woke as well and peered up at him. He lazily scratched at his cheek and mumbled, "Hey. How long have we been asleep?"

Eleksander put his voice under control, he couldn't let it sound like a miracle had just happened. "I don't know. It can't have been that long because Taferia hasn't come down."

His nerves tingled. How would Hale react? Most likely, he'd pretend like nothing happened. The second most likely option would be that he was upset and would act like it was no big deal, just physical release. Neither was good, but there were worse options, and each one rammed through Eleksander's imagination, shattering the spell of happiness.

The Woodlander yawned and sat up. "So. That happened."

Eleksander sat too, pulling his knees up to cover more of his nakedness. "Yes. It did."

"Hm. You know how I feel about Avelynne," Hale said.

Eleksander's heart sank. "Yes, I do."

"I don't know exactly what I feel about you," Hale said quietly, looking lost. "But, like I said before, I care about you. And you mean a lot to me. Like, a *lot.*"

"That's something at least," Eleksander said, being as brave as he could.

"Ah shit. Please don't look so sad!" Hale ran a frantic hand through his mussed hair. "You are the one I'm closest to out of all of the second wave, not just because we're both lads, but because... everything is different with you."

"Different? How?"

Hale groaned, as always when trying to find words. "I guess I mean that you get me? Sabina and I have a lot in common, so she knows a lot about me. Avelynne understands me because she has a weird knack for understanding everyone." He scratched at a cut on his thigh, thoroughly avoiding any eye contact. "You and me, however, shouldn't understand each other because we're so different. Except, you look at me with those big brown eyes and I'm sure you somehow... get me. What I want and what I mean." He scrunched up his face. "Ugh. Listen to me, talking like some silly coin-hoarder poet."

"It doesn't sound silly to me. We are different. I never thought you were the kind of person I would fall for. I've always liked men like me, more sensitive and empathetic."

Hale grinned. "Not rough wildlings with unknown intentions?"

"Oh! Is that how you describe yourself?" Eleksander joined him in chuckling. "No, but seriously. You are not someone I expected to want. But there is," he hesitated, not wanting to scare Hale, "something between us. A kind of connection that grew in those first few weeks sharing a bedchamber, when we went from sizing each other up to learning how to understand each other and care for each other."

Hale nodded.

Now, their eye contact held and the soundless moments passed slow as things settled.

"As I said, there is Avelynne, though," Hale said. "I love her and my love cannot be so flighty. I can't make her think she meant so little to me."

Eleksander couldn't help it, he raised an eyebrow in scepticism. "Ave told you that she chose Sabina over you. That she only wanted to be friends with you."

Hale squirmed and grunted. "Yes. But I swore to her that I loved her. My words are ironclad."

"Hale, I don't think she'd feel that she meant so little to you just because you move on. Sab had a theory, which I'm sure she's discussed with Ave, that you might only have a crush on her because she's your ideal woman and out of your reach?"

"I hadn't thought of it like that." He sounded annoyed. "I don't think it's that simple. That I'm that simple."

Eleksander wished he hadn't mentioned it. "Right. Sure."

"Both you and Ave are too good for me, anyway." Hale ripped at the cut he'd been scratching at, making it bleed. "I tried to make up for my boorish behaviour during first term, but, even with that, I haven't earned the right to have a lover as perfect as either of you."

"Perfect?" Eleksander whispered. He gathered himself. This was about Hale's feelings. Not his own. "Neither she nor I am perfect. What we both are, is capable of deciding for ourselves who deserves us."

Hale spoke down to his cut. "There's also the fact that I never saw myself being with another lad. Now," he held up his hands, "there is nothing wrong with being with a man. Actually, I'd probably like having someone with life experiences akin to my own. Well, at least the physical ones. But it was never something I... saw for my future."

"I know."

"I'll have to give it some thought."

"Yes, and we'll have to figure out what to do about our friendship."

Hale gaped in horror. "Nothing, and I mean nothing, can be allowed to ruin our friendship. If we get to be more than friends, we'll stack that other stuff on top of the friendship, all right? Shit, I need you."

"Thank the waters," Eleksander said on a relieved exhale. "I need you, too."

"Have you been worrying that our friendship could be ruined?"

"Yes."

"No need. I've never been this close to anyone. Nor has anyone put up with my snoring the way you do. You're stuck with me until you get tired of me, soft heart."

"Good," Eleksander said. "Then I'll never get rid of you."

Hale reached out, as if to do his signature punch of the shoulder move, but instead he rubbed at something on Eleksander's collar bone. It stung and when he checked on it, he saw it was a love bite.

With a wicked smile, Hale said, "Sorry about that. But, hey, it's a good reminder that our friendship has a new perk. Now I know what to do if I get too much pressure building up."

Eleksander scoffed. "Oh, you think you can just call on me whenever you get the craving?"

Hale's smile stayed in place as he said, "Maybe? I was hoping you'd be a little bit more generous with that sort of thing than some of the lasses I've been with."

Eleksander tried to keep from laughing as he said, "All lasses aren't like that, just as all lads aren't as slutty as you. While I may want you as much as you want me, I expect to be courted and not taken for granted."

Hale turned serious. "Then that is what you'll get. Goodness knows you deserve that and more." He stood up. "For the record, though, I'm a total slut and proud of it. So, simply snap your fingers whenever you fancy the dirty kind of workout."

"Hale!" Eleksander said on a laugh. He was about to say something thoroughly filthy to catch his new lover off guard when he heard feet moving on the mountain above them.

He grabbed his trousers and began pulling them on, but Hale shushed him. "Wait, that doesn't sound like someone climbing down. Maybe she's just stretching her legs?"

For a moment they listened, Eleksander worrying about any noises they might have made and if they could've been heard up to the top of the mountain.

Then he found that it didn't matter much right now. Not a tenth as much as his new information mattered: Hale didn't regret what had happened. In fact, he wanted it to happen again. And, Hale needed him. They still didn't know what the future would look like for them, but at least Eleksander knew that they'd have a future together. Be that as friends or as a couple, he wasn't going to lose Hale.

The steps quieted down again.

Without needing to confer, the two men quickly pulled trousers on, went out to dive into the waves as a quick overall wash, and came back in to put on the rest of their clothes and try to look respectable.

Hale was clearly going through the motions, and Eleksander wondered if this was all for his sake. Like all Woodlanders, Hale was very happy to speak of sex and to let others know when he had partaken in some. Although, was that still true if the sex had been between two men? Eleksander's thoughts were halted by the clear sound of Taferia clambering down, her footfalls getting closer until they saw her in the cave opening. She rubbed her face and yawned.

He stepped forward to give her a hand. "Did you see anything?"

Taferia waved him away and sat down. "I saw a large landmass to the north. It might be inhabited, it's hard to tell without a spyglass."

Hale headed for the cave exit. "Really? I want to have a look at that! I'll take the next shift."

"All right," Eleksander called after him. "Come down when you need a break and I'll relieve you."

"Promises, promises, pretty lad," Hale shouted back.

Eleksander's cheeks burned even though Hale's reply could be interpreted in several ways.

Taferia was sitting with her head back against the cave wall, eyes closed, seemingly unaware. Or maybe she really didn't care if they'd been having sex in here or not.

Eleksander patted her arm. "How are you feeling?"

"Achy. Worried about the rest of the crew. Mostly, though? Tired to the core."

"I can certainly relate." He studied her. "Are you too worn out to talk more?"

She opened her eyes and gave a tired but earnest smile. "No. Besides, I owe you answers. Having studied the second wave, I know you're not the untrustworthy children the Twelve worried you were. You deserved to know who I was and what my mission was from the start."

"It's all right. The mood of our time seems to be

distrust. It's funny, I had little idea about that growing up in the Lakelands. I trusted we were ruled the way we should be and that the king cared about us."

"I did too. Then my brother was caught 'slandering' King Lothiam and got thrown in one of the labour camps, which they had labelled detainment centres back then. They," Taferia closed her eyes again, "they worked him to death on a meagre diet of turnips and entrails. We know that because he managed to sneak out a letter with a passing messenger raven." Her eyes opened once more, but this time full of rage and grief. "When they sent his starved body back to us, they said he'd died from some exotic infection he had brought upon himself. When you see the lie hidden in plain sight and you keep watching... you can't close your eyes and go back to obliviously living your life."

"No. I guess that's always the case with injustice. I'm so sorry about your brother."

"Thank you. I comfort myself with the knowledge that he would be proud of the work I've done for the Twelve."

"I'm sure he would." Eleksander sat a little closer. "If you're truly ready for questions, may I ask more about the golden magic and Santorine's experiments?"

"Of course. Where were we?" She hummed to

herself. "Atha Santorine, after her experiments and research, believed that the magic of you solstice-born children was stronger than other children's. But more than that, she hypothesised it could be even stronger if combined."

"Hypothesised?"

"Well, she couldn't experiment on you to check. First of all, there's the ethical question since you were children and we couldn't get consent from your parents. Secondly, if there was a generation of stronger magic users, we could utilise that in the fight against the king and so needed to keep it secret."

"The Twelve have been planning all of this since I was a child?"

"Longer than that. This didn't start with King Lothiam. He comes from a long line of kings and queens who treated their people terribly. And yet, somehow, managed to never be dethroned." She ground her teeth. "Lothiam is the worst though. The labour camps. The beheadings. Bleeding his people dry with his tithes. Only pretending to try ridding us of the silver beasts."

"Yes," Eleksander said, twisting one of his wet braids. "We were told about how he doesn't actually let the experts do anything about the silver beasts, as long as the little nightmares are not in the Centre with him."

"Exactly. He claims he's dealing with them, but when pushed further, admits that 'he has more important things to worry about.' Which is short-sighted. If the silver beasts are not stopped, Lothiam will be king over a graveyard and get no tithes." She shook her head. "That is what we of the Twelve cannot understand. Lothiam is stupid and rash. How can he keep a kingdom under his thumb when he doesn't even know how to hold a quill the right way up?"

Eleksander had no reply. He'd wondered many times why people obeyed and revered the king.

They sat quiet for a while, deep in their own thoughts.

"You know, when I saw what you four could do with your magic, I understood Santorine's hypothesis that the more magic users from that mystical solstice put together, the stronger the magic. One of the reasons the Twelve manipulated the king to have four mapmakers in each class, of course."

Eleksander jolted. "No. There are more than one mapmaker/captain to have backups if one dies. And four were chosen because there had to be one from each county, otherwise the four counties would start fighting over who got to send a candidate."

"I know that's what you've been told, but that's not the whole truth. That was the lie we sold to the king to make him ensure that each class would have a larger group."

"Really?"

"Mm-hm. If we thought we could convince him, we would've had more than a dozen together to see what you could do and if you could be our trump card in this game. However, four had to be enough as we had a convincing lie for that number."

"Do you really believe that more solstice magicians would mean even stronger magic?"

"I don't know what to believe. As soon as you solstice-born were all old enough to consent, we tried to perform discreet experiments with anyone born that summer," Taferia said. "But we were always stopped by parents, local authorities, or the solstice-born themselves, asking questions and risking exposing our research."

"Then you got the four of us into the academy?"

"Yes. It was a dream come true. However, until now, we saw no distinctiveness in your group other than that you were extra skilled. We were all questioning Santorine's research." She got a faraway expression. "Perhaps the missing component was always the sea? Or that the four of you had to be in real danger, not just working together in lessons?"

"I think it was that our magic touched," Eleksander said, his fingers stilling around the braid as he pondered it.

"Yes. Perhaps it was just that. But hasn't your magic touched in lessons? When you fought the target practise silver beasts?"

"I suppose it did. I can't remember. But, if it did, I don't think all four streams touched at the same time?" He dropped the braid, fed up with all of these conundrums. "Oh, I don't know. Maybe it does have something to do with the sea? Maybe the golden magic needs sea salt, like a well-seasoned steak?"

Taferia sniggered half-heartedly at the sarcasm. "I don't know why the four of you could do what you did with the golden magic, Eleksander," she said in a gentle voice. "But I really hope I can help you figure it out. That we can all find out together."

Eleksander thought about that and remembered when they were all together last. In his mind's eye, he saw Sabina's face in the moment they went over the waterfall. The moment when he didn't save her. "I can't stand the idea that something has happened to the other two."

"I understand that better than you think. We all undertook this journey with the understanding that we might die." She sighed. "I mean, the Twelve had to prepare for that when we put the queen's son, a possible heir, into danger. You might've been our only hope to get rid of Lothiam, and we had to risk losing you to shipwreck, hostile foreigners, or sea beasts."

Eleksander said nothing, irritated at the comparison of them risking him as a tool to dethrone Lothiam to him missing two people who had almost become a part of him.

"We decided to take that risk but mitigated it by always putting members of the Twelve around you and your solstice-born group," Taferia said. "Something which would've worked better if Hason Rete hadn't gone mad and started a killing spree, revealing our organisation not only to the four of you but to the cursed king. It nearly ruined all of our hard work."

"Tutor Rete wasn't the only one to kill," Eleksander said pointedly.

She glowered at him. "We eliminated *one* person who was a threat, after trying everything to ensure that he, that Thomey, didn't get us all killed. We sacrificed one person to save not only our entire organisation's members but the future of Cavarra."

"Some might say that was an interesting distinction. Or a convenient justification."

"And they'd be wrong, Lakelander! It was a decision we didn't take lightly and that we hated making. What Rete did with that poor girl, however... That was pure, crazed murder born out of paranoia and grief. You know that's not something our organisation would ever condone."

Did he know that? Eleksander didn't answer, so Taferia spoke on.

"We have done a lot for you. Not just to keep you safe but to make sure that you had the best team."

"Do you mean yourself?"

"No. I meant the second wave. We did thorough background checks of the best candidates born during that solstice and the three other best skilled also happened to be good backers if you were to take the throne."

"How so?" Eleksander said, trying to swallow the bad taste of how they were all pawns in a game.

"Well, there's Avelynne with her noble blood and connections. Sabina being a warrior and woman of the people, thereby a true Northern fairy tale hero. And Hale being the embodiment of a Woodlander and therefore likely to appeal to his county and even the Woodlander's Warden. They can win you the acceptance of their individual counties."

"I'm confused. Is that what it's all about, then? Me being a contender for the throne? Was that why I ended up with the Aetholos? To set me up with a high standing?"

Right now, there was nothing he didn't question. If Taferia said he was secretly an enchanted toadstool, he may just believe it.

"No, you being raised by Lakelander merchants was a fluke. If we'd placed you, we would've put you with a noble family, or members of the Twelve. However, a rich merchant upbringing will do. All the public will see is your royal blood anyway." She sighed again. "If we ever get to a stage where we can overthrow the king and put you in his stead, that is."

"If we survive this, is that still the plan?"

"Yes. Step one, find new land and create a safe base for our rebellion there. You and the other solstice-born are the best candidates to achieve that. This also busies the king with dreams of expansion and keeps him supporting you." Taferia held up two fingers. "Step two, overthrow the king by exposing all he's done and his plans, and put you on the throne instead."

"It's interesting that no one asked me if I wanted that."

Taferia scowled, almost baring her teeth. "No one asked me if I wanted to take this journey. I was ripped from my job, my home, my family, and placed on this mission by the Twelve because I was the best candidate. The same happened to you. We all sacrifice to create a better future."

Hale thundered down the mountain and rushed into the cave. "You know that island you spotted, Taferia? I just saw a massive amount of silver magic coming from there!"

Eleksander stood. "Do you think it could be Avelynne or Sabina?"

"We have to check!" Hale panted

"Hold on. What if it's foreigners and they're not friendly?" Taferia asked.

Hale shrugged. "I think we have to take that risk. I mean, we were always going to take that gamble on this mission."

"With a full crew and weapons, yes," Taferia said. "Not the three of us, half dead and unarmed."

Eleksander tried to imitate the scowl she had given him. "If there is even the smallest chance that the magic was sent up from Sabina and Avelynne, or others from the Wolfsclaw crew, then we are going. They might need help."

Hale smiled. "You heard the man. Let's get ready to swim."

Chapter Twenty-Three

REVELATIONS

Halfway through their early lunch, Sabina put down her tin cup and eyed the Hethklish ships. "Aurea. Do you think we might unmoor one of the ships and go searching for survivors, or remains, of my crew?"

She had been wanting to ask this since Avelynne woke up but had been too embarrassed to ask. The Hethklish had helped so much already.

Aurea jerked back. "Oh. How have I, or anyone else, not thought to offer that? Doldrums, we must've all been so preoccupied with having met a new exciting people that we..." She stopped and rolled her eyes. "I'm babbling again. Never mind. Yes. Yes, of course. We'll leave right after everyone has finished their meal."

"Thank you. And don't worry about not offering.

Avelynne needed the time to recuperate and I didn't want to leave her anyway," Sabina reassured.

Leaving when everyone had finished their meals, yes, that was good. Sabina checked everyone's plates. Now that she'd made the request, she was itching to get going. Literally itching, responsibility and guilt prickling under her skin and making her scratch her forearm.

"Breathe. And leave your poor arms alone." Aurea ran a hand over the red scratches, soothing the pain and added, "I'll arrange everything, Sabina, let go of the accountability for a tick. I've got this. Just have another bite to eat. We'll ready the Parataxia to weigh anchor and be out at sea before you know it."

That was the faster and smaller of the ships, it would be perfect for searching every nook and crook of these islands and its waters.

"Thank you. I feel bad for asking for more, considering everything you've done."

Aurea smiled, as bright and beautiful as the sun. "Oh, no need! Hethklish like an adventure and are happy to help." She took a sip from her tankard. "I'm certainly happy to help any stranger in need, even more so for a new trade partner and ally, but most of all for such an enchanting woman as you."

Sabina felt herself smirk and change her tone of voice to more playful when she replied, "Enchanting, huh? Is that what you call all trade partners?"

"Only those who have the personality and looks of you," Aurea shot back with a suggestive tone of her own.

The realisation that she was flirting smacked Sabina in the chest like a shove. Avelynne was right over there, for snow's sake! Innocently speaking to Jero and sneaking bits of meat to Kall under the table. How could Sabina be sitting here flirting with another woman? Hadn't they promised they'd keep to only each other? Wasn't that her own idea?

Clearly feeling the weight of her gaze, Avelynne gave Sabina her full attention. "Are you all right, snowdrop?" she called across the table.

"I'm fine. Just happy to see you up and eating."

"Of course! I'm not going to lay around sleeping when there are such delicious treats to be had," Avelynne said, before reaching out and snatching a piece of dried fruit from the hand of a particularly handsome sailor. He playfully growled at her and she gave him her most charming, innocent smile.

Sabina knew that smile. And how much intention was always behind it.

Her imagined shove to the chest lessened. Avelynne was flirting too. Maybe it was all right, then?

"Why does she call you snowdrop?" Aurea asked, using the handle of a massive knife to crack open a korkorand acorn.

"Um. I suppose it's because I come from the North, where we have snow for almost half of the year. And snowdrops do grow there when the ground is thawed enough."

Aurea poured the acorn juice over a piece of dried canefruit, making it puff up to bright purple fullness, like she was performing a trick of reviving dead fruit. "Ah. I thought it was because of your snow-white skin and hair. Well, I assume it's white as snow, I've never actually seen snow up close." She put the acorn down and looked lost in thought. "I'd love to see snow one day. Not as much as I'd love to see ice wolves, but almost."

Still on the first subject, Sabina replied, "Sure, it could be due to my white hair. We'll have to ask Avelynne."

"My sincerest apologies for accidentally eaves-dropping, but ask me what?" Avelynne said, suddenly behind them.

How did she do that? Hale always said Avelynne moved like water. He was talking about her litheness, Sabina on the other hand, was more concerned with how quiet her footfalls were. Although, when you lived in a castle with parents who wanted you to pretend not to exist— and who would torment you if they found you actually daring to exist in their pres-ence—maybe you learned to move imperceptibly?

"It was referring to you, actually," Aurea said with

her usual open, welcoming expression. "I was asking about the snowdrop nickname you have for Sabina. I like it. I've never had a nickname myself."

"Oh? Why not?" Avelynne said.

She swayed a little on her feet, still not back to normal, so Sabina pulled her down to sit in her lap. Avelynne got comfortable without taking her attention off Aurea.

"I don't really know," Aurea answered with unusual embarrassment. "I do... have a theory, though. My aunt, who raised me, claimed I didn't give anyone a chance to talk to me, which I assume might include giving me pet names? She always said I babbled too much at people for there to be shared conversation."

"Oh, sweetest," Avelynne said, voice brimming with empathy. "That explains why you're always mentioning your tendency to speak a lot."

Aurea spun the empty acorn in her hand and fake-smiled. "I guess."

Sabina sat back. How did Avelynne always manage to find every person's secret pain and then soothe it? For snow's sake, she hadn't even been conscious for very long! Between her tendency to do that and Aurea's knack of making it easy to open up, they should run some sort of clinic for the mentally injured.

Aurea was still fidgeting with that acorn and now

dropped it. Avelynne picked it up and handed it back to her.

"Thank you."

"You're welcome. Aurea, someone has told you, right?" Avelynne asked, her voice as warm and soft as butter.

"Told me what?"

"Told you that it is an advantage, not a flaw."

Aurea laughed mirthlessly. "Of course it's a flaw."

"I wouldn't say it is," Avelynne said. "For someone who has to meet new people and appear friendly and disarming, speaking a lot and being joyfully enthusiastic like you must be a benefit. At least if the person also knows how to listen, which you do."

Sabina had to help and added, "It's cute too." She froze. Was that crossing the line?

Avelynne immediately nodded, though. "Yes, it's very attractive. It puts a person at ease and draws them in. Also, your enthusiasm is so infectious that it almost cures any ill."

"I'll try to save that comment for a rainy day." Aurea cleared emotion out of her throat. "Unlike today, which is turning sunnier for the moment!"

Sabina guessed she was becoming uncomfortably vulnerable and wanted to change the subject, but there was gratitude in those bright eyes.

"Absolutely." Avelynne caught a few stray strands

of Sabina's hair and tucked them into her braid. "Oh, I had almost forgotten what I came over to talk to you two about! That handsome sailor wants to show me, or rather *us*, something he and his friends have been working on with their magic."

"Oh, is it the doldrummed fountain thing again?" Aurea said with a motherly sigh, despite that the sailor in question must be quite a few years older than her.

"I don't know quite what it was since he's not as good at explaining as you are. Yet another perk to speaking more, I'd say. Anyway, shall we go watch?"

The slightly blushing Aurea faced Sabina with a questioning expression.

"Aye," Sabina answered. "After that, Aurea has promised me that we can take the Parataxia out to look for Eleksander, Hale, and all our sailors."

Avelynne lit up. "Yes! Of course. That is an excellent idea. All right, we'll quickly let them show us this trick of theirs and then depart."

Sabina knew she should tell Avelynne to rest and not come along on this journey. Except, there was no way anyone was keeping Avelynne Ironhold from searching for her friends and crew.

It turned out that the sailors wanting to show the trick were three particularly tall and surprisingly big-bellied men—Sabina couldn't get over how well-fed Hethklish sailors could be, there was certainly no starvation here—who used their height to their full extent, standing on tiptoes and lifting their hands to the sky. Through their fingertips, silvery magic shot up like arrows from a bow. Then, the magic burst compounded and split apart again to form ever-changing, intricate patterns so thick and so high in the sky, they covered the sun.

They kept going for so long that Sabina grew wildly impatient to get on that ship. But if the survivors had waited this long, the Hethklish could have their moment.

They tried to form a Hethklish face with their streams of magic, aging scars and all. When they got to shaping the hair, Sabina heard her name shouted from the shore.

She spun around, breath catching, because there was Eleksander, repeating, "Sabina!"

He and Hale were running towards her as if their lives depended on it and it took a beat for Sabina's feet to catch up before she sprinted towards them too. Kall got there first, but she was a close second, and threw herself in the arms of first Eleksander and then Hale.

Suddenly, Avelynne was there too. They were all crying, mumbling about how much they'd missed each other and about worries of who was dead.

Jero arrived as well, giving a traditional Lake-lander bow to his two lost captains. Eleksander bowed back to him, then waved one of his big hands, as if ridding them of formalities, and hugged Jero. Hale clapped him on the back.

"Only you three survived?" Avelynne whispered with pain, looking between Eleksander, Hale, and Taferia Palm. The latter having only waved at them when she wandered up from the waves with tired steps.

"I'm afraid so. Shit. We hoped more sailors would be with you two," Hale said.

Eleksander sucked in a deep breath and began explaining what had happened to them since the waterfall and the currents had scattered the crew of the Wolfsclaw.

Chapter Twenty-Four

CATCHING UP

Eleksander tried to be clear and precise as he told them all about losing sight of people in the water, seeing dead bodies, the island they found, and the orange insects killing three of the crew. In return, Sabina and Jero took turns telling them about their experience and who had not survived the swim over here.

"Perhaps there are survivors on the surrounding islands?" Taferia suggested.

A woman about their age stepped up from behind Sabina. She had a slim face and scars on her cheeks. "The smaller islands around here are full of the orange bug swarms. They live in the korkorand trees." She dipped her gaze. "I'm afraid anyone washing up on the other islands are unlikely to have made it. We didn't pick this atoll just because it's the biggest. It also has the most birds and weasels, both of which eat the orange insects, meaning it's the safest one. Despite the sea serpents, but they attack all islands in this area."

Hale stepped forward, hand on a hidden dagger, eyeing the newcomer.

"Oh, sorry to neglect the introductions," Avelynne said. "This is one of our rescuers, Aurea. She is from a continent called Hethekla."

This woman—Allrheia, Awhera, Aurea?— pointed to a man approaching. "And the commanding bloke with the receding hairline striding over here is Captain Naseer, the leader of our expedition."

The captain glowered at her after the hairline comment, but only in the way you do when a friend is teasing you.

"Uh-huh. What's this *expedition's* purpose?" Hale muttered, dropping his grip on the dagger with reluctance.

"Welcome to our camp! The purpose is exploration. Just like yours," Naseer answered. "Only, unlike you, this is routine for us. I must say, you've done quite well for a first attempt."

"We shipwrecked and nearly everyone died," Hale said through gritted teeth.

"True," Naseer said with a wince. "Nonetheless, you found other life forms and had survivors to tell the tale. Hethklish were on their fifth or sixth journey before we found another race. We lost countless sailors on the first sails, too."

"We were just lucky to wash up on an island with you," Sabina said. "Otherwise, we would have been stranded, trying to survive amongst sea serpents and these orange bugs you speak of."

"Every sailor needs luck," Naseer answered with a paternal smile. "Besides, you're clever and hard-working. You'd find a way off these islands."

Sabina smiled back, it was nice to see her smile again, and began in brief terms explaining that the Hethklish were a people who traced their roots back to Cavarra! In fact, to Eleksander's own Lakelands, which got his attention fast.

Then Avelynne took over, explaining what Naseer had found in their history book, mentioning some of the Hethklish societal advances, and finishing with, "And our very own Northern diplomat here has set up an agreement for a trade deal with the Hethklish."

At which point, Sabina's cheeks went cherry red.

Throughout the tale, Eleksander listened but was eager to tell Sabina and Avelynne about his mother being the queen. And then, confiding to at least one of them in private what had happened between him and Hale. Before he had time to say anything, though, Sabina grabbed his arm and squeezed it, as if checking he was real. "How did you know where to find us?" Her voice trembled, even though she clearly put so much effort into controlling it. Eleksander pulled her into another hug, one that Avelynne joined.

Meanwhile, Hale puffed his chest out and replied, "I saw the silver magic filling the sky. Obviously, I knew it was you."

Sabina pulled away from the hug. "Well," she said, her tone bursting the bubble of Hale's boasting, "it was them." She pointed to a group of Hethklish sailors juggling empty wine bottles and long knives with magic. "But close enough."

Hale shuffled his feet. "Oh. Right."

She grabbed him by the back of his neck and placed her forehead to his. Hale put his hands on her shoulders and smiled so wide that it almost split his face.

"I've missed you, older sister," he mumbled.

"And I you."

Out of the blue, Aurea who was craning her neck to see behind their legs, said, "I see none of you are Northerners with pet companions. Shame. I must admit I was hoping to see an icewolf. Still, we're thrilled to have you as guests!" She stopped abruptly. "Wait. Guests. Doldrums, where's my sense of hospitality? How very un-Hethklish of us to not offer you something to drink or eat. Would you like anything? At least to have a seat?"

"Yes, please," Taferia said.

She still swayed a little whenever she stood still. Eleksander couldn't help but wonder how she and Hale were really feeling. Woodlanders. They were far too prone to put on a brave face.

A while later, Eleksander inspected the Hethklish sailor clothes he and the other had been lent. Loose-fitting linen in browns that was comfortable but most of all clean, mercifully, wonderfully clean! It was a relief to get the dirty and heavy Hall of Explorers outfits off. As much as he and the others loved their uniforms, they were more utilitarian than comfortable. Especially now that the outfits were doused with seawater, sweat, blood, and torn in several places. He even found bits of seaweed lodged in the links of the mail vest.

After the change of clothes, they'd sat down at a large table and were now having goats' milk and something they called canefruit, which had been dried and brought with them from Hethekla. Eleksander couldn't remember anything sweeter than this fruit and ate as much as he dared without seeming rude or gluttonous.

As she sipped at her milk and grimaced at its taste, Taferia sought Naseer's attention. "I am grateful beyond measure for your hospitality, Captain. Especially towards our four young mapmakers. And glad for your company but..."

"You should like to be alone to catch up?" Naseer suggested.

Taferia inclined her head. "Only for a short while."

"Of course," he replied and stood. Aurea followed him over to where their sailors had continued to entertain each other with tricks.

When they were alone, Taferia said, "Sabina, Avelynne, Jero. I may as well be the one to tell you all I told the lads. The time for secrets is over."

And so she did. Everything from Eleksander's parentage, to them being born at the peculiar summer solstice, to how that must explain the golden sea phenomenon. Ending with, "I wonder if the seawater increased the magic's strength."

Avelynne furrowed her brow. "What makes you say that?"

"Normal silver magic tends to simply lay on surfaces, or even vanish, unless the magic wielder shapes it into something, right? When you created that golden magic, it was as if the water helped spread it and amplify it. As if the sea helped you somehow?"

"Be that as it may, what I want to know is why you didn't tell us about any of this before? Why do you in the Twelve always infiltrate, sneak about, and keep secrets?" Sabina said, still in a bad temper.

Taferia slumped. "You know why, dear lass. The king has killed far too many of our numbers for us to take any risks. And even those who you would be sure could be trusted, can be forced to tell truths through torture or blackmail. Not to mention those who do so for coin," she said in a voice laced with sadness. "Which is why they sent to me to keep an eye on you but gave me strict orders not to tell you who you were or why you're important. It was thought better that you remined unaware, giving you a few more years of youth and learning before you understood the weight on your shoulders."

"The weight on our shoulders?" Sabina roared. "We already carry saving our country, creating reliable maps for future sails, finding trade partners, and learning about the flora and fauna wherever we land. Not to mention being in charge of all the sailors." She paused to catch her breath. "Or, you know, *saving the future of our people* by finding them new land to live on. We already had loads on our shoulders! And we failed! Perhaps if we had more information, we wouldn't have," Sabina said, her voice cracking on the last words.

No one spoke for a while.

"You're too hard on yourself, big sister," Hale mumbled. "It wasn't our fault that we were shipwrecked. No one could predict a sea monster and a huge waterfall confronting us at the same moment."

"Still!" She stomped her boot in the sand. "They sent us out to achieve all of this blindfolded. We hadn't even finished our education! Or gotten over all the death and treachery of last term!"

A weight lodged in Eleksander's chest at the sight of her face. As guilty, remorseful, and accountable as they all felt for the loss of those sailors, Sabina would have it twice as hard. Not only because she was the responsible one who took everything on. But because she was the one who had to take Tutor Rete's life, and never recovered. Never allowed herself to recover.

"Yes. Too much has been asked of you, already," Taferia said. "Yet, I'm afraid we'll have to ask even more. You must decide what to do with this gift of the golden magic. Having seen what it can do, I wonder if it may not be the one thing that can defeat King Lothiam."

Avelynne hummed. "Defeat? I believe we must still, somehow, awaken the minds and open the eyes of Cavarrians to what the king is doing. Using our golden magic to... what? Kill the king? That won't work. People, especially his supporters, would rally against us and deny Sander the throne."

Hale smacked his palm against his leg. "First we need to focus on getting back to Cavarra. Being stuck here is wasting our time, golden magic or not."

"Hale is right," Eleksander said. "Before we decide what to do about Lothiam, we have to get home. I believe we need to ask the Hethklish to sail us to Cavarra."

"They would do so happily," Sabina said, still agitated.

"Yes, but—" Avelynne stopped and ran a hand through her hair. "What, or rather how much, should we tell the Hethklish?"

"Hm. I suppose that if we request their aid, we must tell them some of the truth," Taferia said reluctantly. "Not all of it, though. I worry about what they might do if they find out about your golden magic. They may want to use you as fighters. Or experiment on you."

"You Twelve and your cursed secrets! I've observed the Hethklish," Sabina said through part-clenched teeth. "Waiting to see if they seemed to have hidden agendas, like colonising Cavarra or stealing from us. They haven't asked about our amounts of natural resources, our gold, or our defensive powers. The Hethklish are honourable."

"I trust your instincts," Eleksander said. "Nevertheless, the rest of us don't know these people and we can't even trust the people we do know."

"Also, no offence Sabina, but you haven't known them for very long," Hale added.

Before Sabina could snarl anything else, Avelynne put a calming hand on her lower back, and faced the others. "I suggest a compromise. How about we start by telling them the truth about the king and the Twelve, keeping the golden magic and Sander's lineage to ourselves?"

She turned her attention back to Sabina and added, "For now. When we know them better, and we're safely back in Cavarra, we can tell them more."

Everyone agreed, even Sabina.

Avelynne called for Naseer and Aurea to return and explained about the failing nation that their Hethklish ancestors left behind, with its useless and selfish King Lothiam and the long line of cruel royals he came from. How he had infiltrated their studies and about how the Twelve opposed him. That is, the parts that Sabina hadn't already told them.

Today was a day for filling each other in on information. Eleksander's head swam with it all.

"Huh. So Cavarrians need to know what their leader is really like?" Aurea tapped her lip with a forefinger. "Sabina, remember that I told you about the progress we've made with books?"

"Yes," Sabina said. "You have machines that can make books in a fraction of the time of humans copying them out with quill and parchment."

"Exactly. So, we could write down the truth and warnings, then print masses of copies and spread these pamphlets among the people. One village passing it on to the next."

"How will that change our main problem: that if anyone finds out that we're the authors of these warnings we'll be thrown into labour camps or killed?" Avelynne asked.

Aurea shrugged. "Books have authors, but you don't need to sign a pamphlet. Or if you wanted to sign it, you could invent a group. That way, no individuals or the Twelve would be blamed."

"Not officially anyway," Taferia grumbled.

"I like it," Hale said. "It'll be a way to finally take some action!"

"It won't be a quick process though," Aurea admitted. "We have to get you home and write up the contents of the warning. Then sail back to Hethekla, print it and make enough copies, sail back to Cavarra, and then find ways to spread it."

"That will take a long time," Jero, who had been quiet so far, said. "Especially since there will be many things to see to when we get back to Cavarra. They all think we're dead, I bet."

Eleksander peered at his fellow Lakelander, trying to gage how much Jero knew. Sabina or Avelynne must've told him about the king and the Twelve.

Aurea nodded. "Still, drawn out as it is, it's something that can be done on a large scale and a warning that can be kept, not merely spread by word of mouth and then disregarded."

"That's not a bad idea," Eleksander said, thinking hard. "Not everyone in Cavarra can read, but if we spread the pamphlets to noblemen, scholars and merchants, they will pass the word on."

"If we, or at least the pamphlets, can convince them to help people who are different from them, you mean," Hale said.

"And that it's the truth," Sabina added.

Taferia rubbed between her eyebrows. "The groups who have tried to shine a light on the king's and his ancestors' behaviours, have always been thwarted. Even when they wrote the facts down, the parchments it was written on were simply burned or tossed out."

"The people haven't listened?" Naseer asked.

"No," Taferia said on a sigh.

"Strange. Having met different populations, I have found that people are always happy to distrust and complain about their leaders. It is curious that the Cavarrians are so blindly loyal?"

Eleksander flinched. Hearing that from a stranger made it seem so obviously out of the ordinary.

"I remember once, it was on the way to my first

day at the Hall of Explorers, actually," Avelynne said quietly. "I saw a man being hunted down like an animal, he was ragged and starved. He kept shouting about the king being evil and that everyone must know it but no one spoke out. The king's soldiers caught him. I wish now I could've talked to him."

"I remember you saying that your parents didn't like the king either?" Sabina said.

"They don't. I think. One day, they'll complain about him and his high tithes but then it's like... they forget their hatred. Or cannot speak of it?"

Taferia stiffened. "There have actually been rare occasions when a member of the Twelve, who has not been in contact with the rest of us for a while, glosses over the things that the king has done and believes in his absurd, shiny lies."

"Odd! Do you know why this happens?" Aurea asked.

"No. We all assumed it was some sort of reaction or coping mechanism for trauma or grief, which most of the Twelve have suffered lots of. Like burying your head in the sand."

They all stood in silence, lost in their own thoughts.

Eleksander recalled Tutor Santorine once saying that rebellions against the king didn't happen because he kept the four counties too busy fighting each other and everyday people too busy trying to survive. Clearly, there was more than that to it.

So, here was confirmation that the Twelve didn't have all the answers. Good to know.

"This is something we'll have to discuss with the Twelve before we sail again," he said.

"So, they expect us to sail again?" Sabina said. "Not stay and fight the king?"

Taferia rubbed her chin. "I assume so. We still need a place away from the king, to grow our numbers in safety, go through strategies and plan the final attack." She sidled over to Naseer. "Although, we may be able to overthrow the king sooner than expected, especially if we get outside help. May I speak with you alone for a spell, Captain Naseer?"

"Of course," he said, leading her away.

"Aaaaand there they go, the older folks making decisions without us," Hale griped.

From the distance came the sound of an enormous splash. Eleksander hoped it was some sort of whale, he was too tired to worry about sea serpents now.

One of the sailors called Aurea's name and she excused herself to go check.

The four mapmakers and Jero stood watching their feet. Kall sat in the middle of the circle but no one paid attention to him. Eleksander wondered if everyone else was as tired of being used and confused as he was.

He kicked at a lump of dried sand. It split and he wished he could disperse the weight in his chest as easily.

"Are you all right, Sander? I mean, as all right as any of us can be," Avelynne asked him.

"Yes, it's just that I can't stop thinking about my mother. The actual *queen*. Unbelievable."

Avelynne put a hand on his arm. "I'm sorry she was killed before you got to know her, especially for something as silly as vague rumours of adultery."

He stared at her. "That wasn't why the king beheaded her."

"Of course not, it was for starting the Twelve, excuse me. My mind still isn't back to normal after my long sleep."

"No, Ave. I mean, yes, it was, but not only that. Didn't I mention? She had found out some awful secret about the king and he killed her to silence her."

Sabina's eyes went wide. "How did that fact not slip out to the people?"

"The same way nothing does," Hale said. "People must know of the folks sent to labour camps. The people killed as spies. The people silenced for simply disagreeing with the silver beast of a king. Yet, people love him."

"That can't all be achieved by bribes, lies, fear, and propaganda," Sabina muttered.

"I used to think it could. Humans are so easily led. Tell them what they want to hear and they'll give you the blood straight from their hearts," Avelynne said. "Now, I'm starting to doubt it. It's strange how physical distance from your home makes things look different."

Taferia and Naseer returned.

"We have an accord. The Hethklish will help us travel back," Taferia said.

"Obviously," Sabina muttered.

Taferia gave her a recriminating scowl. "Not until I had assured myself that the help came with no other price tag than friendship and a trade partnership. I'm confident of that now."

Sabina called Kall, who was running over to Aurea, back. "I can't wait to get back to Cavarra. To regroup and plan with the Twelve, sure. Most of all, though, to let our families and loved ones know we're not dead. And to have physicians inspect our injuries." At the last words, she caressed Avelynne's head.

Aurea came back, too, out of breath and kicking a sea serpent scale off her boot. "Yes. We'll get you all home safely." The smile she gave Avelynne and Sabina made it seem like it was only the three of them in the world. "Everything else can be decided later. For now, get some rest while we pack up the camp. *And* get a freshly killed sea serpent off the anchor before it rusts the metal!"

While the Hethklish saw to that, the Cavarrians sat and rested. Or tried to, Eleksander wasn't sure he'd ever have a restful mind again.

Hale spat in the sand and said, "I don't care if the Hethklish experiment on us or use us as some sort of hostages for coin when we get home. Or invade us. Or have some other plan that my tired little mind can't fathom."

"What?" Sabina said.

Hale shrugged. "If we're misruled by the Hethklish or by Lothiam, who gives a shit? At least the Hethklish are exciting and don't have toad faces like our lying throne-dweller."

"Right. On that cheerful note," Avelynne said, "let's go help out. Sitting here is not making us feel any better."

Chipper as a funeral procession, they began breaking up the camp.

Chapter Twenty-Five

ART AND BOOKS

Sabina helped a sailor untie and roll up the last hammock and then they boarded the ships.

There was no plan set for whom went on which vessel. Well, there was for the sailors who all had their positions and tasks, but the Cavarrians, Naseer, and Aurea all ended up on the Qetesh, which Sabina found unwise.

She bit her tongue, reminding herself, *you don't have to make sure it's right. They know what they're doing. It's not your problem.*

Sabina scanned the shore. "Is everyone on board?"

"I think so," Aurea said, while checking some ropes.

"I'll go make sure," Sabina said.

Aurea grabbed her arm. "No. You've done far too much already. Besides, you don't know my crew by sight. Stay here and keep an eye on everyone and I'll send one of my most diligent sailors to check for stragglers."

Sabina stood back. "All right."

Not your responsibility. Not your problem. Let it go.

She dropped to the deck instead and did her daily push-ups, Kall watching as he always did.

When they had weighed anchor and were making good speed out to sea, Aurea came over. "Would you mind coming with me?"

Sabina jumped to her feet. "Lead the way."

She followed the Hethklish below deck, trying not to watch the swaying of Aurea's hips as she walked. Everything about this woman was in constant, beautiful motion.

Down there, Avelynne waited by a table, inspecting what looked like a pile of parchment. No, it was thinner and whiter. And there was so much of it! Sabina had never seen a collection of so much writing material in her life and here this stack was, just lying about on a ship.

"Paper," Avelynne said, pointing to them with delight.

That explained it. Just how much cheaper and accessible was that stuff than parchment? She was going to ask but Aurea was busy upending crates and satchels. "Where did I put them?" she murmured over and over to herself. "Someone's moved them, I'm sure of it."

An empty sack flew past, almost hitting Sabina's shoulder, so she got out of Aurea's way and went over to Avelynne instead.

She put her hand on a painfully thin forearm. "How are you feeling, little countess?"

"I'm well, thank you."

Sabina surveyed her. "And if you drop the 'I don't want to be a bother act' and you're honest with me, how do you feel then?"

Avelynne's well-mannered smile fell and she gave a hum of a mirthless laugh. "Fine, I'll tell you." She leaned into to kiss Sabina first, with so much emotion it made Sabina ache. "If I'm honest, I'm bone-tired. Every little thing I do seems to take twice as much energy as it should. I get headaches, too, but that is normal fare for me."

Sabina held her, taking some of the weight off those delicate feet of hers. "Aye, but do they feel like your normal headaches, though? Or are they worse?"

"They were worse, but each one is less debilitating now. The confusion I've had on and off since I woke up has cleared as well. I'm getting better, snowdrop. Please don't worry."

"I'll always worry about you."

She wanted to say more. To tell Avelynne that she loved her and always would, even if Avelynne couldn't love her the same way back.

A small bag of something clinking slid across the deck. Aurea was creating such a mess. What could be so important to find?

"Here!" Aurea pulled out a bunch of quills tied together with string and three pots, one with regular blue ink, one with black, and one with red.

"I'm afraid we only have these three boring colours," Aurea said, handing the inkwells to Avelynne.

"No matter. One can do a lot with black, blue, and red," Avelynne said politely.

"Including making purple. Which is great colour," Sabina enthused in an attempt to get rid of the apologetic expression on Aurea's sweet face.

It worked. Aurea fell back into her usual carefree smile.

Avelynne's gaze moved back and forth between Sabina to Aurea, as if studying them.

"Hm," she said. "Aurea? If we fetched some water for diluting, perhaps we could make the exact shade of purple of that ring in Sabina's eyes."

"There's a ring in her eyes?" Aurea asked.

Avelynne seemed strangely satisfied with the

question. "Yes. Look deep into her eyes. Do you see how the pretty sky blue of her eye has a sliver of pale purple around the pupil?"

Aurea moved a lantern for better illumination and looked right into Sabina's eyes.

Sabina's heart skipped a beat. What was Avelynne playing at? Why was she making them get this intimate?

She could see from the corner of her eye how Avelynne, with a satisfied little smirk, dipped a quill in ink and began drawing. Leaving Sabina and Aurea gazing into each other's eyes, accompanied only by the scratching of the quill.

Aurea hummed, then stepped yet closer. "Yes. I think I can see it," she breathed, ghosting her exhale onto Sabina's lips. "Or? Wait. Hang on."

They were a hairsbreadth apart now and Sabina breathed in the scent of her, all sea salt freshness and something woody underneath.

She had to break this awkward silence before her heart pounded its way out of her chest.

"A-Avelynne is an excellent artist. We all had to learn how to draw to make better maps, but she is particularly talented at it," Sabina spluttered.

The corners of Aurea's mouth twitched, just perceptibly. "Mm. Yes, I think you mentioned that."

"Right. Of course. I did tell you that."

"I see it now! A ring of purple breaking the blue," Aurea said in awed tones, her voice like warm honey coating and calming Sabina's frayed nerves somewhat. It also made her heat up in the most inappropriate places, though.

"Does everyone in the Rosenmarck family have that?"

"I d-don't know. I don't spend a lot of time contemplating their eyes."

"No. I suppose that would be an odd thing to do with a parent or a younger sibling."

"Aye. All of us have blue eyes except my mum, though."

Aurea blinked rapidly and repeatedly, clearly flustered now, too. "I see."

Sabina cleared her throat, searching for something else to say. An embarrassed part of her wanted to leave, although a bigger bit was enjoying the view and closeness. Whatever she did, this was, as Hale would say, a shittingly odd situation. And she was not suited to handle it.

They stood there for a few more heartbeats, then Aurea cut her gaze away and said, "What, um, what are you drawing, Avelynne?"

Sabina walked over to the table, Aurea right behind her.

"I haven't gotten very far yet so don't judge until it

is finished," Avelynne said, quill still moving with the speed of lightning.

Sabina examined the drawing with astonishment. Avelynne had gotten quite far already, actually. How long had she and Aurea been standing over there?

"Oh, tailwinds! That is incredible," Aurea said breathlessly. "You've caught the details of both our faces perfectly."

And she had, because, of course, the drawing was of Sabina and Aurea staring into each other's eyes. To Sabina's discomfiture, Avelynne had also managed to catch what was clearly there when she and Aurea looked at each other. Affection. Attraction. Arousal.

Had she really pushed her chest out towards Aurea like that? Or was that some artistic licence Avelynne had taken? She knew Avelynne had a rather inappropriate fondness for drawing what she called Sabina's "ample bosom." No, knowing how she moved when she was attracted to someone, she probably had done that, and her hips had surely been about to follow. *Shit.* Sabina wanted to jump into the ocean and swim back to the island!

Aurea traced the lines of Sabina's face on the paper, barely touching it, probably as to not smudge it. "I love this. Sabina was right, Ave, you truly are a gifted artist."

Sabina brimmed with pride and awe. Gifted was an understatement. She'd seen multitudes of Avelynne's drawings, but this... it left her speechless. Avelynne was drawing them with such love and attention to detail. From the height difference to the specific expressions on their faces. She was even adding Aurea's freckles now, apparently having memorised their precise placements.

Aurea shook her head in amazement. "We could really use your skillset in my work back at Hethekla. Printers always need illustrators for both the inside and outside of the books."

Avelynne stopped and put the quill down in a bashful manner. "Thank you. I shall keep that in mind if I ever visit there. Oh, and thank you for the compliments. It is easy to draw well when one has such captivating models, though."

Her tone was humble, but Sabina heard the flirtation in it.

The next voice she heard wasn't as sweet. It was a gruff man's voice shouting Aurea's name from up on deck.

Aurea went to the stairs and called back up, "Yes, what is it?"

Sabina couldn't make out the reply. Soon, though, Aurea came back and said, "Right, the quartermaster informs me we are low on fresh water on deck. I'm going to bring up a couple of barrels from deeper in the hold. Care to join me?"

Heavy lifting. This Sabina could do.

"Sure," she said, trailing after Aurea, once more fighting not to stare at those swaying hips. When they passed the next lantern, she noticed that Avelynne *was* staring at them and raking her teeth over her lower lip as she did so.

Sabina stopped in her tracks. Avelynne halted too, noted Sabina's shocked expression and startled, blinking as if waking up from a daydream.

"Sorry," she whispered. "Those hips are mesmerising, though. Like the rolling of the waves."

"That's no excuse. Stop it."

Avelynne nodded, blushing.

"Oh," Aurea said from somewhere ahead of them. "There's a misplaced crate of books here. Do you think..."

She didn't finish the sentence but instead started rifling through the books. Then she held up a thick volume with a triumphant, "Aha!"

When she was met with blank stares, she explained, "This is the second book of Hethklish history. The one Naseer couldn't find."

"I see," Avelynne said, joining her. "Let's have a quick read, then, shall we?"

Sabina ignored how close the two of them were

standing and crowded around the old book as well. Aurea leafed through it until they got to the part where the Hethklish, then confusingly called the Lake-landish, left Cavarra. A lot of what was in this book was the same as in the one Naseer had read from.

But not quite all of it. Not the really significant part.

Chapter Twenty-Six

SACRIFICE, SPELLS, AND SILVER BEASTS

Eleksander and Hale were moving cargo across the deck. Apparently, a certain Woodlander hadn't listened when they got their orders regarding loading everything before they sailed, but simply stacked things where he thought they fit. There was now a dozen crates, boxes, and chests blocking the door to the captain's quarters.

"Thanks for helping me with this," Hale said, gaze down on the crate he'd just moved.

"It's fine."

"No, it's not. I should've listened to where the cargo was meant to go. I don't listen enough. I know that."

"Well, that is progress, knowing your faults and working on them."

"I didn't say I was going to work on it."

"Hale."

"All right, all right. I'll work on listening better."

"Good," Eleksander said with a chuckle. "And it truly is fine. I mean, what are *friends* for, right?"

Hale mumbled something under his breath in embarrassed tones, then stopped to get his balance. All of this would have been easier if it wasn't for the rocking of the ship.

Eleksander grabbed a small oak chest. It was marked "heavy" but his size meant heavy things were rarely a problem. This one must contain lead, though, as he nearly toppled under its weight.

"Hang on. Let me help you with that," Hale said.

Hale had been avoiding making eye contact with him. Although now as they carried the chest, their fingers touched, and their gazes locked. A hesitant smile played at the edges of Hale's lips and the way he blinked was almost... bashful? Eleksander had never seen anything like that in him. He let his fingers brush Hale's again and this time the Woodlander scoffed and said, "You did that on purpose, pretty lad. Stop playing with me."

Eleksander, his heart a little lighter, was about to answer when Avelynne called his name. Then Hale's. They put the chest down and hurried to her, finding her below decks with Sabina and Aurea, gaping over some book.

Behind them came Taferia. "What's all the shouting about? Is everything all right?"

Aurea held up a tome bound in brown leather. "We discovered the lost history volume that Naseer couldn't find. It was in a crate of books. Honestly, he's terrible at searching for things. I must speak to him about that." She shook her head. "Anyway, it mentions the homeland we left behind when we sailed."

"The Lakelands in Cavarra," Avelynne interjected unnecessarily.

"Yes, it says that the violent race who stayed there, whom we now know as Peakdwellers, Northerners, Woodlanders, and Lakelanders, the latter not to be confused with the *Lakelandish*, which is us. Or, rather was us. The Hethklish, I mean."

"Aurea," Sabina warned.

"Sorry, back to the point. They had a ruler. A queen at that point. She made a deal." Aurea made every word have substance. "With a monster. Which lived in a lake. By the Royal Castle!"

She read out loud from the book, describing the lake and its exact location.

Eleksander reeled. This was the lake that the four of them had snuck out to swim in during the first term at the Hall of Explorers!

"What was the deal made with this monster?" Hale asked.

Aurea pointed to a line of text. "That this queen would be liked no matter what she did and believed in whatever she claimed was the truth. That the ordinary citizen would not want to dethrone her." She traced the text with her fingers and read on. "The spell was cast over not only her but all her descendants by blood. There was a price to pay though. Actually, two prices."

Eleksander stood closer to the book. "What were they?"

"Every fifty years a person that one of these royal descendants loves must be sacrificed. The sacrificed head must be thrown to the creature in the lake."

There were at least two gasps in the room. Eleksander didn't look up to see who they came from. Inwardly, he had gasped, too. His birthmother's death. Was this yet another reason the king had her beheaded? On top of her finding out about this spell and therefore forming the Twelve? He rubbed his temples. All these reasons to kill his wife, shrouded under the inane lie of a rumoured affair which functioned as the official crime. Such a vile, confusing mess from a vile, confusing king.

Aurea spoke on. "Secondly, the belief and loyalty of the people comes with another cost. The text gets quite vague here but speaks of the creature warning the queen that such strong magic as this spell leads to a magic surge, a misfiring of magic into the land."

"A surge misfiring magic into the land," Eleksander said. It seemed important. He said it out loud again. Then, puzzle pieces slotted into each other and he voiced his question. "Could that... explain the silver beasts?"

"Aye!" Sabina grabbed his arm. "We were always told that our insects mutated partly due to over-farming, but mostly through overuse of magic, but as the Hethklish didn't have that happen despite using more magic than we do...?" She left the question in the air.

Aurea nodded. "And, as Naseer pointed out, why would it only be insects mutating if this was the flora and fauna changing?"

"I'm certain our over-farming, overuse of magic, and general overpopulation is part of the problem," Taferia said, sounding calmer than the rest of them. "However, I agree that it rings true that there's some sort of magical interference at the bottom of the silver beast problem."

"This would also explain why King Lothiam has stopped fighting the silver beasts," Avelynne said. "Perhaps he knows that they are due to this spell and therefore cannot be hunted to extinction by natural means? It would explain why his only solution is to get new land, he wants to outrun the problem his family has caused."

"We've had generations of our counties warring

by royal decree," Hale roared, slapping his hand on a barrel of fresh water. "Blaming each other for everything from being a drain on resources to causing the silver beasts. And, all along, it was the shitting royalty and their 'love me spell,' wasn't it?!"

Eleksander hummed. "Well, we have to admit to being a rather violent bunch, always looking for someone to blame and to fight."

"Sure, but the blame and the hate has always begun with orders or information from our rulers, hasn't it?" Avelynne interjected. "I never thought that was strange because most things come from the royal court." She toyed with her necklace. "Now I wonder how much of our history has been down to this spell allowing our leaders to make us believe and accept anything. Making us pay for being born."

"Aye, it's disgraceful. All the coin, faith, and power always stayed with the royals. And we all tolerated it, even though a single uprising of the four counties could've given us a better ruler," Sabina said.

"People do seem to have believed and loved the king more blindly lately, though? Despite that his behaviour is getting worse and his deceit and cruelty is more unconcealed. Wonder why," Eleksander mused out loud.

"Does the book say anything about that?"

Avelynne asked. "Maybe something about the spell growing stronger with time?"

Aurea winced. "Afraid not. This is a book of Hethklish history and so it covers the part about being in Cavarra pretty fast and then focuses on our life on Hethekla." She tapped her fingers against a page. "However, it does talk about that part of the spell regarding 'the ordinary citizens wouldn't want to dethrone the royals' thing. Apparently, most people who dislike the royals, will *forget* about their complaints."

Avelynne snapped her fingers as if she'd remembered something. "Taferia, didn't you say some members of the Twelve forgot that they were fighting the king, and why they were fighting him, unless they were in contact with other members who reminded them?"

"Yes," Taferia said.

Avelynne fretted with her necklace again. "Then, perhaps that is one way to defeat the spell, constantly reminding each other that the king is evil and does not have our best interests at heart?"

"I want to know what 'ordinary citizens' means," Sabina said. "Does that mean that those of us who do remember that we hate the king are not ordinary? Or would we also forget if we didn't remind each other? Does the book say anything about that?"

Aurea leafed through the pages. "Hm, let me see.

This book was apparently written by someone whose ancestor was an advisor to the Cavarrian Queen."

"So that's how the author knows so much about this covert matter? Much more than we Cavarrians do?" Taferia asked, a hint of suspicion in her tone.

"Yes. The advisor no longer liked this queen and kept reminding the other Hethklish, or Lakelandish as we were then, and herself of that fact. While sharing everything she had been told by the queen. Whether or not this is all reliable is another matter," Aurea said before skipping to an earlier page. "Ah, here is the segment on what the advisor learned about the monster in the lake. The creature claimed that there are forms of stronger magic that could break the spell and control it, meaning the monster itself, however the writer is quite vague on that too."

"Control it? How? There must be something more," Hale said.

Eleksander was still stuck on the idea that creature in the lake could speak and had magic, like a human. The four of them had been in that lake, half naked and vulnerable. In fact, Tutor Santorine had taken them there for rowing lessons too. Had this creature watched them? Did it know them?

Aurea leafed back and forth through the book for an answer for Hale. They all waited, some with more patience than others, until she looked up again. "No, I'm afraid there's nothing else on that. My people left during those events and everything else in here deals with our life at sea and when we found our new home on Hethekla."

"Shit," Hale said. Then he brightened. "Good thing we of the second wave remind each other about the king and are not ordinary citizens," he said triumphantly.

"How are we not ordinary citizens?" Avelynne asked with a stern expression.

Hale backed down. "I only meant that we have what the book spoke of: stronger magic. The golden magic that spread over the sea, remember?"

Eleksander puffed out a long breath. "Yes, but what does that mean? Is our pooled magic stronger? Or just different? Is it the solution to beating the king?" He put a hand on the top of his head, trying not to sound panicked. "Or are we simply four mapmaking pawns stuck in a dung heap of spells, death, and people who believe the wrong things and refuse to hear the truth?"

"He has a point," Avelynne said while putting a hand on his back. "We are learning more and more but we are also uncovering new questions. Without a clue on how to use all this new information or if we even can do so."

"Ah! You're all so negative and whingy," Hale said.

For some reason, this made Aurea smile. "He's not wrong. Rude, but not wrong. I understand your fears and the pressure you're under, but seeing this from the outside? You can't put all of this on your own shoulders."

"There's no one else to carry it," Sabina huffed.

Aurea watched Sabina with tilted head. "This organisation, 'the Twelve,' that you speak of, they must be able to help and advise? Especially now that you can give them so much more information?"

"Yes. We want to help and I'm so sorry that we made you feel that this was all on your shoulders," Taferia said.

"And what about the leaders of your counties?" Aurea asked. "You know now that the key to cutting through the spell where everyone believes the monarch is to remind each other, right?"

"Right," Sabina said.

"Then, surely, telling people over and over again is your task. Leave everything else for after that. In fact," Aurea gave a calming smile, "leave *everything* for when you are closer to home. Right now, you must live in the present and we all have to ensure we survive the sail to Cavarra without encountering sea monsters or running aground."

No one could argue with that.

They headed back up, the lasses leading the way. Up on deck, the sun pierced through the clouds, blinding him at first. It must've had the same effect on Hale, as he walked flush into Eleksander's back.

He apologised but Eleksander wanted to tell him not to. It had been nice to feel him close again.

He drew up enough courage to whisper, "If you want to bump into me, I won't complain."

Then his nerve failed him. Had that been too much?

Luckily, Hale just grinned and replied, "Noted."

Was that a blush creeping onto those tanned cheeks? It was hard to tell with the beard.

"It's time to trim that shrubbery on your face, I think," Eleksander said. "I can hardly see you under there."

"Ugh. You know I hate shaving."

"I didn't say shave. I said trim." An idea struck Eleksander. "I could help you with that, if you'd like?"

Hale hesitated. "Yes. I'd like that." He shuffled his feet, the usual Hale-bravado nowhere to be seen. "Thank you."

"You're welcome," Eleksander said, shaken by that somehow... he seemed to be the one leading this dance.

From the port side's railing they heard Avelynne gasp with delight. She was pointing to something in the water. "Look!"

They all did. Under the surface swam creatures coloured like the inside of pearl shells in powdery creams, blues, pinks, and yellows. Eleksander squinted to see them clearer, they had a resemblance to seals but were bigger and shimmered, like their skins held a million minuscule candleflames in those pastel colours instead of dull greys.

"I'm going to guess those aren't dangerous?" Sabina said, not sounding sure of her assumption.

"They're not. We call them moon seals," Aurea said with a tender smile at the animals. "They're safe unless you eat them, their skin contains a poison which kills sea serpents and other carnivores who are desperate enough to try."

"Humans too?" Hale asked.

"Oh, yes. My people learned that the hard way." One of the animals stuck its nose up above the surface so Aurea paused to say hello to it before the seal went back down. "Moon seals are rare because they live off a sort of plankton which we see less and less of out here, but they have no natural predators. Hence their showy colours and the bold behaviour. Most other creatures out here are grey, greenish, or blueish and hide in the depths."

The moon seals kept pace with their ship as though they were racing. They undulated through the water, gliding like currents more than swimming. They did gleam like moonlight, making Eleksander understand why the Hethklish named them after the moon. Some of the seals had their young by their side, little cylinders in paler colours. Like faded, rounder-bellied, and smaller copies of their parents.

Avelynne leaned closer to Eleksander. "Nice, isn't it?"

"What?"

She had a marvelling expression. "To see something beautiful and peaceful out here."

"I suppose so," he answered, unconvinced.

She laid her head on Sabina's shoulder, and the taller lass put her arm around her, seeming equally enthralled by the discovery of these animals.

Eleksander watched the moon seals with the nagging thought that their beauty and novelty wasn't worth all the danger and death the sea had given him. That was a problem, though, wasn't it? He had a future built on sailing the seas, exploring and finding new things, like these seals. Where did it leave him that he wanted to do anything but that?

Chapter Twenty-Seven

WOMEN BY STARLIGHT

Sabina should be asleep. It was far into the night and the stars twinkled above while waves lapped against the Qetesh's hull. She calculated that they were six days into the journey. She couldn't be sure, though, her whole life had lost its predictability. Out here at sea, on this smooth-running ship, every day slipped into the next.

It was nice in a way. She didn't have to mark off the days, didn't have to remember when she had what lesson at the Hall of Explorers or when which of her little siblings would have to attend their weapons training or practise their fishing. It was hard to feel her ability to tell—and control—time slip from her fingers though.

She enjoyed working with the sailors and watching the sea change. One day it was dark madness with waves crashing, and the next it was soothing swells in blues and greens. Unlike on the Wolfsclaw, this ship had all she could need. She slept in a nice hammock, ate plenty of varied food, had a new ship to explore, books to read, she even had a mirror to check the progress of her new sailor's tan in. She could play boardgames with the other sailors, spar with Hale, and win every time Aurea challenged her to a push-up competition on the spacious deck.

Aurea.

Sabina's mouth went dry.

The second in command of these impressive ships. The enthusiastic printer. The passionate learner. The funny conversationalist. The woman who saw everything that Sabina counted as a flaw in herself as something interesting.

Aurea was on the night shift and stood right over there by the tip of the bow, studying the night sky with Avelynne. The ship's lanterns swayed in the growing wind, showing Sabina that the two women were smiling as they spoke. She moved closer, needing to be near them.

Aurea leaned in to Avelynne to point up at the sky. "What do you call that constellation?"

Avelynne didn't move back as Aurea entered her personal space, she closed the gap further and followed Aurea's pointing. "The archer. You see how those stars there resemble an arrow in a bow?" Now it was her turn to point.

Aurea wasn't focusing on the archer though, she was watching Avelynne's perfect face. Avelynne looked back at her and Aurea tore her gaze away, obviously embarrassed.

"Isn't it peculiar?" Avelynne said in an awed whisper. "That we have grown up with the same stars, but from a different angle and with different names?"

Sabina knew how that reverential whisper and that intense gaze of Avelynne's affected a person. Aurea's chest must be filled with a warming sensation and her mind must be firing in a million direction, trying to find a way to impress this woman, to speak of the same sort of magic as Avelynne spoke of. To romanticise the small things until they were as unique and eye-catching as Avelynne was.

"Yes," Aurea croaked. "Peculiar."

"Are you all right?" Avelynne asked, as always unaware of the effect she had on people. For someone so intelligent, she was slow-witted when it came to attraction. No, that was unfair, Sabina decided. Avelynne was filled with the self-loathing her parents instilled in her. It would never have occurred to her that she was this charming, this beautiful, or had this magnetic pull on people. Sabina had once heard her refer to herself as "tolerably good-looking" which was like saying the sun was a tolerable light source.

"Tails, yes, I'm fine. I—" Aurea interrupted herself to stare over Avelynne's shoulder. "Turn! Quickly!"

Avelynne did and must've just caught what Aurea and Sabina could see. A shooting star, carving a line across the breadth of the velvet-black sky.

Avelynne gave that sweet, marvelling gasp of hers and Sabina wanted to kiss her so much it hurt.

Aurea must've felt the same, she surged towards Avelynne but stopped herself.

She cleared her throat and pointed to another cluster of stars. "Hm. What do you call that one? We call it the Nine Mothers."

Avelynne squinted at the constellation. "Why?"

Aurea began explaining and as she did, Sabina realised that she wasn't meant to be here. Wasn't meant to eavesdrop and watch others. Wasn't part of this moment. She should go.

But.

The two women she adored stood so very close and whispered such romantic and interesting notions about the stars. They were sharing something that every bit of Sabina ached to be a part of. Would she be welcomed if she asked?

Sabina shifted her weight from foot to foot, fidgeting with a button on her greatcoat as Aurea and

Avelynne smiled at each other again, that sort of intimate smile that means something. Avelynne's pretty dimples were out in full view, showing off.

Perhaps it was merely physical attraction. Avelynne didn't do romance, after all. She did like to bed people, though, and didn't put as much significance in sex as Sabina did.

But what if it was something more than that?

What if they ended up liking each other more than they did her?

Sabina shivered. A brisk wind was sweeping the deck. Although, she wasn't sure the wind was why she shivered, not the only reason anyway.

She wrapped her arms around herself. It didn't feel like a hug at all.

Kall rubbed his big head against her leg. That helped a little.

Jero appeared next to her, bending at the waist to pet Kall. "Hi, Captain Rosenmarck."

He refused to call her Sabina, no matter how many times she asked him.

"Oh, hello, Jero. You're awake too? Everything all right?"

"Yes, I couldn't sleep. Just... in a pensive mood, I guess."

Must be something in the air, she thought.

Out loud, she asked, "What are you pensive about? If I may ask?"

He delayed his reply, still petting Kall. Finally, he stood and said, "When I signed up to journey with the second wave, I wanted to see new lands and meet exciting foreigners. Experience fun adventures to tell my grandkids about one day and all that."

Sabina opened her mouth, about to apologise for the monsters, the shipwreck, their dead friends, the plot over the leadership of Cavarra that they had pulled him into, their current uncertain fate.

Except he spoke first, his gaze on the dark sea where the wind now whipped the waves. "I'm glad I got to experience that."

Sabina's mouth closed. Glad? He *did* get to experience those fun adventures he'd wanted? He wasn't dissatisfied?

He didn't blame her?

A loud wave crested against the ship behind her. Then another. Her hair began to blow out of its braid as a howling wind came upon them. The wind wasn't cold anymore, instead it was hot against her skin, like steam from a boiling cauldron.

A crack of lightning split the darkness. Sabina turned to watch it and realised that, behind them, there were no starry skies or beautiful women. Behind them raged a strange storm. One worse than she had ever seen, one that had skulked up behind them without a sound until it was too late, one that headed for them with a speed she had never seen a storm on Cavarra possess.

Sabina called a warning to brace, knowing it was all she could do.

There was no time to prepare.

Chapter Twenty-Eight

BRACE AND HOLD FAST

Eleksander awoke to the clash of thunder and squalls like he'd never heard. He got out of his hammock and threw some clothes on.

He stumbled up on deck right as the ship pitched. It was hard to see anything with the ocean the same blue-black as the night sky and the rain lashing onto his face. The candles in the lanterns flickered and some went out as they were swung in the oddly warm wind. The nearest one fell off its hook and crashed by his feet, Eleksander had the clarity of mind to stamp out the flame. Not that the rain or the seawater coming over the side wouldn't have doused it soon enough.

This tempest was unnatural in its strength. Dread made the blood run cold in his veins.

He had never wanted to be home so much in his

life. Even with the conspiracies and death and lies awaiting them in Cavarra, right now, Eleksander Aetholo was very done with the sea.

A sailor stumbled into him, apologising before climbing the rigging on Captain Naseer's shouted order. Eleksander heard Naseer call out something about the topsail but he had no idea what the procedure in a storm was with such an advanced ship. Nor what a topsail was.

Lightning struck the waves and soon the following thunder drowned out the shouts, the whistling wind, and the painful creaking of the ship. Hale rushed past with the quartermaster, carrying what was probably a barrel of freshwater to be secured. Eleksander went to help them but lost them in the darkness and the hubbub.

After ringing the ship's bell, Aurea called, "All sailors on deck!", and the turmoil got worse. The deck became full of sailors, half asleep and barely out of their hammocks, some of them not even properly dressed. Everyone started seeing to the sails and other parts of the ship in a dizzying array. Eleksander noted the other ship, the Parataxia, come alongside. Captain Naseer picked up one of the ropes of the rigging and swung himself over, having no time or opportunity to lay out the gangplank to walk across.

This much Eleksander understood, he knew nothing about these ships but obviously they'd need to have an experienced leader on each ship to survive this.

Where were the other Cavarrians? Eleksander stumbled about, trying not to get in anyone's way but to see if he could help. The rain that came down was hot, adding both to the confusion of the situation and Eleksander's sweating.

The sea roiled as if it was furious with them, trying to knock them over with every wave. Eleksander held on to whatever he could as he moved around, though it didn't help that the soaked deck made him slip with every step. He needed to hunker down somewhere. Or find something to do. A massive wave crashed, flooding the deck to the point where the water was up to his ankle.

A brawny sailor next to Eleksander sobbed and wailed something about never getting to see his newborn daughter. Eleksander put a hand on the man's shoulder but had no words of comfort.

Aurea shouted, "All hands to attention!", and the sailor, still crying, got to work. Aurea was staring at the other ship and Eleksander understood why. The Parataxia was too close. Pulling near to its sistership had been fine in calm seas and a good way to transfer people or objects between the vessels. With these waves, however, it was a different matter. How had the Hethklish not known that? They should be used to these strange storms, right?

Aurea screamed, "Brace and hold fast," before taking the wheel and heaving the Qetesh to portside to avoid its sistership.

But it was too late.

Both ships sloped towards each other and what Eleksander thought was called the topmast tangled with the one on the other ship. He was certain they would get stuck and plunge both ships straight into that ink-dark water.

The creaking of the wood was awful and the screaming from the sailors grew worse. Eleksander recognised one of the shouts. Sabina, standing out with her white hair glowing eerily in the light of a thunder strike, was screaming out curses while securing herself and Kall against the wall of the captain's quarters. The snowtiger roared, sounding more angry than frightened.

Eleksander crawled over to help a female sailor who had been struck down by flying debris. They grabbed on to the port side railings together, hanging almost horizontally from it as the ship tilted further and further.

He closed his eyes as the sides of the two ships dashed against each other with a screeching that could be heard crystal clear even over shouts of sailors, the rough winds, and even the roar of the waves. He was certain the Qetesh was going to stave her smaller sistership's side in.

A sailor clinging to the highest mast yelled something inaudible and then must've untangled part of the sail or some rigging, as the two masts went their separate ways with a whipping sound.

The sailor hanging next to Eleksander gave a wail of relief. He was still too panicked to even do that.

The ships stayed tilted toward each other, leaning dangerously close to the depths of the ravenous sea.

Then, mercifully, the waves and currents separated them. The ships righted themselves, as much as could be expected with the high waves. A complete collision had at least been avoided.

Eleksander could only hope it had been worth getting the ships so close to one another to send Captain Naseer over to the other one. Deep down, he knew that if he'd been in charge, there would've been an able captain on each ship to start with.

His moment of pondering what he would've done as a leader didn't last for long. Free as they were from the other ship, they weren't out of the storm yet. The Qetesh rose to the top of a towering wave, as if she was aiming for the sky, and everything on deck rocked with the rising motion, sailors and all. Eleksander was holding on to the now upright railings for dear life, remembering when the Wolfsclaw went over the waterfall. He'd been sure it was the last day of his life then and he felt equally certain now. The cruel sea beneath them, still pelted with rain and occasional lightning, seemed to be taking its anger at this out on the ship. The wave dropped and they went with it, rushing along too fast and too wildly against the roaring of the gale-force winds.

The sailor next to him was shrieking something about the state of the mainmast and the stays.

He placed a hand on her arm and tried to make his voice authoritative. "Listen to me. You're doing well and we *will* survive this. Now, didn't your captain issue orders?"

She blinked away the rain, staring at him. "Yes, I was to help make fast the crates at the aft."

"Then that is what you'll do, sailor. Let someone else worry about the mast and stays."

"Yes, Sir." Some of the panic on her face abated. She went about her task as ordered, much steadier on her feet than Eleksander could ever hope to be during these circumstances.

He watched his own trembling hands, now both back on the railing, in amazement. Somehow, that little pep talk had worked and made them both feel better. Perhaps he was growing into the role of leadership. A fine thing to do when he no longer had his own crew, and fine timing to do it right as he faced death. Again.

Chapter Twenty-Nine

QUITE THE WOMAN

Sabina balled her hands into fists. What could she do against an end-of-days tempest like this? On the Wolfsclaw, she'd been taught what to do when it stormed. Protect the sail, get the sailors further in on their benches, and make sure everyone was ready if they capsized. On a ship like this, there were so many working parts and they were all a mystery to her!

She checked the skies. The wind, rain, and thunder did seem to be easing, but she couldn't be sure. The ship pitched on another wave. Kall was growling at the water and jumped up on some crates to escape it.

Sabina's searching gaze found Aurea leaving the wheel and shouted, "Aurea, what can I do to help?"

"Use your magic to plug the holes in the broken barrels over there until someone can mend them with wood and nails," Aurea called back, wiping rain out of her face. "We can't lose all the fresh water or the wine."

Through a lightning strike, Sabina saw Hale, Jero, and a bunch of sailors crowding the barrels and food crates. "Someone's already doing that. There must be something more important I can do?"

Aurea handed out brooms to some sailors, who all began sweeping water into buckets and emptying them overboard. "You can help these sailors get the water back in the doldrumming sea where it belongs! Or you can check on the injured, like Avelynne and Eleksander are doing."

"Sure, but those things are all being done, I..."

Aurea stopped and gave her a stern look. "You don't have to do more than that, Sabina. The worst of the storm is passing and we Hethklish have seen much worse in our years at sea. We have it under control."

Sabina was about to argue but Aurea grabbed her hand and said, "I have no time to help you realise that you don't have to fix everything, Sabina. You'll have to come to that conclusion yourself." Then she rushed off to confer with the quartermaster by the main mast.

Everyone around her was bustling about, mending, securing, and seeing to a million things she didn't understand. Things she didn't need to understand.

Sabina stood there for a moment. Then she nodded, once, to herself.

All of this? It wasn't her problem to solve. It was all right.

She lowered her shoulders from her ears, called for Kall, and the two of them began helping clear the water off the deck. Kall mainly by showing the water his enormous teeth, growling, and swiping at any bit of kelp the waves had brought up.

As they worked, Sabina experimented with ways of clearing the water faster and found it was the same as with shovelling snow, you couldn't hurry the process but just had to put your back into it, empty your mind of stress and thoughts, and keep everyone's spirits up while you toiled.

One of the sailors was humming and she bumped him with her shoulder. "That's nice, that is. What is that?"

He told her it was a sea shanty and she soon coaxed all the sailors to sing it. It helped the time pass and the singers all basked in her appreciation.

By the time the deck was cleared, the lightning had stopped and the thunder subsided to a distant rumbling. The storm dwindled to only hot rain, wind, and frothing waves. People stopped clamouring about, too. They returned to the composed, normal working of the ship and began assessing the damage, both to the ships and to its crews. Naseer and Aurea called updates to each other across the two vessels while the sky showed signs of dawn's approach. This awful night was finally ending.

Avelynne came stumbling towards Sabina, her hair a wet mess, blood spray on her clothes, and her eyes wild with worry.

"Snowdrop, are you all right?" she panted.

"Aye. What about you, my countess?" Sabina heard her own voice, hoarse from shouting to be heard over the storm and less confident than she'd like.

"Oh, unharmed, but soaked to the bone and not a little shaken."

The rain finally ceased, making everyone cheer.

Kall padded over to Avelynne and licked her fingers. Avelynne threw herself on him, cuddling him close, fists bunched in his thick fur.

Great. Now Sabina wasn't just jealous of Aurea. *And* Avelynne. But also of her own companion. Smashing.

When Avelynne stood again, Sabina gave up any attempt to be stoic. She took Avelynne's hands and pulled her into a rib-crunching hug, burying her face in the crook of the Peakdweller's slender neck. She smelled of rain with a hint of cat fur.

Avelynne tightened the hug, caressed her hair

and said, "Sander was with me, so I know he's all right. Have you seen Hale?"

"Yes, he and Jero were securing the food supplies. I think Taferia was with them. All the Cavarrians are safe."

She felt Avelynne release a long-held breath. "Good. And Aurea?"

"Oh, she saved the day. Steered the ship and kept both crew and vessel from coming undone. Commanding, calm, and very impressive. And she'll probably be modest about all of it."

Avelynne laughed. "Of course. She's quite the woman."

"Aye, that she is."

Avelynne moved back so they were face to face. "And so are you."

Not sure what to say, Sabina kissed her.

Soon the first hesitant light of dawn illuminated the ship, showing how most of the rubble and excess water had been cleaned up. Many repairs were being made, ripped sails sewn, ropes re-tied, and lost nails replaced. There were injuries amongst the sailors but nothing too bad and no lives lost, expect for two goats that had fallen overboard at some point.

Naseer came over on the gangplank and Aurea told him both ships had taken damage but were still seaworthy.

"We'll do what we can as we sail and then make

more extensive repairs in the Cavarrian shipyard after docking there, Captain."

She sounded a lot more hopeful about the success of that than Naseer did when he muttered, "We can make minor repairs, but we're not shipwrights and the Cavarrian shipwrights have never seen a ship like this. Who knows if Cavarrian wood will even be compatible!"

Mournfully, he held up a large wood splinter from the Parataxia with the frown of an anxious puppy.

"It'll be fine, Naseer. And if it's not, we'll find a solution together," Aurea said, shaking water out of her tousle of hair in a way that was far too attractive.

When they all dispersed, Sabina allowed herself a short break.

She sat down with Kall and took stock. They had made it through another disaster. And, this time, there had at least not been any deaths, sea monsters, or waterfalls.

Most of all, none of it had been her fault. Or her responsibility.

She scratched her snowtiger's chin and mumbled, "Not bad, huh, old friend?"

He purred and looked every bit as comforted as she felt.

Chapter Thirty

CAPTAIN ON DECK

Eleksander couldn't help it, the first thing he did when the storm was over was take Hale aside and check him for injuries. When he used a fingernail to scrape off some dried blood from Hale's neck, the Woodlander yowled, "Ouch! Mind my cut."

"Oh. Sorry!"

"It's all right. *I'm* all right, so drop the worried wife act."

"Husband," Eleksander corrected with raised eyebrows.

Hale snorted but grinned. "Fine. You'd make a fretful *husband*, you know, always searching your spouse for wounds."

"Only if my man took risks and didn't check himself for injuries."

"Mm. Fair enough," Hale said, cutting his gaze

away in a manner that showed how uncomfortable this conversation suddenly made him "Anyway, I'm fine. You're fine. The ship's been beaten up, though. What are the odds we'll end up marooned on a shitty island again?"

"Low," Captain Naseer said from their side. "Sorry to eavesdrop. I'm just going around assuring everyone that we're safe and making sure everyone has a job to do."

"When did you swing back over?" Hale said.

"A tick ago. The Parataxia took less damage than the Qetesh so I thought I'd come over here and see things for myself."

Eleksander cracked his knuckles, unsure if he should say something. No, there could be no doubt. He had to say something.

"Captain Naseer, may I ask a question?" he ventured.

"Of course!"

"Have you and Aurea ever considered the idea that there should be an acting captain on each ship?"

Naseer knitted his brows. "The Hethklish always have their first and second in command on the main ship, as it leads the way and therefore is where the decisions need to be made."

"Yes. I see the sense in that, and I know that Aurea's task is to help you with those decisions, as well as managing the sailors." Eleksander eyed the battered Parataxia sailing behind them. "But for moments like last night, where both ships need a person in charge. Well, getting so close to one another to transfer a captain over seems too big a risk?"

Naseer scowled, more at the conversation than at Eleksander. He hoped.

"Most of the time, the ships aren't in danger though," the older man said. "Meaning the two officers in command should be together on one ship to confer."

Eleksander knew what he was getting at. He'd learned that the Hethklish valued the fairness in decisions being made together by dissenting voices, to make sure no one person had too much power.

Naseer scratched his chin before adding, "And there's the breach of etiquette. It would be seen as me being contemptuous of Aurea if I sent her to another ship in times other than emergencies."

"Really?" Hale asked, sounding as sceptical as Eleksander felt.

"Yes. It's the way it has always been."

"And perhaps it is the way it must stay," Eleksander said. "But I only wonder if there might not be a better way? Just to ensure that when things get rough, you don't have to worry about leaving one of the ships without a leader."

That sparked a new idea in Eleksander's tired

head. "Actually, if having your second in command on a different ship would be demeaning to them, perhaps you need the next in command. The, um..."

Eleksander looked to Hale for help and the other lad helpfully suggested, "The quartermaster?"

Eleksander focused back on Naseer. "The quartermaster or someone like that to be on the second ship? Promote a talented sailor, even? Perhaps that is how you honour your traditions but still have someone in charge on the smaller vessel?"

Naseer laughed. "Well, look at you, mapmaker Aetholo! Telling the seasoned sailors what to do with their ships."

Eleksander felt the blood drain from his face. "No! Uh. I didn't mean—"

"Don't fret, Cavarrian. I'm only joking. It's a good idea and certainly food for thought." He inspected Eleksander for a moment. "You ought to trust your instincts more. There's a strategist and leader in that head of yours. You should let it out more."

"He sure as shit should," Hale agreed.

Eleksander only watched his salt-stained boots, too embarrassed to speak, but taking in the praise like a parched plant does with the first drops of water.

Chapter Thirty-One

LOTHIAM'S CONSEQUENCES

Sabina stood with Aurea, overseeing some repairs. Well, Aurea was overseeing. Sabina was listening in and trying to learn the terms for things. She was just about to ask what a jib was when they were interrupted by a shout from a sailor somewhere up in the rigging.

"The thunderstorm's brought in heavy debris on starboard side!"

"From this storm or an earlier one?" Aurea called back. She turned to Sabina. "This area is known for severe and repeated gales this time a year."

"Afraid I can't tell!" the sailor replied, his words nearly whipped away by the burgeoning wind. Luckily, this felt like a normal cold wind, nothing like the mad tempest.

Aurea waved at him. "That's all right, back to work, sailor. I'll go see to it."

She and Sabina went to the ship's starboard side. Naseer, a couple of sailors, and all the other Cavarrians stood there. They were mesmerised by a grouping of cliffs peeking out from the water, jagged and sharp, but barely visible due to some sort of ocean-blue seaweed covering them. Around them drifted flotsam from a ship, there was even half a keel speared on a long spike of rock.

"I know what that is," Hale said, his voice low. "I recognise that Cavarrian sail and that dragon figurehead."

So did Sabina. And it made her stomach sink.

"By all the waters," Eleksander gasped. "This must've been the first wave's ship!"

They had capsized, then. Sabina subtly grabbed onto Aurea's shoulder for support. The first wave had never been kind to the second wave, they'd been aloof and superior. Still. Under all that, they had been much like her and the second wave. Young. Academic. Naïve. Adventurous. And... unprepared.

She clenched her jaw as she added another word to that list: *sacrificed.*

They had been alone out here with a mission they were not armed for. All to get to new land just a little faster. The king and his grand schemes, this was the end result.

"Can you see sign of life? Any survivors?" Avelynne shouted with panic.

Aurea hummed, not sounding optimistic. "Follow the currents around the rocks to over there. If anyone is still alive, that's where they should be."

Moments passed in vice-tight silence.

Then, Sabina's heart sank, joining her stomach.

Bodies. Lots of them. Floating face down and bloated. Most of them severed into parts, either by the capsizing of their ship or by predators' teeth.

The Qetesh sailed on, showing fresh horrors with every new body Sabina spotted.

Something floated forth from behind the rocks. It was a set of planks that had been clumsily tied together to form a raft. On it were two bodies. One of them, a male sailor, looked more dead than anything Sabina had ever seen. His clothes were drenched with blood, his mouth gaping open, and his eyes stared up sightless at the sky, one even being pecked by a small bird. Eleksander threw the piece of dried fruit he'd been holding at the bird, making it fly off and leave the dead in peace.

Next to the dead sailor lay a woman on her front, wearing a Hall of Explorers uniform. She held the sailor's hand. In sympathy with a crewmember? Or had they been lovers? Unlike him, she could've been sleeping, her eyes were closed and her face cradled in the crook of her arm. Her torso didn't seem to be moving with breaths, though, and her skin was the dull grey of death.

Hale dove in and headed for the raft, getting to the woman first. She was the first wave's Lakelander if Sabina remembered correctly. Well, she *had* been the first wave's Lakelander, as Hale looked back at them and shook his head after searching for her pulse.

Sabina was sure no one had expected there to be one. But it felt right that Hale had checked.

"I'm afraid survivors are unlikely. There's no landmass for quite a distance. Nothing to swim to," Naseer said while helping Hale back up on deck. "Besides, by the looks of these bodies, they've been here for quite a while and all manner of creatures live and feed here. These young people stood no chance."

Sabina wanted to scream. They had dallied and so not found the first wave in time. Perhaps she could've saved them? If it hadn't been for that monster and the waterfall! Or, no, perhaps they'd been on the wrong course earlier than that? She'd been so busy with their own journey, if they should claim land for the king or the Twelve, and her attraction to two different women, that maybe she hadn't made enough haste and effort to find the first wave.

"They shouldn't have been out here," Eleksander murmured. "They hadn't finished their training or been given all the materials and crew they might need. They weren't prepared."

"Like us," Avelynne said, quiet and shivering.

Sabina didn't know if the woman she loved trembled out of emotion or the chill in the wind, but she went to the crates where she'd stashed her greatcoat and picked it up. She draped it over Avelynne's shoulders while still watching the bodies in the water. It felt wrong to avert her gaze.

"This is your Hall of Explorers uniform coat," Avelynne protested. "*You* should wear it. Or keep it safe and as clean as possible until we arrive back home."

"You're cold. What that coat symbolises doesn't matter anymore. What matters is to keep you healthy and warm."

The greatcoat had been useful, but not quite fit for purpose. That thought gave her pause. Who gives sailors clothes that become extraordinarily heavy in water? Their leather and mail uniforms had nearly drowned them all. How much of all of this was Cavarra's lack of experience and how much was due to the king and his followers not caring if their disposable mapmakers lived or died?

No, they hadn't been prepared for this mission, any of them. However, it wasn't their fault. Not *her* fault.

Avelynne must've been thinking the same

because she said, with iron creeping into her voice, "They made us run into danger before we were equipped, all because the king got impatient."

"And probably frightened of the Twelve exposing his secrets," Taferia said.

"Aye. Most of all, though, because we're expendable." Sabina planted her feet. "Well, every wave of young people he ships off into danger won't die. Nor are the second wave the easily manipulated child soldiers he thinks we are. We'll show him that when we get back."

Kall growled at her feet and she wished she could send her snowtiger to rend Lothiam's cruel and reckless arse into pieces.

"What a doldrumming villain you have for a leader," Naseer said, crossing his arms over his chest. "I see why you're so eager to show your people his true nature."

Sabina was lost in sadness and anger but distantly heard Avelynne agree with him and then say, "We were asked to find the first wave and bring them back if possible. I don't know if that included their remains."

"We should have asked," Eleksander said.

"That's not fair. They should've *told us* when they gave us our orders," Hale countered.

"What does it matter at this point? We've failed in our orders. We didn't even bring our own sailors home. Dead or alive," Sabina mumbled. "Or even find them all."

That quieted everyone. She knew those words had cut her co-captains as deep as it had her, but it was true. They were so woefully unequipped for all of this.

Avelynne cleared her throat. "Well, we can try to do what's right for these people at least. Captain Naseer, may I ask for yet another favour, one quite gruesome and time-consuming?"

Naseer sucked in a breath through his teeth. "I don't think we have room in the hold, unless we do some undignified stacking. Nor that these remains would survive the trip without something to preserve them. Furthermore, I'm afraid the Hethklish believe corpses on board bring bad luck as well as disease; my sailors would rebel."

"Oh," Eleksander said.

He was surely thinking what they all were, that they couldn't ask anything else of the Hethklish, but that they had a duty to the first wave and their crew.

Sabina was still lost in emotion, but fully aware that she would dive off this ship and collect the bodies for some sort of burial herself if no one else volunteered. Avelynne was right, there was nothing Sabina could do for the second wave crew, but she could do something for this one.

Naseer hummed. "What we can do is what we

Hethklish do with sailors who died while sailing. Gather up what pieces we can, place them in weighted burial bags, and give them all a burial at sea with speeches and songs."

"Yes," Hale said. "We'll do that. And mark the spot on a map so their loved ones know where they are."

Naseer ordered the ship brought about and the anchor dropped.

Sabina didn't hear the rest of the conversation, she was focused on her thoughts and the feel of the Hall of Explorers compass, heavy in her pocket. The first wave would've had the same sort of compass weighing down their pockets.

Life punished the victim too shittingly often. Not this time. She'd find a way to make King Lothiam pay for this when they got back. She'd make him explain his decisions. Make him see the blood he'd spilled.

And yes, she'd expose him to the world. Even if it was the last thing she ever did.

Chapter Thirty-Two

GILDED HEART AND EMERALD RAVEN

On a quiet morning on their way back to Cavarra, Eleksander uncharacteristically fell during his equilibrium training. He and Jero had set up at the stern and stood in the whitengale pose when he lost his balance. This ship moved so differently than their longship had. Smoother but, because of its size, Eleksander felt like he couldn't predict every turn and wave the way he could on the Wolfsclaw. Jero laughed, completely falling out of the pose and saying that he was calling it a day and going to get some rest.

It was wonderful that another Lakelander had survived so he had someone to equilibrate with, but it still made Eleksander think of all the sailors they lost, and the funeral for the first wave crew a few days ago. It was unfair that the second wave's four captains should survive when so many of their sailors died.

It was a luxury to be a leader, but a burden, too, filled with guilt, anxiety, and regret. They hadn't been taught about that at the Hall of Explorers. When they sailed, he had naively assumed that the four of them being captains meant they'd be the ones to plot courses, navigate, and steer. Every other decision they would share with the sailors and their physician. Debating and deciding together to ensure everyone felt happy, safe, and heard.

Being a leader wasn't always like that, though, and now he wondered if he'd been even a little ready for it. No, he worried that he'd never be ready for it. He hadn't inherited that trait from his mother, had he? Queen Lea had been a good ruler whenever her husband was not around, which was often in those days as the king liked to spend most of his time in alehouses with ladies paid for their company. The queen's leadership skills were what had made it possible for her to form the Twelve. People listened to her, trusted her with their lives. And she had not gotten them all killed, like he had with his sailors.

He felt cold and heavy, from his toes all the way into his soul.

Was it too late to give all of this up and become an apprentice merchant with his father? He remembered Taferia's words about how the second wave was unique with their augmented magic and let silver strands play at his fingertips. Had he and the other three been chosen for a certain destiny?

Thinking about Taferia's words made him seek her out. She was standing with Captain Naseer, using magic to move a crate back and forth in what must be an evaluation of magic skills. It was clear that Sabina had been right when she said that the Hethklish had stronger magic. At least it was greater than Taferia's and Jero's magic. Was it stronger than his own and that of the others of the second wave? Was that perhaps a key to this whole mystery, that those born in that mystical summer solstice somehow more related to the Hethklish?

No. It was more likely to be unrelated.

Not everything fitted in neatly with a simple explanation. There were so many questions in life and Eleksander, having grown up with more of them than most people, had learned that you didn't get all answers. Often there were none to be had. He was thrilled to have gotten the answers about his parents and now aimed to find out what the king was truly up to and how he could be beaten. Everything else could wait, or perhaps not be answered at all.

Hale joined him, his face—so tanned it was almost golden in the sunlight—wore a troubled expression. "Water, and water, and more water. I never get used to it."

"To not seeing land, you mean?"

"Not just that. It's... the sea is so different. And indifferent. We're so far away from everything. Isolated. Like we're in a void where no one can find us."

"I suppose I see what you mean." Eleksander perused the endless ocean, a green-blue opaque soup today. "Our bad connotations may stem from that we've had bad experiences when being this far out at sea, though?"

Hale scoffed. "Shit, I'd welcome a sea monster right now. Or a storm. Maybe even a big-arsed waterfall. I just hate that everything is so... vast and quiet. I like a busy jungle or forest. Not this," he waved his scarred hands at their view, "eternal water."

"Hey." Eleksander grabbed one of the hands. "You know it won't last forever. We'll be home at the academy soon, and you can train with all the weapons in the armoury. Or eat all the newly-made oakenberry pie in the great hall."

Hale peered down at their intertwined hands and then pulled his away.

"Oh. Right," Eleksander said.

Hale looked distraught. "No! I mean, um. Don't be sad."

Eleksander waited to hear the rest but nothing came. His lover was his usual uncommunicative Hale Hawthorn again.

Eleksander sighed with every fibre of his being. "You cannot just ask me to not be sad. You need to explain why."

Hale groaned. "But it's so hard!"

"I know, but this is how human relationships work. You have to talk. You have to explain what you're thinking and feeling."

"Fine. I just..." Hale looked around. When he found no one was watching, he took Eleksander's hand again and kissed the knuckles. "Loving another man is new to me and being affectionate in public was never my thing in general."

Eleksander drew his hand back and raised his eyebrows. "Really? You always responded fine when Ave cuddled you."

"Yes, exactly! With everyone else I've always been more comfortable with a slap on the back or a punch on the shoulder. It's what I'm used to from back home. But with her..." He rubbed his eyes with the heels of his hands. "Shit, one of the reasons I fancied the living daylights out of Ave was probably that she got me used to being touched with tenderness."

"I see," Eleksander said, unable to keep envy out of his voice.

Hale didn't seem to notice; he was lost in making sense of things. "Now, everything is different. And I'm realising that I want to get used to you touching me. All the time. With tenderness."

"Just me?"

"Just you."

Eleksander didn't let his love-drunk heart run away with him. He wasn't going to be anyone's dirty secret, so he had to ask, "Even in public?"

"Yes. I mean, sure. Or, I suppose so? At some point?" Hale said, sounding like his brain was arguing with itself. "I need time. And, I still think I owe it to Avelynne to explain..." He scratched his head violently. "Shitting silver beasts, I don't even know what I'm going to explain. I don't know what I feel. Or what to do. Or if I'm capable of doing it or, anything really!"

"It's all right, my sweet gilded heart." Eleksander couldn't stop himself from placing a hand on Hale's cheek. "Take your time. I'm not going anywhere, and neither are you. We're stuck on this ship, on this endless sea, and have plenty of time to figure out what we're feeling and how we're going to handle it."

Hale nodded, leaning into the hand on his cheek, then murmured, "Don't let Sabina hear you call me *gilded heart*. She'll tease me for days."

"Then you'll tease her back." Eleksander put his hands in his pockets. "And say that there's nothing wrong with having a heart of gold."

Hale snorted. "I don't."

"You do. You merely work very hard to ensure no

one sees it because you think being kind and generous makes you vulnerable."

"Stop analysing me," Hale muttered. "You're as bad as Avelynne. Or Aurea."

"Speaking of Avelynne, I think you talking to her is a good idea. You need closure, right? And, if nothing else comes from it, she has a lot of insight into emotions and relationships and will probably give you some good advice."

"You don't think she'll be," Hale rubbed his newly trimmed beard, "angry that my love for her was, I don't know, changeable? Fickle? Maybe she'll be disappointed?"

"No," Eleksander said, trying not to laugh at his clueless Woodlander. "I think she'll be relieved. She was terrified that she'd broken your heart when she told you that she didn't want a relationship but was going to have some sort of friends with benefits arrangement with Sabina."

Hale's features tightened. "Yes, but this isn't about her emotions or commitments. I promised her my undying affection, even if she doesn't want it, I swore it to her." He paused. "Granted, it was scribbled on the back of a blacksmith's receipt for copper ore, since I sent it one night when I was drunk and facing my feelings, but I did write that she had my love until I took my last breath."

"Oh." Eleksander weighed his words. "Well,

that's very gallant of you, but you cannot lock your-self into that. That would serve neither her nor you."

"No. I guess not. I'm just so confused."

"I know. As I say, take your time. We'll get there together."

Hale examined him. "You're the one with the golden heart, Lakelander. And you're far too good for me. I couldn't deserve you even if we lived a thousand years. You know that, right?"

Eleksander grew warm all over but tried to sound carefree when he said, "Sure."

"Shit, I love that lopsided smile of yours," Hale rasped. Then he reached in and gave Eleksander a rough kiss on the lips with a moaning grunt, before hurrying off.

Still reeling from the kiss and the passion in it, Eleksander felt a new confidence in this relationship creeping in. He'd help Hale get used to them being a couple. Now that he knew that Hale wanted him, he'd make this work somehow, no matter how long it took. No matter how patient he had to be.

He checked that no one was watching and then punched the sky in triumph. Looking up at his fist, he saw a bird coming towards the ship. He knew that type of bird. It was a messenger raven, one of the ones the Hall of Explorers bred specially to have emerald green feathers for identification.

"Hey, all Cavarrians," he shouted at the top of his lungs. "Come look at this!"

They all came over, joined by some Hethklish, and followed his pointing finger up to the sky.

Avelynne gasped. "One of our messenger ravens! It's all the way out here? We must be closer to Cavarra than I thought."

"Quite close, yes," Naseer said. "Our ships are faster than your longship was. Following your rough coordinates, I reckon you'll be home in around five days."

"Wait," Taferia said, suddenly interested in the bird. "See that white band tied around its neck? This is not only a Hall of Explorers raven; this one was sent from one of the Twelve's covert agents!"

She moved as close to the bird as she could, whistled, and held her arm out to let it land. The raven clamped onto her arm and she winced, the birds were trained to land gently but Eleksander knew it still hurt.

Taferia checked the message rolled up around its foot. Ravens had been chosen as messenger birds due to their size, able to carry large letters. This one only had a small note, though, filled with strange lettering that Eleksander assumed was code.

"What does it say?" He asked.

"It's from one of our members stationed in the North, meant for our agents at the Hall of Explorers.

It enquires about news regarding our expedition and mentions a labour camp infiltrated up there, as per the agent's orders."

"It came from the North?" Sabina asked with some eagerness.

At her feet, Kall yawned, seeming less excited about his former home.

"Yes." Taferia's eyes were lit with hope. "And while it has taken a long way around, probably avoiding a forest fire or something, it will reach the Hall of Explorers. You know how unstoppable these ravens are. I'll simply attach another message to the old one. May I have some parchment?"

Aurea fetched some paper instead. Taferia jotted down a note with her free hand, the raven cawing impatiently on her other arm. She attached the missive and the raven flew off, steadfast and quick.

"What did you write?" Eleksander asked.

"I kept it brief, vague—and coded, as we always do—and explained that we're on our way back on a foreign ship and should arrive in a few days. Also, that we suffered heavy casualties and that I have news about a new weapon."

Hale tapped her shoulder. "What new weapon?"

Taferia whispered, "Your golden magic," so only the second wave could hear.

They all stood rooted to the spot and watched the raven fly away, each lost in their own thoughts.

Aurea and her cheerfulness broke the reflective mood. "Right, who wants to help sewing the rips in the sails? Or assist me in doing repairs to the masts and rigging?"

They all volunteered and were told which tasks they should go help with.

The distraction was welcome. Eleksander could only hope that his remaining days to Cavarra would fly by in a haze of repairs, rest, and yes... flirting with Hale.

Chapter Thirty-Three

CLOSE TO HOME

Sabina blinked up at the stars which had just deigned to show their little faces and light up the moonless night. A day of repairs done. Four more days until they reached Cavarra. What would they do then? Go straight to the academy? Travel home to their families? Get the Hethklish settled in the ship-yard for their more extensive repairs? She was too tired to plan.

She surveyed the tools used by her, and those sailors who'd worked with her but left long ago. She should carry a few things back down to the hold at a time, taking two or three rounds.

Shitting silver beasts to that, she thought, loading her arms up with the clawed hammer, bench hooks, rough sewing kit, the bucket of nails, and a caulking mallet that she wasn't sure what they'd wanted her to use for. Caulking presumably. Whatever that was.

She stepped forward and there was Kall, slinking in front of her feet. How? He had been behind her a mere tick ago!

With reflexes honed throughout years of sparring, she sidestepped in an intricate dance move and just managed to avoid falling.

Then there was something solid and bearded bashing into her.

"Hale! What the—" she had time to scream before she toppled.

Down she went, armful of things flying in a cascade. Including all the nails. Obviously.

He bent over her. "Sorry, mate! I saw you struggling and wanted to help."

"By getting in my way?"

He shrugged. "It's dark. Didn't see properly. Are you hurt?"

She moved about to check. "Only bruised and annoyed. Help me up."

He did and then they checked the snowtiger wasn't hurt. He wasn't. He was washing as if nothing had happened.

Footsteps rang out and soon Eleksander and Avelynne appeared, asking if she was all right and bending to pick up tools and nails. The lantern light, barely helped along by the stars, illuminated some of the deck. Still, finding the nails was a slow, frustrating task.

As they worked, Eleksander said, "I can't believe we're days from home. It's surreal."

Sabina called Kall to her to ensure he didn't step on the nails. Or trip anyone up. "Aye, it's like we've been out here for years, not weeks."

Avelynne halted midmovement. "Weeks? I know I was unconscious for some of it, but hasn't it been months?"

They all quieted, counting days in their heads.

Hale grunted. "Who cares? I'm more focused on what we'll find when we get back home."

Sabina plonked the last handful of nails into the bucket, not caring if they pricked her skin. "Do you mean Lothiam, the Twelve, the spell, creating the pamphlets to inform everyone of the king's true nature, or having to tell the families of all of our sailors that they'll never see their loved ones again?"

"Not to mention breaking the bad news about the first wave," Avelynne said.

They gathered up all the tools in a pile and stood.

Eleksander ran a hand over his face. "I've got the added fun of figuring out what to do about my biological father and how to relate to the fact that my mother by blood was the late queen. And," he sighed, "that the Twelve want to put me on a throne.

Me. I can't even lead some sailors. How could I rule a whole continent!"

"I can't imagine how you're feeling," Avelynne said, "And I know this won't be easy, but I promise that you won't be alone."

"No," Sabina said straight away. "We'll be there to support you every step of the way, no matter the cost."

Eleksander smiled, but even in the dim light Sabina could see that the smile was forced. "The second wave sticking together might be more important than ever."

Sabina swallowed at that. He was right. And this was a terrible time to have confusing feelings for Avelynne. And for Aurea. What would that do to their team?

"Yes. Although, this is not all about us four." Avelynne fretted with her necklace. "Did any of you know Taferia is betrothed?"

Hale's eyebrows shot up. "No."

"She is. To a man working undercover for the Twelve in the Peaks. She hasn't seen him for over a year but doesn't complain about it."

Eleksander mumbled, "In the cave, she did talk about how the cause is more important than the needs and wants of individuals."

There was a tightness in Sabina's chest. She flexed her muscles there instead, their strength reassured her and the tightness turned to firm resolve. This wasn't just about them. It was about all of Cavarra. Perhaps it wasn't fair that so much would lay on the shoulders of four nineteen-year-olds. But it did. It was time to make the best of it.

"Aye, the cause is more important right now," Sabina said. "And we'll fight for it. We'll win. And then I intend on living my life the way I want."

Avelynne wrapped her arms around herself but kept her posture proud. "Agreed."

"Aren't you... frightened?" Eleksander asked.

"Of course I am," Sabina replied. "Frightened and unsure and angrier than a rabid ferret in a sack! It doesn't matter. We'll still do what's right." She turned to smile at the other three. "Together."

"Hey, anything that gets me off this shitty sea," Hale said with his boyish grin.

Avelynne laughed. "Now there's a point. At least the dangers we faced at sea are over and we survived. That's something."

"It's a shitting lot!" Hale corrected. "Also, as soon as we're back, we get to take the fight to Lothiam. Let him pay the price for once and expose the useless maggot-brain for what he is."

"That will be a good day," Sabina agreed, her fighting blood heating up.

Avelynne stepped back, with a sudden cheeky expression. "Say, after we've replaced the tools, does anyone want to borrow a bottle of wine from the Hethklish and play Bottletop?"

Hale punched his fist into his open hand. "What do you think? Fun and booze sounds perfect tonight."

Eleksander didn't reply at first, but he looked like he wanted to say something.

They all waited.

He cleared his throat. "Yes. In a moment, though, if that's all right? I'd like to watch the sea."

"Are you looking for Cavarra?" Sabina wasn't sure why she was speaking so low and quiet.

He gave a small, timid nod.

She leaned her head against his shoulder and set her gaze in the same direction as him. From the corner of her eye, she saw Avelynne do the same on his other shoulder.

Hale took a step towards them, then hesitated.

"Oh, go on, little brother," Sabina said to him.

He obeyed with an air of relief.

Eleksander held his arms out in front of him and Hale, after some fidgeting, stood in his embrace. He was stiff as an iron rod and probably ready to run if anyone saw them, but he did it. Eleksander's height must've meant he could see above his lover's head, at least when Hale leaned his head back against his chest like that. It was mad that Hale hadn't realised the obvious before: he was so in love with Eleksander that it must shine all the way to the Hall of Explorers. Sabina hoped with all her might that he'd dare embrace it soon. They deserved to love each other without fear or shame.

The four of them stood nestled in comfortable silence, watching the pitch-black sea in the direction of Cavarra. They were not nearly the same people that they had been when they were last there. Nor were the rules of the game, or even the game itself the same. If this could be called a game.

But they were together. And soon they'd be home.

Once again, the question came to Sabina. At the start of something new, was it right to be excited or terrified?

She decided on both.

REVIEWS

I sincerely hope you enjoyed reading Golden Sea.

If you did, I would greatly appreciate a short review on your favourite book website.

Reviews are crucial for any author, and even just a line or two can make a huge difference

SUPPORT ME ON PATREON

Being an independent author writing LGBTQIA stories you don't always get the exposure and financial support that other authors achieve.

Because of this, many of us rely on support from the reading community through sites such as Patreon.

As a patron of mine you will receive exclusive behind the scenes news, updates, my latest book releases for free before anyone else, and even free audiobooks!

If you are interested in supporting me then I'd be extremely grateful.

https://www.patreon.com/emmasternerradley

ABOUT THE AUTHOR

Emma Sterner-Radley is an ex-librarian turned fantasy writer. Originally Swedish, she now lives with her wife and two cats in Great Britain.

There's no point in saying which city, as they move about once a year.

She spends her time writing, reading, daydreaming, exercising, and watching whichever television show has the most lesbian/sapphic subtext at the time.

Her addictions are reality escapes, coffee, protein bars, sugary snacks, and small chubby creatures with ridiculously tiny legs.

www.emmasternerradley.com

Printed in Great Britain
by Amazon